SCYTHIAN TRILOGY

BOOK 1:

LION OF SCYTHIA

By Max Overton

Writers Exchange E-Publishing
http://www.writers-exchange.com

SCYTHIAN TRILOGY BOOK 1:
LION OF SCYTHIA
Copyright 2012 Max Overton
Writers Exchange E-Publishing
PO Box 372
ATHERTON QLD 4883

Cover Art by: Julie Napier _www.julienapier.com_
from an original concept by Ariana Overton
Lion photograph by Julie Napier

Published by Writers Exchange E-Publishing
http://www.writers-exchange.com

ISBN ebook: 978-1-922066-54-1
    Print: **978-1-922066-83-1**

Prologue

The field hospital was little more than linen cloths strung between poles to alleviate the worst of the midday sun. Scores of wounded soldiers lay packed beneath them on the bare earth, spilling out to each side of the shade, where the suffering of the battle's survivors had thirst and heat added to the plague of flies that had arrived to torment them. Now the hum of insect wings provided a background to the moans of the conscious victims and the muted clatter and murmur of overworked physicians and their blood-spattered assistants.

Through the scene of devastation walked a young man with fair hair and an aura of authority. His two companions towered head and shoulders above him, but nobody had eyes for them. Every eye turned to watch the young man, and even the dying stifled their groans as he drew near, pale bloodless faces turning to him as if his very presence could turn back the remorseless march of death.

The young man stopped at every wounded soldier, stooping to grasp a hand or touch a shoulder, murmuring a word of thanks or praise, often using the wounded man's name. With some, the young man dropped to his knees and spoke at greater length, remembering past deeds, but no man was ignored – even the unconscious or dead warranted a look or a sigh. His companions stood in silence behind him, watching in pride and awe as their commander gave of his own strength in an effort to strengthen his men.

"How does he do it, Hephaestion?" one of his companions murmured. "He knows every man by

1

name. Even I don't know the names of half the men in my troop."

Hephaestion smiled, his eyes never leaving the fair young man on his knees beside a grizzled, blood-soaked soldier old enough to be his father. "Perhaps when you do, Philippos, you too will be Alexander."

The trio continued onward, the long day slipping toward nightfall. Outside the confines of the field hospital, the Macedonian army cleared the battlefield of the fallen, separating out the bodies of their comrades from those of the Sogdian enemy, and setting up camp for the night. Alexander took no sustenance as he communed with the wounded, taking neither food nor drink, but he looked none the worse for his labours, feeding off the strength of his spirit.

Toward sunset he arrived beside the last handful of men and looked down at a tall fair-haired Macedonian clad in the remains of antique armour, a bloodied band of cloth wound around his head.

"What's your name, soldier?" Alexander asked softly. "You're one of few here I don't know."

"Nikometros, sir."

"Son of Leonnatos, from the hills behind Pella," Philippos added. "He's in my troop. Brave, if a trifle inexperienced."

"Indeed? I know Leonnatos and as his son you are welcome."

"I...I met you once, sir. At Mieza."

Alexander stared at Nikometros for a minute, and then nodded. "I remember – the white fox cub, wasn't it?"

Nikometros essayed a smile. "Yes sir. And again at Siwa."

Alexander nodded again, the faintest of smiles creasing his tanned face. "How's your head?"

Nikometros lifted a hand to touch his head and bit back a wave of pain. "It will mend, sir," he gasped.

Alexander squeezed the fallen man's shoulder and passed on to the next man. Shortly after, but only when he had comforted the last of the survivors, he accepted a cup of watered wine and a piece of bread. Refusing a seat, the young king looked out over the campsite and then turned to the east, staring hungrily toward the unseen horizon.

"We move out at first light."

"What of the wounded?" Hephaestion asked. "Many will not be fit to travel for days."

"Leave a company to guard them, and half the physicians. They can catch up when they've recovered."

"The more severely wounded?"

"Have them taken to the settlements and outposts. When they recover, they can join the men who govern these lands in my name."

At dawn, the Macedonian army moved on, toward the east once more, leaving over a hundred wounded behind them. Days later, most of them were well enough to start in pursuit of the vanished army, but Nikometros and a score of the others found themselves sent to tiny military outposts scattered in the wake of conquest, where small detachments of soldiers strove to keep the peace, a handful of Macedonian soldiers amidst thousands of newly subjugated tribesmen. By the time the wounded recovered fully, the army was far to the east and their duty now lay with the garrisons that had taken them in.

One such outpost lay on the southern borders of the great rolling plains of grass known as Scythia.

3

Chapter One

Razor-sharp shadows cast by the harsh sunlight made the landscape unreal and forbidding, adding to the feeling of unease that had been gradually washing over Nikometros, son of Leonnatos. The patrol had been following the tracks of the bandits for half a day – tracks that led into the stony, barren hills near the Oxus River – without finding them. It was as if they had sunk into the dry ground or taken wing. Desolation met Nikometros' eyes in every direction as he scanned the valley and rock-strewn hillsides – the desolation of a largely lifeless land. The few signs of human existence, crude stone and timber dwellings, were now in smoking ruins.

The stench of burning flesh hung heavy in the still, hot air, and the sounds of his horse picking its way between the stones on the uneven path were flat and muted. Flies, ever-present, rose in swirling clouds as the horse's shadow fell over nameless carrion, settling again a moment later. His horse shied as a vulture squawked and beat its way slowly into the air, and Nikometros leaned forward, patting the stallion's neck, soothing him. "Easy, Diomede, easy!"

Horse and rider picked their way slowly over uneven ground past a burned out hovel. A dirty, unkempt figure moved slowly on foot alongside him, kicking aside bits and pieces of pottery and other debris that lay scattered by the side of the track. The buzzing of flies, the soft clop of hooves and the muted jingling of harness were the only sounds invading the silence. Nikometros scanned the rocky ground ahead, seeking the danger he knew must be near but finding nothing. His head ached, bright sunlight spearing his red-rimmed eyes, and he removed his antique bronze

4

helmet, raising a hand to touch the scar that lay beneath his sweat-soaked hair. He looked up to where a few kites circled high above, almost lost in the intense blue of the mountain sky, the sight reminding him of the cold airs above the mountains of his homeland. The crush of heat as he lowered his eyes to the Scythian mountain wastes was almost too much for him.

Nikometros shifted his weight when his stallion fidgeted, stamping and trying to turn as another horseman came up alongside him. He turned to see his friend, Eumenion, smiling at him.

"There's nothing here, Niko. We should head for home."

Nikometros felt again the pang of injustice as his friend spoke. They were of equal rank, but Eumenion was his superior by a month. That was enough to give him command of the patrol, even though Nikometros had seen more fighting than his companion.

"I disagree," Nikometros murmured. "The bandits obviously passed this way and recently, but I don't trust our guide. He keeps assuring me they are nowhere near."

Eumenion glanced at the figure of their guide standing stolidly by Nikometros' horse's head. Short and solidly built, clothed in dirty rags, and reeking from accumulated filth, his body blended in with the desolate rocky ground. His dirty face gazed vacantly at the hills around them.

"I'm not sure he's capable of guile, Niko," he replied. "He hardly seems aware of us."

Nikometros reached down and tapped the guide on the head, grimacing as he did so. He was sure the man was covered in lice.

"Raiders...where are?" he said, twisting his tongue around the recently learned syllables of the Scythian tongue.

The guide looked up at him with a blank stare then shrugged and pointed once more up the valley.

Nikometros cursed softly. "A plague on this language, 'Menion. I wish I knew enough of it to really question him and find out where he's leading us. I'd also feel happier if we had enough men to send out a proper scouting party."

"All the more reason to head for camp then. There's nothing happening here."

"But they've been here. You can see the bodies, the pillaged huts."

Eumenion looked around and yawned. "They're only natives, when all's said and done. Oh, all right, Niko, a compromise." He pointed up the valley. "We'll go as far as the crest of the ridge. If we see nothing, then we head home. Agreed?"

"I'll move them ahead then."

Nikometros snapped off a sardonic salute, wheeled his horse, and galloped back to the men waiting further down the dusty track. The body of horsemen broke into a trot when Nikometros beckoned them forward, clattering forward over the rough ground. They displayed little discipline, joking and chattering to one another as they rode. Nikometros upbraided the first of them but the men, mostly older recruits, took no notice. Instead, he contented himself with examining the men as they passed, putting a name to each face, scrutinising their equipment, noting how each sat his horse.

"Ten only," he muttered to himself. "And only half-trained recruits at that. May the gods keep us." His right hand went to the ornate gold armband around his left arm, as it always did when he was worried. The armband had been his mother's, and her mother's before her, a trophy of some long forgotten war with the Illyrians on Macedon's northern border. It featured a woman's upper body merging into the coils of a serpent. A prized possession, Nikometros felt that some daemon of good luck resided within it. He rubbed it absentmindedly, hoping his luck held for them today.

Spurring his horse forward Nikometros took up a position near the head of the column, the guide running alongside and holding onto his horse's mane. The valley narrowed, the path steepening, and the rock walls drew together in a short but narrow defile before rising to the ridge crest, marked by two large boulders. When they entered the mouth of the defile, Eumenion raised his hand, and slowed the column to a walk. Nikometros scanned the rocky hillsides, looking for any sign of movement. Only the sun-baked earth met his intense gaze, waves of heat distorting the air. A few scraggly trees sprawled over the boulder-strewn ground, casting harsh shadows in the bright sunlight. Sweat trickled slowly down his back. Flies gathered in a small cloud around him, settling around his stallion's eyes and mouth. It tossed its head irritably, snorting. Nikometros shifted uncomfortably, the worn, leather straps of his armour digging into tensed muscles. He slipped his helmet back on, immediately feeling the sweat pour out and soak his hair.

The column moved slowly forward, penetrating deeper into the defile. Eumenion moved up beside Nikometros, his brown gelding whickering softly at the golden stallion.

"It's too quiet, Niko," Eumenion said nervously. "We should turn back."

Nikometros frowned. "You said the ridge crest. It's not far."

"It's a good place for an ambush."

"Then we will have achieved our purpose and found the bandits." He stared at Eumenion. "We continue?"

Eumenion hesitated, and then nodded.

Nikometros searched the pass in front of him with his eyes, before turning to the fidgeting column of men and horses behind them. "Move forward slowly, and as you love your lives, stay alert as we go through there."

He pointed his sword at the guide, who looked up at him impassively, scratching his armpit. Nikometros leaned down, gesturing with the sword.

"There up take," he said then cursing, tried again. "Take us up there, but if you lying, I kill you, no make mistake."

The guide looked sullenly at him before turning away. The column of horsemen, with the two officers at its head, moved slowly up the path and through the defile in single file, passing between the larger rocks at the crest of the ridge. Nikometros looked keenly about him when they topped the ridge, but could see no sign of danger. The shade cast by the large boulders was a short but welcome relief from the heat. Nothing stirred on the slopes, on either side, as the column moved slowly over the ridge crest. The path before them descended steeply for fifty paces before leveling out.

Nikometros pointed to the level space. "We can rest there before we turn back." He found himself rubbing his armband again, and dropped his hand self-consciously. The horses' hooves slipped in the loose scree, the clatter of the rocks and the jangling of metal sounding loud in the baking immobility of the bare hillside. Nikometros slowed and looked back to check on the men, seeing the last of them emerge from the shadows of the rocks on the ridge crest.

"That cursed fool's half asleep," he muttered to himself. Nikometros opened his mouth to shout at the soldier swaying on his horse. A shadow flitted across the sun and something whispered in the still air. He glanced upward, glimpsing swift movement above. Eumenion grunted beside him, and Nikometros swung round to face his companion.

Eumenion stared back at him; a wide-eyed empty look of horror, and his hands scrabbled at his throat. He opened his mouth and blood cascaded down his chin. The officer slid slowly back off his horse, falling limply to the ground. Nikometros watched all this in numbed disbelief, the silence and lack of awareness of danger making the events seem unreal. Eumenion lay on his side on the stony ground, an arrow shaft in his neck propping his head up. His dead eyes seemed to be looking back up the trail.

Unthinkingly, Nikometros glanced in the same direction. So little time had passed that the trooper swaying on his horse in the shadows of the rock was still falling, and two others began to fall with him. A shout of warning left his lips as reality flooded into his mind. Nikometros jerked his horse's head round, seeking the guide, but the man had disappeared. As another volley of arrows whistled overhead, he saw figures moving on the far slope, many more than he would have expected. Nikometros looked back at his friend's body for a moment then shook himself back into reality, cursing as he realised the folly in delay.

"Men, to me!" he yelled. "Form up on me...shields over your heads."

One of the soldiers surged back up the path, whipping his horse frenziedly. A man stepped out from the shadows on the ridge crest, and cast a spear, taking the horse low down in the neck. The horse screamed and reared, throwing its rider. Before the man could rise, two youths were upon him, hacking downward with short swords.

The remaining men closed on Nikometros, jostling his horse. Strained faces peered around shields as they struggled to maintain a position close to him. The clatter of arrows on the shields brought back an instant memory of hailstones on the wooden roof tiles of his uncle's hall near Pella, and of safety. He felt a strong desire to lose himself in pleasant memories as the weight of his responsibilities fell upon him. His friend Eumenion was dead. Unless he took some action – instantly – he would be joining him in Hades, as would his men. It was now his duty to care for the troopers. He looked quickly around, taking in the situation.

"Listen, men," he cried, pitching his voice to carry over the din. "We are going to have to break free, and we can't go back through the pass. Follow me down the valley. Keep in close formation, shields up!"

Nikometros kicked his horse in the ribs, pulling his head towards the slope and urging him onward. The powerful stallion leapt forward, plunging down, scattering rocks, and slipping in the loose rubble of the scree slope. High-pitched cries came from the hillside when the ambushers saw their prey escaping. Another volley of arrows followed, but these already fell short as the surviving troopers fled. Aware of riders close behind him, Nikometros spurred his horse on harder, fighting for control on the steep slope, the angry cries of the archers fading rapidly as his small troop raced onward. Down onto the valley floor they fled and, eventually, out onto a broad grassy plain at its base. The Macedonians fled onward, only slowing as their mounts tired.

Pulling his horse up, Nikometros turned to look back at his men, afraid of what he would see. Only five remained. Sweaty, dirt-streaked faces stared back at him, eyes wide, seeking reassurance from their only surviving officer. The men wheeled their mounts round, looking back the way they'd come, quaking at the thought of pursuit. Horses panted and snorted, their coats covered with foam, muscles trembling from the effort of their flight. Nikometros flicked his eyes over his men, registering who remained. He recognised Timon, an older grizzle-bearded Macedonian.

"You, Timon...I saw Doriskos and Thyses fall. What happened to Leonidas and...who was that new man, Periscus was it?"

"Fell in the first volley sir," Timon grunted. "And another three of us took wounds. What do we do now, sir? We can't go back through that valley."

Nikometros did not want to think of what must be done. His mind cringed at the responsibility so suddenly thrust upon him. *Five of the men dead...gods! And Eumenion too...*He put his shock and grief aside, thinking furiously. *We can't risk going back over the ridge, but the hills are low at this end of the mountain range. Perhaps we can go around them. The Oxus River must be close too, and there's a small garrison on the river, closer than our fort. Maybe two days ride.* Lifting his head, Nikometros raised his voice so they could all hear him.

"We go around the hills, to the west. That will bring us back to the Oxus River. Then we go south, upriver." He paused, and his voice took on a gentler tone. "There's nothing we can do for our fallen. We'll be back in force later. We can honour our dead then..."

His voice trailed away when a memory he fought to forget pushed unbidden into his mind. He saw again the ghastly stare on Eumenion's face when death took hold of him. Nikometros gathered his thoughts, and then addressed his men again.

"All right, listen to me. We have a long ride to the river and we can't push our horses much more, but if the gods are with us, we can make it. Keep close together, and don't be tempted to fight if we run into more of the enemy. This time we run." He quelled one or two murmurs at this with a fierce look. "We'll be back and we'll avenge all our comrades then." Nikometros looked into each man's eyes as he spoke, seeing pain and doubt in some, exhaustion in all, but also a desire to survive. "Timon, lead out, double file. At a trot." He kicked his horse into motion and the six remaining troopers formed a rough double line, their shadows long behind them.

Shadows were gathering around the tiny column when at last they rounded the low remnants of the hills. In front of them, though still many miles away across a plain that resembled a sea with the wind rippling the grass like waves, lay the river. Nikometros reined in, letting his horse rest. He gazed over the plain, searching for any trace of the enemy. The ambush by archers and spearmen worried him, though he tried to conceal it from the others. The rabble of local tribesmen owned no horses, and none had been in evidence at the ambush, yet they had followed the tracks of at least twenty horsemen for the last three days.

Where are they now? Nikometros wondered. *Have they come through the valley ahead of us? Are they waiting for us somewhere?*

Nikometros looked around slowly then pointed towards a small rocky outcrop about half a mile away, nestled beneath the last of the hills. "We camp there tonight," he said, "and try for the river at first light."

The men were reeling with exhaustion as he led them toward the pile of rocks. He wished they could risk a fire tonight but he knew it could easily be seen on these featureless plains.

At least we have some basic rations, and a warm blanket apiece.

When they drew close to the rocks, a motion beyond caught his eye. Involuntarily pulling back on the reins, his spirit plummeted at the sight of a large body of true Scythian horsemen coming around the edge of the outcrop. They rode easily, men in trousers and jackets, hide boots and Phrygian caps with gaily-coloured material hanging down around their horse's legs. More ominously, they were armed with the short double-curved bows that could cut them down long before they could get to grips with their enemy.

They had no choice. Nikometros' weary band had nowhere to hide, nowhere to run, and they were heavily outnumbered. His men and horses, tired already, waited for his command, though one or two were already edging away from the oncoming enemy. Nikometros knew that to sit and do nothing meant certain death. To flee, though, was but postponing their fate a short while. *But what choice do we have?* Wheeling Diomede, Nikometros gestured towards the distant river.

"Ride for the river," he yelled, "we'll be cut down if we stay."

13

The horses reared, jostling and bumping each other when his men hauled on their reins. Before they could move more than a few paces, loud cries told him they were seen. Nikometros kicked Diomede, forcing him into a gallop, in spite of the horse's great fatigue. His men strung out behind him, thrashing the sides of their horses, hoping for more speed. He glanced back, his throat tightening to see the Scythian horsemen only a few lengths behind. They screamed excited war cries while they rode, their horses moving easily, fresh and full of energy. Nikometros snapped his attention back to his men, urging them onward, but he could see their efforts were hopeless. Already, their horses were faltering, stumbling, their sides streaked with lather. As he watched, the Scythian horsemen swept by on both sides then curved around in a double line to block them. Nikometros cursed volubly. His men hauled at their horse's heads, desperate to avoid a collision with the encircling warriors, but Nikometros knew that surrender meant death.

"Ride through them," he screamed, "we cannot stay here to die."

Nikometros' horse swerved violently, almost unseating him, and he realised it was too late, there was no way through. The gods had turned their faces away and death must surely follow swiftly. His men sat slumped on their jostling horses in the middle of a ring of screaming and laughing riders. The Scythians, brandishing weapons, tightened the circle. At some unseen signal, the ring of galloping horses came to a stop amid clouds of billowing dust, and a complete silence fell. Every Scythian horseman sat staring in at the small group of Greeks. All held a bow at the ready, arrows pointing toward the Macedonians. The soldiers stared back at them, in no doubt that their deaths lay only a few breaths away. The moment dragged out and still the encircling Scythians sat silent and motionless.

"Fight, you sons of whores!" yelled Nikometros. "Come and find out how Macedonians can fight!"

Three riders detached themselves from the ring of horsemen and moved slowly towards him, halting twenty paces away. Two of the men were typically short and squat, but the third, tall and slim, sat his horse silently. The tall man wore a close fitting leather jacket and trousers, with a cloak over his shoulders. Gold ornaments and jewels hung from his neck and encircled his arms. An ornate felt cap of Phrygian design with inlaid metal rings covered his head. Nikometros locked eyes with him, acknowledging him as the leader. The other two, far more plainly dressed, remained slightly behind him and to each side. They exchanged a few words, too low for him to hear then, at a gesture from the leader, one of the others drew his sword and rode forward slowly, shouting at Nikometros.

Nikometros stood his ground. He resisted the temptation to draw his own sword. Their lives were in the balance and he knew he must not precipitate a massacre by any sudden action. The fact that they had not been killed immediately told him they still had a chance of survival. Maybe the Scythians meant to ransom them. Nikometros dredged up every Scythian word and phrase in his memory, preparing to bargain for their lives.

A high, clear cry came from behind him, lifting the hairs on Nikometros' neck. A soldier pushed past him, still calling out in a high voice. Agamis, the young Thracian, pushed past his companions toward the Scythian leader. He called on his gods to accept his spirit, to know he had lived and died well.

"Agamis," Nikometros shouted. "Halt!"

A glazed look in his eyes, Agamis spurred his horse, calling on his Thracian gods again and launched himself at the trio. An unseen signal from the young Scythian leader released the ring of horsemen and Agamis died, transfixed by several arrows. The ring of horsemen surged inward, swallowing up Nikometros and his men in a confused melee. Nikometros dragged his sword from its sheath and holding his shield high, he dug his heels into Diomede's sides. He swung his sword at a horseman on his right, slashing him across the chest, while blocking another blow with his shield. A spear caught him in the left shoulder, knocking him back and another in his thigh threatened to unseat him.

I die with honour, father. Pain flared in the side of his head, dizzying him, and his bronze helmet tumbled to the ground. The figure of the Scythian leader loomed in front of him, and Nikometros swung blindly, determined to take him with him in death. A jarring shock in his arm swung him around when one of the leader's guards parried his blow. The man shouted and thrust his spear at Nikometros' midriff; the bronze point striking his breastplate and glancing off. Nikometros swung his sword, pushing the spear aside then again, hacking at the guard's neck. The blow connected with the man's shoulder, slicing through the thin leather. The guard cried out shrilly, blood soaking his chest and his face pulled taut in agony. Nikometros pushed his horse past the dying guard, seeking the Scythian leader as horses milled around him, confusing him. Sounds of combat fell away behind him, but he could not spare a look when another

16

spear came at him, searching for his life. His men's cries and shouts faded then ceased and Nikometros knew death had come for them all.

"I will not die alone," he cried out.

His stallion pressed closer to the leader, and a startled look crossed the Scythian leader's eyes when Nikometros swung his sword again. The man jerked backwards, pulling sharply on his reins and half turned his horse to escape the raging blood-covered Macedonian. Nikometros swung wildly at the arms clutching at him and ignored the spears probing his armour. Dropping his shield, he threw himself at the man, falling on the other horse's rump. He slid off, clutching at the man's leg with his hand as he fell, dragging him off his horse. Nikometros fell to the ground, amidst flailing hooves and dust, coughing and clutching his sword and, with an effort, pushed himself up on his knees. Horses stamped and moved around him, bumping into him and churning up the dust, making him cough. A stray hoof thumped into his side. Nikometros looked around wildly, seeking the Scythian leader.

They can't see me for the horses.

The young Scythian leader lay half-stunned on the ground in front of him, making feeble efforts to rise. Nikometros threw himself forward, chopping down awkwardly with his sword. The blow hit the man on his metal-ringed cap, knocking it off and away under the horses' hooves. The leader cried out and raised himself on an elbow, eyes wide as he faced his death. The horses parted momentarily and Nikometros gathered himself for the killing stroke, knowing his own death would closely follow. He raised his sword, his eyes locking with the fallen man's – deep green eyes, wide and staring. Something stirred deep within

17

them as they gazed at Nikometros' own pale blue ones. Long locks of black hair framed a delicate, beardless face; a face too soft, too gentle to be a warrior's.

Awareness flashed through Nikometros' mind at the same moment he started the killing downstroke, "Gods," he croaked, "a woman..." His arm jerked the blade to one side, missing her and burying the blade in the rocky earth. Nikometros' sword slipped from his hand and he knelt in front of her. His right hand crept across his body, fumbled awkwardly with his armband again. The young woman's eyes followed the movement of his hand, her eyes suddenly widening in shock. A shadow crossed his face as a horse moved up beside him and a stunning blow to his head sent blood cascading over his face. Blinded, Nikometros was briefly aware of someone shouting in a clear high-pitched voice before he slipped gratefully into oblivion.

Chapter Two

Rocking...swaying...darkness...where? What?
Wrapped deep in swaddling furs to keep out the
winter cold, his old nurse Helonika rocked him gently
in her arms. As awareness seeped back into Nikometros' mind, he clung to memories of comfort, unwilling to face those vague, unsettling thoughts skittering
around his head. It was much more pleasant to lie
here feeling the strong arms of his nurse cradling him,
murmuring reassurances. Formless noises from the
household only dimly penetrated his senses. A steady
beating noise, keeping time with Helonika's rocking
motion, thrummed against his ears. Nikometros felt a
dull pain. He groaned. The strong smell of horses
grew in his nostrils...

...Nikometros waited for his uncle's groom to
come and pick him up from the hard earth. His body
ached with the pain of the fall, and his head throbbed,
though he did not remember hitting it. He knew he
had disobeyed his uncle by trying to ride the new
horse. It was such a noble beast; he just had to try,
though he knew an eight-year old boy had no business trying out an unbroken horse. *I suppose I'll be beat-
en now*, he thought. Most of the time, he felt happy to
be ignored, to go his own way, but it was sometimes
difficult being without a proper father. As a child, he
called his mother's uncle Leonnatos, father. A few
years later he came to realise it was not true. His nurse
eventually told him the gossip. He was a child of Ptolemy, son of Lagos, begotten on his mother in a moment of passion. Ptolemy wasn't there as a father, but
he was a generous man. He provided well for them,
and sometimes a small gift would arrive on the anni-
versary of his birthing day. Later still, he found out

Ptolemy was supposed to be a bastard half-brother of the prince Alexander, son of King Philip. That made Nikometros close kin to the king himself. He felt very important for a few days, until a son of one of the household warriors told him, that as the bastard son of a bastard son, he would never be recognised. His world lurched under him again. *Where is the groom?* Nikometros wondered. *I can't seem to move, and my head hurts...*

...he lay draped over a rock, or at least something hard, but why it should be moving he couldn't tell. He realised he must have fallen from the cliffs behind one of his uncle's farms in the mountains. *I remember, the falcon's nest. I fell.* Flashes of light told him it was daytime, but he couldn't make out any coherent image. *Where is Polynices? He was climbing with me. Has he fallen too?* Nikometros struggled to move when he heard horses' hooves approach. *A body of mounted men this close to my uncle's farm can only mean Illyrian raiders. I must get back quickly.* At thirteen, he would be allowed to help defend the farm. He would be able to prove he was a child no longer...

...rough voices, not understood, filled with menace. He was sixteen, standing shoulder to shoulder with other youths and men in a rough line facing twenty or thirty sweating men in leather armour. Nikometros looked down at himself, seeing his body clad in leather breast piece, shin guards, and sandals. A leather belt with a short sword hung from his waist. An old bronze helmet rubbed against his scalp as he turned. A round shield with a lion's head emblem hung from his left forearm. He gripped a spear, grimly staring at the approaching warriors, fear gripping his entrails, threatening to shame him. The line of youths swayed back as the armoured men charged, thrusting with

20

their spears. His own spear broke and he drew his sword. A young man beside Nikometros went down, clutching his stomach in agony. The line closed at once, and Nikometros hacked at the oncoming warriors. Life concentrated around him as he sweated and laboured to stay alive. Terror and exultation swept through him in opposing waves. The clamour and clash of metal told him he was part of a larger battle, raging unseen around him. More men joined the line. They started advancing. Nikometros saw a gap in front of him and thrust with his sword, taking his man in the throat with the point. Blood gushed into the man's grizzled beard. He fell. The coppery stink of blood mixed with sweat filled Nikometros' nostrils. *Why do I smell horses too?* he thought. *There is no cavalry here. That came later...*

...the sound of hoof beats beat louder, almost deafening, and the motion was more pronounced as Nikometros thundered across the floodplain. He rode with Alexander's Companion Cavalry, cleaving deep into the left wing of the Persian army. He felt godlike and invulnerable astride his powerful stallion. Their momentum carried them toward the enemy commander, slashing and stabbing. The enemy folded in front of them, their will to fight sapped by the wild charge of the Macedonians. The fighting became general. Nikometros could feel dried blood crackling on his skin as he moved. The fierce pain of wounds filled him. His head throbbed unbearably and nausea brought a sour taste to his mouth...

Nikometros opened his eyes to darkness, lit only by the flickering orange glow of a small fire. As he grew accustomed to the dark, he saw he was in a tent of hides open on one side, bodies and baggage lying beside him. Figures armed with spears moved across the front of the tent, and the sound of horses came from the darkness to his left. He sat up and cried out in agony before collapsing, clutching his head, and waiting for the waves of pain to subside. Memory returned of the fight and of the Scythian leader. *What was it about him that was so strange?* he dimly wondered. Nikometros put the thought aside for consideration at another time. A figure loomed beside him and a hand slipped under his shoulders, raising his head slightly.

"Drink this, sir; it'll make you feel better."

"Who is it?" Nikometros croaked, aware suddenly of his dry throat. The voice was familiar. "Is that you Timon? I thought everyone was dead."

"No, there are three of us left, sir. I don't know why they didn't kill us all. I can't understand a word these savages say to find out what they intend either." He spat to one side. "Here, this'll help." Timon proffered the horn cup again.

Nikometros sipped, and gagged on the bitter liquid.

"Sorry, sir, I should've warned you. It tastes foul, some barbarian brew, but it helps with the pain."

Nikometros drank again; keeping it down this time then lay back groggily, half listening to Timon talking softly beside him.

"We've been traveling a night and a day sir. Mostly north into the plains. They slung you over the back of a horse at first but you were bleeding something awful, so they put you in some sort of hide bag and slung you on the side of a horse. Treated your wounds too. Not much food for us yet but water at dawn and dusk. Couldn't give you more than a sip but I managed to clean your wounds, sir. They look bad but they're not deep and they'll heal clean if the gods smile on us." Timon paused for a moment. "Thought they were going to kill you at first, sir. That chief of theirs, a woman of all things, stopped them. Get that woman into proper clothes and she might be worth a look, for all she's a barbarian savage."

"I remember her, I think," Nikometros muttered. "And she's worth more than just a look. There's something about her I can't quite place." He rolled his head and looked at Timon. "You said three of us. Who is the other one? And where is he?"

"Mardes, sir. He's over there." Timon jerked his head toward a far corner. "He's hurt bad, though. Looks serious. It's a wonder he's still alive." He gave a low laugh. "His head always was his strongest part."

Nikometros looked where Timon pointed but could only make out a vague shape. Mardes, he remembered, had volunteered. A native Persian – with some unpronounceable name they had shortened to Mardes – he had enlisted after the satrap, Bessos, was captured. A good man, and a good cavalryman too. There was some grumbling in the ranks after he joined – trouble between Macedonian soldiers and the people they regarded as barbarians was commonplace – but he was loyal.

"Trouble is," Timon went on, "I can't understand a word of this heathen tongue, so I don't know where we're going, or what they mean to do with us. You speak Scythian, don't you sir?" he added hopefully. "Maybe you could find out."

"I know a few words," Nikometros replied. "Have any of them tried to question you yet?"

"No sir. Do you think we should try to escape? Before they decide to save themselves the trouble and just kill us?"

"Where would we go? And how? The chances of getting out of a camp full of armed men, who know

23

the area, without horses..." Nikometros let his voice trail off. "Anyway, I'm not leaving Mardes behind." Deep weariness washed over him like a flood. "Get some sleep, Timon. We are in the hands of the gods. Let them do as they will." Nikometros rubbed his eyes.

Timon moved away then hesitated. "One other thing, sir. Another party of Scythians joined our lot yesterday. Led by somebody important. He had an argument with the woman. Real angry he was."

Nikometros sank back onto the hides beneath him and closed his eyes. "Worry about what it means tomorrow, Timon. Get some sleep now." He rolled over. Presently he slept, as the first light paled the eastern sky.

* * *

A kick awakened Nikometros shortly after dawn. Already, the camp bustled with activity, the hide tent being dismantled around him. When he opened his eyes, a Scythian warrior loomed above him, prodding him with the haft of a spear. He struggled to rise, and the man grunted, put a hand under his arm and lifted him to his feet. Nikometros stood, swaying slightly, and his head throbbing. He rubbed gummy eyes and looked around. Timon and another man were loading baggage onto horses. Mardes lay motionless in a folded bag of hides slung on one side of a placid looking mare.

The pressure in his bladder became urgent. He turned to the spearman, pointing off to one side. Not knowing the proper words, he lifted his tunic and mimed what he hoped was a suitable action. The man grunted again and nodded, standing watch while Nikometros walked off a few paces and relieved himself. He moved back to the tent and asked the guard for water. The man handed him a water bag and waited while he drank. The water was tepid, tasting and smelling of badly cured animal skins. Nikometros gulped it down as if it was the sweetest wine, lowered the bag, belched, and then dashed a few handfuls of the water over his face. *All I need now is a hot bath, an oil-rub by a competent slave, and a good solid meal,* he thought with longing. He handed the bag back to the Scythian and made eating gestures.

"Food...eat?" he said hopefully.

The man shook his head and pushed him good-naturedly towards a horse. "Get on," he said, "But not try escape. He watch and will kill." He pointed at another man on a nearby horse, armed with a small double-curved Scythian bow. Nikometros had seen those in action enough to know he would be dead before the horse moved ten paces.

Despite the ache of his wounds, he gripped the mane and vaulted up onto the horse's back, gripping its sides with strong thighs. Then he sat holding his head, waiting for the throbbing to subside after the exertion of mounting. A Scythian rider reached over and took his reins in hand, kicking his own horse into motion. Looking back, Nikometros saw Timon, also astride a horse, and a whole troop of Scythian riders surrounding them both.

They rode north, further into the long rolling plains, grass-covered, and dotted here and there with tiny sparks of colour, wildflowers that painted the scene with a subtle beauty. The sun rose higher, bringing with it swarms of biting flies feasting on his wounds. Nikometros brushed them off continually but they returned within moments, and after a while he gave up, stoically enduring the torment. A gentle breeze picked up, blowing out of the west, sighing as it swept over the plains and rippling the long grass. A solitary bird sang somewhere high above in the azure sky, notes impossibly sweet as if from the lips of some unseen god. The only other sounds were the muffled movement of the horses mingling with the low voices of the riders.

The sun burned high overhead when they finally stopped. At a signal from his captors, Nikometros eased himself off his horse gently and sank to the ground. He felt giddy, his wounds were aching again and he felt ravenous. *Do they mean to starve us?* he wondered, *or are they short on supplies themselves?*

A group of horsemen approached from the southeast. As they got closer, a rider detached from the group and trotted over. The guard shouted and prodded Nikometros with his spear, forcing him to his feet. He looked towards the approaching riders and recognised the tall Scythian leader; the woman he had been so surprised to see when he had been captured. She dressed as before, astride a fiery red mare and controlling it expertly with small movements of her slim legs. The woman looked down at him for a moment then turned to her companions and spoke briefly. The rider next to her fumbled in the bundle tied to his horse, extracting a small package. He made as if to throw it to Nikometros but a shout stopped him. Heads turned as another rider galloped up, coming to a halt in front of the group. The new rider gestured sharply with his right hand and his harsh voice barked a command. The other horsemen turned and trotted off, leaving the woman to face the angry man. Nikometros could only make out snatches of conversation.

"...weak...needs food," the woman was saying.

"No! He...dead man...why you want?"

"...chosen...Great Goddess...sign." The woman pointed to her upper arm then held her hand low, flat to the ground. Angry Man snapped a short, sharp remark at her then savagely wheeled his horse away. The woman took a small package from a bag tied to her horse and tossed it to Nikometros.

"Eat," she said. "Tomorrow Great Goddess decide." She turned her horse with a twitch of her feet and rode away. Nikometros picked up the package from the grass and opened it. Inside were a hunk of foul-smelling cheese and a small piece of dried meat. The stink of the cheese made his stomach rebel, but after a moment's hesitation, Nikometros gulped the cheese down then chewed on the meat. He sank to the ground, and lay back on the long grass, feeling the warmth of the sun soothe him. *That man must have been the chief Timon saw,* he thought. *He seems to have authority, but maybe not complete authority. And what is her position?* He looked over at his guard.

"Who man?" he asked, "...angry man?" The guard looked over his shoulder before answering.

"Man is Areipithes son of Spargises, our king." He shrugged. "Maybe kill you, maybe you be slave. Probably kill."

"And woman, who she?"

"Daughter of Great Goddess. Holy. No concern of you." The guard turned away and started grooming his horse. Nikometros lay back on the soft grass, listening to the sighing of the wind, and the song of the birds. He thought of the tall leather-clad woman with the green eyes and wondered who she was. The warm sun and the food in his belly conspired to relax him and he dozed.

He awoke again with a start when the guard kicked him. Nikometros glanced at the sun but it didn't ap-

27

pear to have moved much. With much shouting and laughter, the horsemen swarmed up onto their mounts, starting to move away even as Nikometros dragged himself onto his horse. The long, monotonous journey resumed across an ocean of grass. Nikometros imagined himself a hawk, hanging motionless in the cool air, looking down on the tiny forms of man and horse lost in the limitless plains. *I never thought there could be so much grass. It must stretch to the encircling Ocean.*

The man guarding him seemed friendly enough, so Nikometros started asking the names of common objects as they rode along. Body parts and weapons were simple enough, but there was an element of doubt whether the words he was getting for sky and ground were not really for air and plains, or wind and grass. It was all a bit confusing, but gradually Nikometros absorbed a small vocabulary and spent the next hour or so stringing words together into sentences amidst much merriment from his captors.

When the sun sank toward the western horizon, the mood of the horsemen changed. Voices rose and excitement gripped them, individual horsemen peeling off the group to gallop away and back again, whooping and calling. A pounding of hooves off to the left drew Nikometros' attention. The angry man and a group of riders rode past, heading off into the setting sun, and a few minutes later, the woman and another rider set off in their wake. The rest of the party changed course behind them but continued their slow pace.

Nikometros called to the man in front of him. "What happens?"

The man turned and grinned. "Urul, home...feast," he said. "For you, maybe not good." He shook his head and grinned again.

The setting sun threw long shadows in a land that was no longer flat. What Nikometros had initially thought was a line of low hills, became raised earthworks. A long low wall of earth extended across their path, and the riders angled to the east, passing the wall. Presently they came to a gap in the earthworks and rode through into a town that unfolded before Nikometros' amazed eyes. *I never realised Scythians had towns. And so many people.* A multitude of tents vied for space among wooden and stone buildings. The streets were haphazard and narrow, thronged by women and children who greeted the horsemen, yelling and screaming, as they rode into Urul.

The town surrounded a large cleared space. A low, brightly coloured circular hut of felt and hides faced the open ground, with armed guards standing at the entrance. People gathered as the main body of riders approached, people whose bearing and clothing identified them as persons of importance. Guards hauled Nikometros and Timon off their horses and pushed them to the front. As they were hustled up to the waiting group, Nikometros glimpsed Mardes being carried to one side, still unconscious, but he could pay him no more attention as he was roughly brought to a halt in front of the waiting men. A hush descended on the mass of people.

One of the men holding Nikometros' arms pushed him forward yelling, "Kneel!"

Nikometros caught himself and drew upright again. Timon was thrown down on the ground and a spear held to his back prevented him rising. Again Nikometros resisted being forced to kneel, and now the crowd murmured and the men behind him shouted in anger. He stared straight ahead, ignoring the angry looks, until a savage blow to his head knocked him down. When he struggled to rise, two men leapt forward and gripped his arms. Twisting them behind his back, they forced him down again. Silence fell once more as a tall, powerful man stepped forward. He wore leather trimmed in furs with a brightly coloured cloak flowing behind and his height was accentuated by a tall felt headpiece. A large ornate gold pectoral hung down his chest, with gold and enamel armbands and brooches decorating him.

The tall man walked slowly around the two prisoners then turned to the group waiting by the tent. "Why have you spared them?" he asked. "These barbarians should have been killed at once. Who decided to bring them back?"

"He carries the sign of the Great Goddess on his arm. He must be given to her."

Nikometros craned his neck to see the owner of the soft, clear voice. The woman stepped into view, long flowing brown and green robes sweeping the ground around her. A band of gold encircled her raven-haired head and a large gold and enamel pectoral hugged her breasts. The woman walked slowly to the tall man. She looked slight beside his massive body but stood fearlessly almost eye to eye with him. Smiling, she pointed at Nikometros' armband. The man peered closely then straightened, holding his right hand flat to the ground. The crowd murmured and the man glared round at them. "Very well then. He goes to the Goddess tomorrow. The others..." he gestured at Timon and Mardes, "...will die afterwards. Hold them secure."

Nikometros' spirits sank. His guards hauled him to his feet and marched him off, Timon by his side. Two men carried Mardes, almost tenderly, and the silent crowd parted to let them through. The guards escorted them to a stone building on the other side of the open space, and then pushed them through its low doorway into a small room. The unconscious body of Mardes was laid at their feet and the guards turned and left. The wooden door slammed behind them and a bolt dropped into place. Stygian darkness enveloped them, leaving them alone with their thoughts to prepare for death.

Chapter Three

The sun had risen halfway to its zenith, sending strips and puddles of gold creeping over the floor, when the warriors came for them. The door was flung wide and half a dozen men crowded into the hut. They hauled Nikometros and Timon to their feet, binding their hands behind their backs and hustling them outside. Mardes now conscious but groaning softly, was slung over the shoulder of a warrior. The morning light dazzled them after the dimness of their prison and they stumbled, almost falling. A low laugh rippled through the waiting throng, and coarse jests assaulted their ears.

By the gods, thought Nikometros, *are we to be mocked? Let them see how a Macedonian soldier dies.* He straightened, standing tall then half turned to Timon. "Have courage, Timon. Show them we are men."

Timon grunted and a wry grimace passed swiftly across his face. "Aye, sir...for a while at least."

The crowd on their right parted and a push from the warriors sent them stumbling into the gap. Men and women, and hordes of children, straggled behind and to each side while the procession moved through the town. Although his wrists were bound, Nikometros flexed his arms as he walked, trying to get some of the stiffness out of them. His shoulder and thigh still ached from his wounds and his head throbbed slightly. *At least my wounds are not serious.* He laughed quietly to himself. *Yet.*

At last, the procession breached the earthworks and they emerged onto the wide plain outside the city gates. In the hot morning sun, a cool northerly breeze tempered the heat, rippling the grass out to the horizon. *It looks like the sea.* Nikometros marveled anew. *A sea of grass, stretching forever.* He closed his eyes and breathed in cool air, the breeze bringing him the pungent scent of horses, reminding him of the Macedonian horse lines. For a moment he forgot his situation.

A tall structure of cloth and poles loomed ahead, seemingly featureless, but when they came closer, Nikometros made out designs on the cloth. They appeared to be just random swirls and lines at first, but then his mind recognised a distorted horse's face and the designs leapt out at him. They were beasts – fabulous beasts. He saw many horses and a lion leaping onto the back of one of them. Other beasts were represented but were harder to identify – *a deer perhaps? And a boar?* The guards shouted at him and roughly pushed him. His escort halted, lowering Mardes to the ground.

The cloth hangings formed a backdrop behind an ornate throne of carved wood richly inlaid with beaten gold designs. On the throne sat an imposing figure in long felt robes dyed deep red with a tall headpiece almost obscuring the face. Shuffling and fidgeting, the crowd spread around the small group of men standing before the throne. An expectant hush fell. Movement to his left drew Nikometros' eyes, and he was startled to see the tall figure of the chieftain stride out from behind the screens. His gaze whipped back to the sitting figure. *Who is that then*, he thought, *if not the chieftain?* The figure raised its eyes as if in answer to his thought. Two deep green eyes gazed back at him, fluttering slightly as they met his gaze. The woman flushed slightly then focused her gaze on the approaching chieftain.

The chief strode to the seated woman, stopping a few paces in front of her. Stretching out both hands to her, he intoned a complex series of phrases, its cadence rising and falling in a sonorous chant. When he fell silent, she rose to her feet, putting the fingers of one hand on the chieftain's forehead, she raising the other to the sky.

"Great Goddess, bless thy people, lead us through thy chosen one." She dropped her hands and walked out into the space in front of the assembled tribe. "See, O people. See thy mighty leader, Spargises, son of Masades, chosen of the gods to lead his people. The Great Goddess blesses him once more." A sigh swept through the crowd at her words. She turned back to the chieftain.

This is a man who dominates any group of warriors, Nikometros thought. Powerfully built and tall, Spargises' eyes moved slowly over the crowd. A crimson tunic fell to his thighs with deeper red leggings tucked into brown felt boots. Gold thread woven into patterns of animals ran along both arms and legs. A short coat of metal scales covered his chest, overlain by an ornate gold and enamel pectoral, and a round gold helmet covered his head with felt flaps falling over his ears. A sword hung from his waist in a golden scabbard and a ceremonial mace hung by a leather thong from his right wrist. His intense gaze came to rest on Nikometros and Timon.

By his side, Nikometros recognised the angry man, Areipithes son of Spargises, from the day before. He too, was dressed in gold-adorned felts and armour, and though smaller than his father and less strongly built, he nevertheless exuded an essence of danger. Areipithes smiled viciously at Nikometros then leaned over and whispered to his father. Spargises nodded.

"Let them be offered," Areipithes declared. Pointing at Nikometros, he turned to the woman. "If he belongs to the Great Goddess then send him first. Let him go to greet her and bring blessings on her people."

The warrior behind Nikometros undid his bonds. Another removed his breastplate, leaving him clad only in tunic and boots. They hustled Timon to one side and dragged Mardes away and the other warriors drew back to the encircling crowd, leaving Nikometros alone with the woman in a circle some fifty paces across.

The priestess approached him and spoke softly. "Do you know the ways of the Great Goddess?"

Nikometros shook his head. His breath caught at her nearness. *By all the gods, she is beautiful*, he thought. He smiled inwardly at the thought that even so close to death he could appreciate a woman's beauty. "What is your name?" he asked.

"That is not for you to ask. I am a daughter of the Great Goddess. I serve her for the people." She paused, looking at him through long lashes. "But as you are chosen by the Mother...I am also Tomyra, daughter of Spargises."

"Why you say I chosen?" Now that he could talk to her, Nikometros wished he knew her language better. He could understand basic words and phrases tolerably well, but his tongue still stumbled over the syllables.

"You bear her image upon your arm. How did it come to you?" Tomyra pointed at his armband. When she saw his confusion she pointed at the golden armband again. "It is the image of the Goddess."

"Gift was from my mother and from hers before her."

"A gift from The Mother," she breathed. "Gifted to your mother."

"Image not as beautiful as you."

35

She shook her head and a shadow crossed over her face. "You must not speak to me in this manner. It is unseemly. Because of this image, you were spared in battle. You must now face her chosen warrior and go to her in death. It is our way. She must be shown her people are faithful." She turned to the screens and beckoned. A heavily armed warrior stepped out from behind them and moved ponderously toward her.

"I wish you were a man of the People," she murmured, "But I think you are a courageous man at least. Fight bravely and earn a warrior's death." She paused, a hint of sadness in her eyes. "What is your name that I may pray to the Goddess for your worthy death?"

"Nikometros, son of Leonnatos, of Macedonia."

"Nikomayros? Niko...a strong name, a name for a warrior."

Nikometros grasped Tomyra's sleeve when she started to turn away. A growl of anger arose from the crowd.

"With what I fight? What weapons I have?"

"Unhand me, Nikomayros," she said. "To touch me is death." His hand dropped from her sleeve and she looked at him with an unfathomable look. "You have no weapons. It ends with a death for the Goddess - your death." She turned away quickly and walked back to the throne to seat herself.

Nikometros gazed after her, his mind in turmoil. Shadows flicked across his vision and without conscious thought, he flung himself to one side as a heavy mace swept through the air close to his head. He rolled over swiftly and scrambled to his feet. The warrior grinned at him and advanced and Nikometros backed away slowly, watching the man's eyes. Although death was the expected – and likely – outcome, he refused to just submit to it. If death was his fate, then he would go down fighting. Besides, the woman – Tomyra – was watching. For some reason, Nikometros wanted to look good in her eyes.

Wait, he thought. *Look for an opening.* The warrior came in confidently, swinging his mace, aiming a blow at Nikometros' head and forcing him to retreat. Besides the mace, the warrior carried a short spear in his left hand and a sheathed bronze sword at his waist. He wore no armour or helmet, just a greasy leather tunic, felt trousers and boots. He continued to grin, shouting coarse comments at the crowd. The crowd responded, cheering their champion on.

Nikometros continued to back away until a sudden push on his back took him by surprise. He stumbled forward and the warrior swung his mace again. Desperately Nikometros threw himself to the right but the mace caught him a painful glancing blow on the side. Nikometros' breath escaped in a rush. He scrambled on his hands and knees, trying to find a purchase on the slick grassy ground. The mace thumped into the ground beside his head and shouts of joyful encouragement erupted from the crowd. Nikometros regained his feet with difficulty, the warrior thrusting his spear at his face. Nikometros ducked under it and kicked out, feeling his boot connect with the man's thigh. The warrior stepped back, the smile disappearing from his face, his eyes narrowing in a thoughtful look. As Nikometros edged back, slowly circling round, the man tucked his mace into his belt and took the spear in his right hand. He shifted his grip on it and hefted it, preparing to throw.

I must attack. Get in close. The warrior drew back his arm to cast and Nikometros threw himself towards the man, feeling the spear brush his shoulder. He crashed into the Scythian's broad chest, grappling for a hold as they both fell to the ground. They rolled, grunting and gouging, hands slipping on sweat, the man's fetid breath nauseating him. Nikometros found himself on top, pinning the man down. His hands found the man's throat and squeezed, but the warrior jerked his knee upward into Nikometros' groin, unseating him and bringing tears of agony to his eyes. Fighting back the pain, he lunged at the warrior, butting him in the nose with his forehead – blood spurted and the Scythian howled with pain. Nikometros brought his head down again but a fist crashed into his temple, almost stunning him. His vision swimming, he rolled off the man and staggered to his feet. His opponent rose slowly too, blood streaming from his nose. Face contorted in a snarl, the warrior dragged his bronze sword from its sheath and lurched towards Nikometros.

Limping from the pain in his groin and from his reopened wounds, Nikometros retreated. His head pounded and the image of the advancing man doubled and faded in and out of focus. The man shouted at him and slashed, just missing Nikometros' leg, then slashed again, almost overbalancing in his desire to end the fight.

He's no swordfighter, Nikometros thought. *Now if I can get him to...*

The Scythian lunged. Nikometros feinted to his right then grabbed for his sword arm, and for a minute or two they swayed back and forth, fighting for control. The man kicked him in the shins, throwing Nikometros backwards, and as he stumbled back, the man aimed a sword blow at Nikometros' neck. He threw his arm up despairingly to ward off the blade, knowing as he did so that it was all over. A roar went up from the crowd when the sword connected with Nikometros' arm.

Nikometros fell to his knees. He stared up at the man, agony shooting up his left arm. The man dropped his sword and massaged his hand, swearing. Nikometros dragged his unwilling gaze to his arm, dreading the sight of ruin, but for a moment, he stared uncomprehending. The gold of the armband on his upper arm was marred, scarred by a great slash, revealing the dull blue gray of iron beneath the precious metal.

My armband, he thought, *the blade struck it. It saved me.* The man standing above him swore again and reached down for his sword. Nikometros threw himself forward, knocking the man's legs from under him. His right hand found the sword hilt and he scrambled on top of the struggling warrior thrusting the blade downward. The man stared wild-eyed up at Nikometros, his hands clutching the blade, blood pouring from them as his hands were sliced open. Nikometros pushed until the point of the sword pricked the skin at the base of the man's throat, the metallic stench of blood filling his nostrils.

Keeping the sword carefully in place, Nikometros looked up, seeking the chieftain and Tomyra. *Now to see if I can save our lives,* he thought. He cleared his throat, calling out to her.

"Great Goddess has my life spared. Her token, her gift, fights for me. Goddess chooses me to live. What say People?"

In the silence that followed his words he caught sight of Tomyra staring at him, the glittering green of her eyes revealing her shifting emotion. *What is she thinking?* he wondered.

* * *

Leaving the barbarian in the circle, Tomyra walked back to the throne, her head held high, showing the dignity proper for her station. Her father, though chieftain, bowed to her, deferring to her as priestess of the Great Goddess. He took a position to one side of her throne, a solemn expression on his face, while on the other stood her half-brother Areipithes. The young man spoke politely but, looking at his face, she could read the jealousy and hatred poisoning his life. As she sat down, the crowd roared and she looked up swiftly to see Nikometros evading the first blows. Her heart leaped in her chest and she frowned, examining her feelings. *Why do I feel this? What is this man to me? I am a consecrated priestess of the Great Goddess, protector of the People, while this is a captured barbarian. He must be sacrificed.* She watched Nikometros back away from the warrior. *He is handsome, though, even dressed in those outlandish clothes. What? You think of him as a man? He is a sacrifice...yet...*Nikometros went down under the blow of the mace. She held her breath, releasing it only when he rolled clear. *Why do I feel this way? I feel as if I should know him, have always known him. O Great Goddess, why have our lives crossed?*

Tomyra's mind went back to her first sight of him, less than two days before. She sometimes went out with one of the regular patrols along their southern borders. Riding out was not unheard of for a woman but was unusual, except for Tomyra and her maidens. Her mother had been a Sauromantian – called Amazons by some – from the western lands beyond the Great Sea, and her wildness and independence had been passed on to her only child. Some people frowned on Tomyra's desire for adventure – her half-brother Areipithes, in particular, tried to keep her at home, as he resented her influence over their father and the love the tribe bore for her. When she became consecrated as priestess, he became more circumspect in his opposition, but lost no opportunity to contain and control her.

The barbarians from the west posed a recent problem, proving to be formidable horsemen. They crushed the Persian Empire in only a handful of years, yet the open plains and the People still stood unconquered to the north. *We will remain so as long as the People remain true to the Goddess*, she thought. *Mobility is our strength. That and a refusal to come to battle except on our own terms.*

Although unskilled in arms, Tomyra liked to accompany the patrols whenever possible. She used her own personal bodyguard and was never in any great danger. *Except this last time*, she thought. *This sun-haired barbarian with the token from the Goddess got past Araxes. I almost died at his hands. What stopped him? He definitely stayed his hand.*

The thought of her bodyguard, Araxes, brought her attention back to the sacrifice being performed in front of her. It was only fitting that Araxes should be her champion in the battle of sacrifice, but the victim was putting up more fight than anyone had anticipated. Araxes rolled on the ground now, grappling with the barbarian.

Honour him with his name, she reproved herself. *A brave warrior deserves honour. What was his name? Nikomayros?...something like that.* Her mind went back to the moment when he looked at her with those pale blue eyes of his. Then he had touched his arm and she caught sight of the holy image. *The Great Goddess herself on the arm of a barbarian.* She had to know why; know what it meant. It was with difficulty that Araxes had been prevented from killing him and then Areipithes

41

tried to sacrifice him before she could question him. *The Mother must have a purpose for him.* She flushed faintly at the thought that her feelings for him were not solely due to respect for the Goddess' token on his arm. He excited her in a strange manner, making her feel like a young girl again, instead of a mature woman of twenty summers and a priestess of the Goddess. *A virgin priestess consecrated to the Great Goddess,* she reminded herself. *So why does he make my heart beat faster? Is it just that he has been sent by the Goddess?*

The roar of the crowd brought her back to the present. The two men were circling each other and Araxes looked angry, his drawn sword in his hand.

Areipithes spoke across her to his father. "Now he'll finish him. He's been baiting him so far. There's no other way the barbarian could last so long. These outlanders dress like women and fight like them. Now we'll see if he dies like one too."

"I think not," her father murmured. "He has the look of a fighting man. But when the gods weigh the balance he is still unarmed and Araxes has always championed the Goddess well." He looked down at his daughter, sitting still, hands folded on her lap. "The barbarian is marked by the Goddess and he will serve the People well by his death."

The roar of the crowd jerked their attention back to the fight. Araxes swung his sword. The barbarian flung up his arm in a useless effort to block the sharp blade, falling to his knees. Araxes dropped his sword, standing above his victim for the space of several breaths and then suddenly their positions reversed. Incredibly, the barbarian was sitting astride Araxes' chest, the warrior's own sword probing for his life. The barbarian looked up, keeping the point of the sword pressed against the fallen champion's throat, his gaze searching and locking with hers. Tomyra's heart leapt into her throat.

"Goddess chooses me to live," called the barbarian. "What say the People?" Though his accent was execrable, the words were understandable.

Tomyra started upright. Her half-brother grabbed a spear from a warrior, roaring with anger. "Father, stop him," she cried. "He must not be hurt."

Her father, used to instant battle decisions, did not hesitate. "Hold!" he bellowed.

Areipithes stopped dead then turned with a thunderous look on his face. He stalked back to the throne where, standing in front of his father, he thrust the spear into the ground. "That man must be killed," he ground out. "He should have been killed in battle. Now he has bested the champion. Kill him, or I will kill him."

Tomyra stood white-faced beside her father, her thoughts in turmoil. *How can an unarmed man best Araxes, unless the Goddess wills it? What does it mean?*

Her father turned to her, a carefully neutral look on his face. "Well, priestess of the Great Goddess? How do you read the will of the Goddess in this? Is he chosen to live or does Areipithes kill him?"

Tomyra fought for control of her thoughts. "I...She..." She took a deep breath and looked her father straight in the eye. "The barbarian wears the symbol of the Great Goddess. He came by it not as plunder but as a gift from his mother. Such gifts are sacred. This is a sign." She gestured to where Nikometros stood over Araxes, sword in hand. "Now the blade of Araxes is turned by this same symbol and leaves his hand for the barbarian's. The Goddess speaks clearly. His life must be spared."

43

"No!" Areipithes turned on her furiously. "He is not of the People. Since when does the Goddess favour a barbarian?"

"Father, trust in the Goddess."

Spargises looked carefully at his daughter for a long moment then turned and strode out into the circle. He stopped a few paces from Nikometros. He pitched his words so all could hear. "Barbarian, can you understand me?" he asked. Nikometros nodded. "Very well then," the chief went on. "The Goddess spares you for a reason I do not know. Yet the goddess must have her sacrifice. Do you choose to live?"

Nikometros paused; looking puzzled then carefully enunciated his reply. "Yes, I choose live."

"Then the sacrifice lies before you." Spargises watched him carefully. "Do the bidding of the Goddess."

"It is not my custom to kill helpless men," the barbarian said.

"Yet you will do it or your men may still die. There must be a sacrifice."

Tomyra watched Nikomayros consider her father's words. The barbarian slowly bent down, kneeling beside Araxes. He murmured something to him and paused, listening for a few moments to something Araxes said before suddenly leaning on the sword, pushing it deep into the throat of the fallen man. Araxes kicked violently, and his limbs shook for a few moments before falling into the stillness of death. Leaving the sword embedded in Araxes, the barbarian rose to his feet.

Shaking with rage, Areipithes turned to Tomyra, giving her a look of hatred. "What is this man to you? If you were not priestess..." He turned on his heel,

44

pushed through the excited tribesmen and disappeared toward the town.

Tomyra breathed out raggedly when he left. *Why did I save the barbarian? I could have ordered him killed without fear of offending the Goddess. He is not of the People. Yet this Nikomayros...my soul knows him...somehow.* Tomyra looked towards the man standing over the body of Araxes. *I wonder what he thinks? Does he know me too?*

* * *

Nikometros felt an intense distaste. To kill an unarmed man went against his idea of honour. The gods knew he had killed many men in battle but never in cold blood. *If it was just myself...but I must be responsible for my men.* He dropped on one knee beside the fallen man, keeping the sword carefully in place. The warrior looked up at Nikometros, a patient, resigned look in his eyes. Slowly he took his bleeding hands away from the blade. He moistened his lips with his tongue.

"Send me to the Goddess, barbarian."

"Release me of it then."

The man looked puzzled. "What mean you, barbarian?"

"I would not have your shade, your ghost, angry with me. Tell your gods you went willingly." The man nodded faintly and closed his eyes. Nikometros took a deep breath and pushed down hard on the sword. He felt the blade slice through flesh and gristle as blood spurted. The man shook violently for a few moments and then stilled. Nikometros got to his feet and faced the chieftain.

The chief watched him carefully as he got up then nodded and signaled to his bodyguard. "Take these men back to town," he said. "Put them in one of the royal..." Nikometros cursed to himself at the unfamiliar word. Every word and nuance could be important.

45

"...food and drink but guard them carefully. I will see them at sunset."

The warriors marched up to Nikometros and gestured, politely but firmly, in the direction of the town. Nikometros caught a glimpse of Tomyra standing quietly to one side, watching him. He said nothing when the guards closed around him, feeling not only a weariness deep in his bones but also elated. *At least we are still alive! We may yet get out of this.*

Chapter Four

"Sun's going down, sir." Timon stood by the door to the hut, holding the horsehide covering to one side. Nikometros looked up from where he sat cross-legged on the floor, talking to Mardes. The remnants of a meal lay scattered around them, barely discernible in the dim light of an earthenware oil lamp.

"Then they'll be coming for us." He looked down at Mardes, noting his sallow complexion. "It's hard to believe you have recovered so fast," he said. "I would not have thought food and rest could have such an effect."

Mardes grinned up at him. "I was seeing double there for a while sir," he said in strongly accented Greek, "And I'm still weak. It'll take more than these cursed barbarians to kill me." He touched his bandaged head gingerly.

Nikometros got to his feet and stretched. He ran his fingers through his rumpled hair then brushed down his tunic, grimacing as he imagined how he must look and smell. Never a stickler for neatness, he nevertheless appreciated the opportunity he had been given to have a brief wash and a cursory shave. Despite the lack of a good bronze mirror, he had managed well, though small patches of golden stubble still marred his jaw and throat. Spots and streaks of dried blood and dirt marred his tunic. *Thank the gods not much of it is mine.* He rubbed his armband absentmindedly, feeling the deep groove that cut through the gold into the iron of its serpent coils. *Without this, I'd be dead.* He shivered as he recollected how close he had come to death. *I...we might still die.*

An armed warrior pushed the horsehide door hanging aside and entered. He carried a stick bound with rags soaked in pitch. Setting the stick into a metal holder in the middle of the floor, the warrior lit it from the oil lamp, sending curls of black smoke spiraling into the still air of the hut. He looked at Nikometros and grinned.

"You fight well. When you hit Araxes with your head, I laughed much." He shook his head. "Maybe we will fight someday?" he added hopefully.

Nikometros nodded at him. "Maybe."

"I go now. They will come for you soon." The man grinned again and left, dropping the hides behind him.

Timon watched the man go then remarked, "Real humorous lot, aren't they sir? I agree with him though, that was a good fight. It's not often you see an unarmed man get the better of a swordsman. Not that he was much of one, mind you."

"Thank you for your confidence," said Nikometros wryly. "I'll try my best to fight a more worthy opponent next time."

The sound of footsteps outside interrupted Timon's reply. They turned towards the door as a group of armed warriors pushed into the hut. One of them faced Nikometros and touched his right hand to his forehead, gesturing towards the doorway. "Come, it is time."

Two of the men raised Mardes to his feet, supporting him while the others formed up alongside Nikometros and Timon. They walked out into the gathering twilight, where smoke and the aroma of roasting meats lay heavy in the air. The town was in darkness, lit only by smoking torches and cooking fires. Small groups of men were sitting or standing around fires in the open, eating and drinking amidst general merriment, but silence fell over the nearest ones as the prisoners were brought out. Men stopped talking and heads turned, silence spreading like ripples in a pond, people turning to stare – and a few made the placatory sign to the Goddess of a hand held low over the earth.

A hundred or so paces away Nikometros spotted a large round hut with butter-yellow light shining brightly out of cracks in its wall. The small escort moved closer, shepherding Nikometros and his companions toward the entrance of the hut. A pair of fully armed guards stood at the doorway, spears at the ready and as they approached, one of the guards stuck his head through the hide curtains and spoke. He listened for a moment then swept the hides aside and beckoned them in.

Large and richly appointed, the hut clearly belonged to the chief. Rich carpets covered the floor and scattered hides and furs lay in heaps. Heavy cloth, richly embroidered with abstract designs and animal shapes, decorated the walls, the complex woven designs drawing the eye. A small fire blazed in a clear space at the centre of the hut, smoke coiling out through a hole in the roof. The smell of roasting meat tantalised Nikometros' nostrils, making his mouth flood with saliva and his stomach grumble in protest. Despite the meal he had eaten earlier, he still hungered. Shadows flickered, almost hiding the small group of men sitting on the far side of the fire. As the escort brought Nikometros round the fire toward them, the chief rose and gestured towards a pile of furs near him.

"Sit." He waited until all three Macedonians were comfortable. "You have eaten and rested? My men have seen to your wounds?"

Nikometros inclined his head towards the chief and smiled. "We thank for hospitality," he said. He hesitated a moment then asked, "May I ask you what intend us?"

The chief turned and reseated himself on the cushions. He sat looking at them for a few moments before answering. "I have discussed today's sacrifice with my advisers, my counselors." He gestured to the seated figures on either side of him. "Nothing like this has happened in the memory of the oldest man of our tribe. Always prisoners have been sacrificed without problems. The priestess of the Great Goddess tells us that the Mother has spared you for a reason, but cannot say what that reason is." The chief shook his head then leaned forward, a hopeful look on his face. "Do you know the reason? Has the Mother spoken to you?"

Nikometros sat silently as he spoke, thinking hard. "I speak slow, not your language speak well." He paused, gathering his thoughts. "Greeks have many God, Goddesses. We have Chief God, king of God, name Zeus. God of sun, Apollo. God of sea, Poseidon. Also, have Goddesses. One who is huntress; strong Goddess of wild place is Artemis. I think Great Goddess is Artemis."

The chief leaned forward again. "If your Artemis is the Great Goddess, why does She save you? What has your Artemis to do with you?"

"Mother of my mother offer at shrine of Artemis when girl. Given this." Nikometros touched his armband. "Mother tell me it old image of Artemis, hunter Goddess. Mother gives to me."

A half-suppressed sigh went through the group of seated men. Spargises nodded and muttered something to the man beside him. The man rose at once and left the hut.

"So, we wait," said the chief. "Your men," he said to Nikometros after a pause. "Do not look the same as you. You have hair like gold and are as tall as me. Your men are shorter and dark haired. Yet, they fight for you. Are they both from your tribe?"

"This is Timon, son of Kerobates." Nikometros gestured. "He is Macedonian cavalryman, like me. In my land, he lives near, on horse farm in village called Messa near city called Pella. Not what you call same tribe, not kin, but close." He turned to look at his other companion. "This Mardes, son of Oxartes. He Persian volunteer. Join me half year. Good horseman. Fight with Macedonians now."

Spargises now looked closely at Mardes. A man sitting next to him said something in a low voice. Spargises turned to Nikometros, laughing. "Ah, Persian. We fight the Persians sometimes. It is always good sport. We attack, they run away. Now you new people come from the West conquering the Persians. Then you attack us." He shook his head then continued more seriously. "We fight you people sometimes...but always at a time of our choosing. This is our land. When your people have given up and returned to your homes, this will still be our land."

Nikometros remembered when the Macedonian forces first entered Scythian country. The empty rolling plains seemed heaven-sent for the mobile cavalry of the Greeks but the Scythians melted away in front of them. Try as they might, the Greek army could not bring them to battle. The Scythians preferred to harass the Macedonian infantry and baggage trains with lightning raids. In the end, Alexander offered to his gods and marched on, leaving small numbers of troops under experienced junior officers. A handful of men trying to control a hostile country larger than all of Greece. *I wonder if our commanders have any real idea of the nature of our foe,* he thought.

The hide curtain over the door was pulled to one side, admitting the priestess Tomyra, five warriors walking attendance on her. A long plain robe covered her from head to foot, a circlet of gold in her raven hair alone proclaiming her rank. She glanced at where Nikometros and his men sat, but her face remained impassive as she crossed the hut and stopped in front of the chief. "Greetings father. How may the Great Goddess help the People?" she enquired.

"Greetings daughter...and priestess. I have need of you to speak to the Goddess for the People. I have discussed this unprecedented situation with my counselors. They cannot agree. Never before has the sacrifice overcome the Mother's champion. I would have you cast the willow sticks for me. Tell me what the future holds for the People and this man."

Tomyra gave a small bow and then turned to look at the barbarian. Her deep green eyes bored into his blue ones as if seeking to read his soul, but her face remained impassive, remote. She turned away, walked calmly to the far side of the chief and sat down, cross-legged on the carpet. Removing a small bundle from the folds of her gown, she carefully undid the wrappings and rearranged the contents. She bowed her head, becoming very still, and Spargises and his counselors shifted uneasily, watching her.

Time dragged out and Timon started fidgeting. "What's happening?" he whispered to Nikometros.

"I think she's going into a trance. I've seen priests do this before but they usually drug themselves with smoke first." Nikometros watched as a tremor rippled through her body, and the shadows in the hut seemed to gather around her. Nikometros shivered. "There is power here, I can feel it," he muttered.

Tomyra lifted her head. Her eyes snapped open but remained oddly expressionless. She picked up the contents of the bundle with her left hand, revealing twenty short bare willow sticks, glistening wetly in the firelight. Raising her right hand she muttered a few phrases and lightly tossed the sticks to the ground in front of her. Spargises and his advisors leaned forward eagerly, trying to read the message lying there in front of them, but Tomyra seemed to just pick idly at the sticks, moving one or two, removing another. She raised her head and looked at Spargises, speaking in a monotone, as if from a great distance.

"The Mother Sea. A tribe without a head. A king. Conquest. Change." Tomyra fell silent, picking up the sticks with her left hand. She raised her right hand again and muttered some more phrases and Nikometros stiffened as he heard her mention his name. She threw the sticks and bent forward, stirring them with her forefinger.

"From the blood of kings comes a warrior of the People. Great glory. A golden king lies in his future. Death, and..." She looked up, a look of shock on her face. "I...I cannot see more. The Mother hides her face."

Spargises stirred and coughed. His face reflected worry as he whispered to his advisors. One of them argued quietly but with vigour, waving his arms in agitation. The chief looked back at his daughter. "Priestess, you have, to my mind, prophesied both good and ill. What do your words mean?"

Tomyra sat still, visibly collecting her thoughts before arising and addressing the group. "I see the People moving north to the Mother Sea, warfare with northern tribes. A tribe of the People is without a leader. I see a king and new lands for the People, and great changes." She looked down at her father fondly. "Do not be concerned, Spargises son of Masades, the Great Goddess holds you dear. You are neither the leader who is lost, nor your tribe the one without a leader. For you, I see glory all your days." A shadow crossed her face. "Changes will come after you and I fear for the future of the People."

Spargises greeted the news with a broad smile. Around him, his advisors nodded and chattered. Tomyra turned to Nikometros, a strange look on her face. Her voice cut through the noise.

"For you, Nikomayros of the Greeks, I see great dangers and great glories. A warrior you are and a warrior you will be. A great king of gold lies in your future. In addition, deaths, many deaths...and other things. The Goddess clouds the future here."

Nikometros felt the hairs rising on his forearms. He shivered, feeling the shadows in the hut beat around him. The power in her voice was not that of a young woman but of a priestess in the grip of divine prophecy. Unlike many Macedonians, he believed that the Gods of other races were as real as his own. When the opportunity arose, he sacrificed to his own gods and to the gods of other people. Who knew where luck might come from? *What does she see in my future? She is hiding something.*

Spargises cleared his throat and got to his feet, his counselors rising with him. "The words of the Goddess are pleasing, daughter." Turning, he went on, "Nikomayros of the Greeks, it seems the Mother holds you dear. Your future lies with the People. Much glory and much gold...for your king." He smiled

54

broadly, rubbing his hands together. Looking at his advisors he continued, "Have I not always said that great things would come to the People under my leadership? Now the Great Goddess sends a mighty warrior to the tribe, one who will bring glory and gold." He laughed loudly. "By all the Gods and Goddesses, he took Araxes unarmed. Could the People ask for a better warrior?" Turning back to Nikometros, he looked serious again. "Nikomayros, you must be made one of the People. Our ways will be your ways, our Gods will be your Gods, our enemies will be your enemies, our friends..."

Nikometros felt uneasy as Spargises went on. He held up one hand and waited until the flow of enthusiasm slowed and dried up. "I aware of honour done to me and my men," he said slowly. "However, I am a Macedonian officer, I cannot join a people who war with mine. I will not fight against my people."

Spargises frowned, and a babble of comment broke out behind him. "You are choosing not to be one of the People? You cannot refuse this honour. The Mother has chosen you. You must join. You no longer have other people."

"I am sorry, my lord," Nikometros bowed slightly, "I cannot join your people if it means breaking faith with my people and my gods." He waited, holding himself erect. Behind him, he heard mutters of agreement from Timon and Mardes.

A look of baffled fury came over the chief. "No! You will make your oath to the People or die. If you refuse this honour then we have mistaken the will of the Goddess. We will sacrifice you again." At a gesture, the warriors raced to their sides, gripping Nikometros and his men.

"Father. My lord, please wait." Tomyra crossed to her father's side and gently put her hand on his arm. "There is another way. If you will but hear my voice, I believe we can all obey the will of the Mother and travel on the path to glory."

Spargises growled and shook her hand off his arm. He glowered at Nikometros then turned and sat down again. Nodding at Tomyra, he waved a hand in her direction.

"Very well then. Tell me of this other way."

"My lord, this day we saw this man," she pointed to Nikometros, "A great warrior, defeating the champion of the Goddess, turning his own arms against him. We saw by the casting of the sticks how the Goddess chooses him to be one of the People. He says only that he will not fight his own people, the Greeks, nor be unfaithful to his gods. I ask him 'If you are never asked to fight your people, never asked to forsake your gods, will you join us?'" She looked at Nikometros, a silent plea in her guarded expression.

He thought over her words carefully before addressing Spargises again. "I not fight against my people. I not break faith with my gods. Nor I ask my comrades to do so. I will not shift on that. In all other ways I be of the People until I go back to own land. I take oath if you agree."

Spargises looked thoughtful. One of his counselors bent and whispered in his ear. He nodded. "Daughter, the western barbarians attack the People as they move about their own land. How can he be a true member of the People and not fight them? In honour."

"Father, the sticks tell of the People moving north to the Mother Sea. If we move north early – now – we will not encounter the western barbarians. An oath given by this man, by Nikomayros, can be held in honour by all."

Her father contemplated her words for a long moment then grinned suddenly.

"Daughter, you are worth ten of my counselors." Some of the men behind him scowled at his words. "It shall be so. This man shall be made a brother. He and his men will not fight their own people. They may keep their gods if they wish. We will move north to find glory and gold." He gestured at the warriors holding Nikometros. They stepped back, bowed and moved to their places. "Bring wine. The oath shall be taken!" he shouted. A guard detached himself from the others and ducked out of the hut. Spargises turned to his advisors and spoke in a low voice, using emphatic gestures. They bowed in turn and stepped back a few paces. Nikometros turned to Timon and Mardes, who stood just behind him, looking worried.

"Sir, you know I will follow you anywhere," muttered Timon, "but I don't feel comfortable joining these savages. I cannot give aid to the enemies of our people. I won't be a traitor."

"Nor I, sir," agreed Mardes. "My gods are not the gods of these savages. I cannot sacrifice to false gods. I'm not a Macedonian but I have sworn an oath of loyalty to the Great King, whether Persian or Macedonian. I won't be foresworn."

Nikometros nodded and held up his hand. "I understand. I ask only for your trust on this. They don't ask, and I won't ask you to worship any gods but your own, nor fight any of your own people. I won't ask you to act in any way against our own countrymen. I will, if you agree, act for you with these people. We shall return to our own some day, I swear."

57

Timon nodded at his words. "All right sir. I can go along with that. As long as they don't ask me to make a sacrifice to one of their heathen gods, eh Mardes?"

"Yes. Sir, I agree with Timon. I must keep my own gods but I will keep faith with you."

"Thank you, Timon, Mardes. We'll find our path through this and return to our homes, if the gods will."

A commotion at the doorway drew everyone's attention. The warrior who had been sent out for wine entered bearing a wineskin, closely followed by the chief's son, Areipithes. He strode into the hut, a thunderous look on his face. He stopped, gazed round at the counselors and then crossed to Spargises, halting just in front of him.

"Has everyone in this tribe lost their minds?" he hissed. "They tell me you mean to bring this barbarian offal into the People, to make him one of us."

"You forget yourself, Areipithes. How dare you question my decisions? Have you forgotten I am your father and your chief?"

"When you endanger the People then I question your decisions. These men," he gestured at the group of counselors and warriors, "Follow you like cattle. But they know I lead the tribe at war while you stay in Urul. When I am chief..."

Spargises stepped forward and grasped his son by his tunic, pushing him back.

"You whelp," he growled. "You will never be chief if you cannot lead in peace as well as in war. You know the People choose their own chief. Being my son does not give you the right to be chief. The People will choose the best man to lead them...after I am gone. Remember that, Areipithes. As long as I live...I am chief and you will obey me." Spargises thrust him back then added softly, "Unless you think you can best me in battle."

Areipithes stood shaking with emotion. With an effort he took control of himself and calmed down, looked up at his father who towered above him. A thin smile appeared on his face, though his eyes remained cold. "Of course you are right father. You are chief still. I will obey your wishes." He glanced at Tomyra. "If they are, in fact, your wishes, or has my sister been leading you along with her personal interpretations again?" He looked Tomyra up and down. "I see you are still infatuated with this barbarian," he sneered. "You tread a dangerous path, sister. Well, we shall see." Areipithes turned to his father once more. "With your permission I will withdraw. I feel unclean in the presence of so many live barbarians." He nodded at the counselors then turned and strode out of the hut.

Spargises stared after him, his face showing a mixture of anger and sorrow.

"If he wasn't my son..." he sighed. He turned to Nikometros. "I'm sure he will come to accept the decision of the Goddess in time." Spargises gestured towards the warrior with the wine. "Bring the wine and the sacred vessel." Turning to Tomyra, he held out his hand. "You have the sacred knife, daughter?"

Tomyra produced a short dagger from her cloak and handed it to him. The warrior came across the hut, holding a sloshing wine bag and an ornate horn cup. Spargises took the horn and lovingly stroked it, the gold and silver images on it gleaming in the firelight. He handed it to Tomyra. The warrior undid the stopper on the wine bag and poured a stream of rich red wine into the horn. The sharp sour smell of the wine made Nikometros' mouth clench. Spargises took the dagger in his right hand, holding his left arm out toward Tomyra. The metal flashed and dark blood welled on his forearm, and he held it out above the horn, watching as the blood dripped into the wine. After a moment he let his arm drop, ignoring the blood as it continued to flow.

"Come," he said, turning to Nikometros.

Nikometros stepped up to the chief and bared his arm. Spargises ran the tip of the dagger lightly across his forearm, blood flowing behind the blade and into the cup underneath. Nikometros stepped back, letting the blood slowly congeal in rivulets between his fingers.

Spargises slipped the dagger into the mixture of wine and blood. The dagger clattered against the sides of the horn cup as he stirred. "Bring the weapon of the warrior Nikomayros," he cried.

One of the guards rummaged at one side of the hut. Nikometros recognised his sword in the man's hands.

Spargises took the sword and dipped the tip of it in the cup. As he removed it, the glistening drops of wine and blood ran down the iron blade. Despite himself, Nikometros shivered slightly at the symbolism. The chief drew his own sword and repeated the action, laying both blades down at Tomyra's feet. She held the cup aloft and in a low voice intoned an oddly cadenced prayer to the Gods of the tribe.

Nikometros tried to catch what she said but her voice was too low to catch more than the odd word. He recognised an invocation to the Great Goddess and strange names. *They must be the names of other gods*, he thought as the prayer droned on. Nikometros felt his head start to swim and his vision blurred. The walls of the hut slowly receded. He saw, within a mist,

Tomyra in the arms of a tall man. He felt the stirrings of jealousy then with a shock he saw the man with Tomyra was himself – an older self but there could be no mistake. The scene misted over as he heard his name called repeatedly.

"Nikomayros...Nikomayros..." Spargises looked at him strangely. "Come Nikomayros, it is time to take our oaths."

Nikometros shook his head, dismissing the vision. "I am ready, Spargises son of Masades. What form do oaths take?"

"Listen to what I say then repeat my words. Change the names though." He grinned. "Hold up the cup of Oaths when you speak, and look our priestess in the eye. When you swear, you are swearing for yourself only. I take this oath of brotherhood with you alone, not your men. I am a chief, I do not take this oath with common men. They will be bound by their oaths of loyalty to you as their chief. You understand?"

Nikometros nodded and listened attentively as Spargises started his oath.

"Hear me Great Goddess; hear me Gods of the People. I, Spargises son of Masades of the Massegetae swear allegiance to the death to Nikomayros of the Greeks. I hold his ways to be my ways, his friends to be my friends, his enemies to be my enemies. He enters my household as one of my family, my goods are his goods, my horses his horses. He is my brother in all things. He will fight by my side in battle. His arm will be my shield and my arm will be his shield. I will lose an arm, an eye, or my life before I let harm come to my blood brother. I swear this before all my gods. Let my shade wander without rest if I break this oath." Spargises stepped back and smiling, waved Nikometros forward.

Nikometros stepped up to Tomyra and placed his right hand on the cup. His fingers brushed hers and a tremor ran through her body, bringing a flush to her cheeks. Nikometros locked his eyes with hers. "I, Nikometros son of Leonnatos of the Macedonians do swear allegiance..." His memory brought the phrases to his mind without effort. Nikometros gazed into her deep green eyes as he spoke. He felt as if he talked to her alone, as if he swore allegiance to her. "...before all my gods. May my shade wander forever if I break my oath." He smiled, letting his fingers brush against hers softly as he withdrew.

Spargises moved alongside Nikometros and took the horn cup from Tomyra. He knelt on the floor, pulling Nikometros down beside him. "Now we drink to seal our oaths. It is important that we drink together, so come close." He laughed at Nikometros' expression. "We are brothers, Nikomayros! Come, embrace me."

Nikometros grinned and put his arm around the chief. Taking the cup in his other hand, he raised it to his lips. His face pressed up against Spargises' bristly moustache and he caught a faint odour of meat and milk on the chief's breath. Spargises tipped the cup and the mixture of blood and wine gushed into both mouths. Nikometros swallowed, tasting the sourness of the wine and the slimy smoothness of blood. He felt a moment of nausea but suppressed it, swallowing again. The red liquid spilled out around their mouths, cascading over chins, staining garments. As the last of the blood and wine left the cup, Spargises lowered it and belched loudly.

Rising to his feet, Spargises hauled Nikometros up and swung him around to face the knot of men standing around the walls of the hut. "Behold my brother Nikomayros. Now bring more wine, koumiss...and meat. Let us feast together to honour my new brother!"

At once, voices broke out in excited conversation, the news being carried beyond the confines of the chief's hut, spreading among the people outside. Men moved to take meat off spits, to carve it and to pour out wine for the chief and his guests and fermented milk for the Scythian counselors and warriors. Nikometros raised a hand to his mouth and belched discreetly. He looked at Timon and Mardes – the older man nodded his approval, the younger man grinned and looked appreciatively at the roasting meats. A warrior brought them a platter heaped high with smoking joints of beef and barley bread. Nikometros' mouth started watering and he realised how hungry he felt.

So, it starts, he thought. *And only the gods know where it will end.*

Chapter Five

"Ho, barbarian! Are you going to sleep all day?"

Nikometros groaned and rolled onto his back. He opened his eyes and instantly regretted it. The early morning light stabbed into his head, sending his senses reeling. *Gods, how much did I drink last night?* he thought. He sat up slowly, and looked around, rubbing one hand over the golden stubble on his chin. *Where are the others?* Nikometros occupied a more richly appointed hut than the one he shared with Timon and Mardes the day before – the rugs and furs on the floors were of far better quality.

The languid voice came again from the doorway. "Barbarian, are you going to waste the whole day?"

A Scythian warrior stood framed against the sunlight. His short, stocky body, dressed in the usual tunic and felt trousers, partially blocked the bright morning sun. His hair hung long and dark, merging with a luxuriant beard and moustache.

Nikometros struggled to his feet. He rubbed his eyes and yawned. "Where are my men?"

The man looked at him. "They are well. They have been up since daybreak earning a living. Spargises told me to look after you, show you the tribe. I am Partaxes. The man you killed yesterday, Araxes, was my mother's sister's son."

Nikometros tensed, his hand slipping to his waist in search of a weapon. His eyes searched the man's face, trying to read his intentions.

Partaxes looked amused. "I do not seek your life, barbarian. You fought well. Araxes died honourably, as a gift to the Goddess. I must tell you though, that not all feel as I do. Some among us think taking you in is a mistake." He shrugged and thrust out his hand, "Come, the day is wasting."

Nikometros smiled uncertainly and extended his own hand. He grasped the man by his forearm briefly. "I need...not know name...midden?" He mimicked his actions of the other day. Partaxes roared with laughter and clapped him on the shoulder, pointing. Nikometros hurried off, guided by his nose.

He returned a few minutes later to find Partaxes sitting by the hut. He rose and handed Nikometros a cup of sour milk, a slice of meat and a hunk of bread.

"Your name is what...Nikomayros? I heard it last night, but these impossible barbarian names are hard to remember and more difficult still to pronounce."

"Nikometros." he said. "Nikomayros close enough. What we do now?" He swallowed the last of the meat and bread, drained the cup of sour milk.

"Spargises told me to show you anything you want. What do you want to see?"

"Where are my men, Timon and Mardes? I like to see them first, make sure they all right."

"They are well, working in the horse lines. If you are concerned, we can go there. Come." Partaxes swiveled on his heel and set out towards a gap in the earthworks. The two men strode along in the bright morning sun, weaving through groups of busy men and women, the rich smells of massed humanity strong in their nostrils.

A small crowd of children soon attached themselves to Nikometros' heels, chattering and pointing. Nikometros found it difficult to tell boys and girls apart. Almost everyone he saw wore a tunic and trousers. The children tumbled and leaped around, laughing and playing, their long hair swinging. "What they saying, Partaxes? I cannot understand them."

Partaxes grunted. "They think perhaps you are a woman, or maybe a gelding. You are clean shaven and wear a skirt like some barbarian women." He turned and spoke gruffly to them, cuffing one of the older boys lightly. They grinned and raced off, laughing and shouting. "I ask you to forgive their lack of manners, Nikomayros."

"They are only children, Partaxes. I do not take offence at the words of children."

He nodded and smiled. "Children are a delight. At least other men's children. Do you have children, Nikomayros?"

Nikometros shrugged. "Not that I know. At least no girl was unwilling..." He turned towards Partaxes and smiled. "One day when I have conquered lands and have much riches then I marry and raise many sons."

Partaxes nodded. "Yes, a man needs riches to support a wife and children. I have good mares that produce many foals. I shall marry soon, I think."

The two men continued walking toward a gap in the earthworks. On the far side of the gap, they came to rough lean-tos, housing no more than fifty horses. Nikometros looked round. "Are these all?" he asked, puzzled. "I thought tribe have many horses."

Partaxes shook his head. "No, Nikomayros, these are only the horses that are sick or ready to foal. We look after them here. The main herds are out there somewhere." Partaxes pointed out to the horizon. "There is little food for them close to Urul. Soon we must move north again. Already we must go out two days travel to find good pasture."

"That is something else I wish to ask. I thought Scythians were nomadic people, yet you live in a city – in Urul."

Partaxes snorted. "We are Massegetae. Maybe other Scythians live in cities, but we do not."

Nikometros looked back through the gap in the earthworks. "Yet here you are – living in a city."

"Urul is for short time, Nikomayros, not for always. It is winter place – you understand? When snow covers grass, we come back here to trade and...and...how you say? Make things new again? Mend?"

"Refurbish your equipment?"

Partaxes screwed up his face. "Maybe. I not know Greek words."

Nikometros moved down the horse lines, examining horses and equipment. He found Mardes about halfway down the lines, in a stall with an expectant mare. "Mardes," he exclaimed. "What happened to you last night? Where is Timon?"

Mardes looked up, a delighted look on his face. "Hello sir. Good to see you. We slept in the main barracks with the chief's bodyguard. They seem a good sort, for all I can't understand a word they say." He got to his feet and looked around. "Timon is here too, somewhere. It seems our duty is to be with the horses. Suits me, I've always loved working with horses."

"How do you get on if you can't understand them?" Nikometros asked.

"Oh, signs usually. I think some of them understand a bit of Persian if I talk slowly too. One of the guards, Scoles, understands quite a bit. He's around here somewhere too. Ah...here's Timon, sir."

Nikometros looked around and saw Timon walking towards them, wiping his hands on a cloth. Bits of straw clung to his clothing. A strong but pleasant smell of horses wafted from him as he approached. A small Scythian walked beside him.

"Greetings sir. Things are looking up, aren't they?"

"I think so, Timon. Are they taking care of you?"

"Yes sir. Food's good, bread and meat, some vegetables. The sour milk they drink is a bit hard to take though. Some of it smells as if it's been fermented. I thought after last night it was going to be wine every day." Timon laughed. "They're a bit odd in some ways too. They think it's a real joke how you bested that man yesterday." He shook his head. "This is Idanthes, by the way." Timon waved in the general direction of the other man. Idanthes nodded his head slightly but said nothing. "He looks after me." Timon glanced in his direction, lowering his voice. "I'm not sure if he's here as a guide or a guard." He shrugged. "Well, we must all make the best of it I suppose. If you have any influence here sir, would you ask them to give me other work? There's an injured horse back there that needs attention but all they'll tell me is, it's lame. I'd really like to work on weapons sir. I know metals. I used to be an armourer."

"All right, Timon. I'll mention it to the chief when I see him next."

"Thank you sir." Timon saluted and turned to leave.

Mardes stepped forward, an eager expression on his face. "I'd like to have a look at this lame horse, Timon." He left with Timon, disappearing into one of the stalls. Idanthes muttered something under his breath and followed.

Partaxes touched Nikometros on the arm. "Come Nikomayros. Let us go on, we have much to see."

"All right. By the way, do you know what became of my horse? The big golden stallion I was riding?"

"A fine animal." Partaxes nodded approvingly. "The priestess claimed it when you were captured. Is it one of your family's horses from your homeland?"

"No. It's army mount, but I ride it for nearly two years. We used to each other. I'd like to get him back."

"You must talk to the chief then, or the priestess."

Nikometros nodded and walked slowly on down the horse lines, looking at the activities of the horses and men. Every stall was filled. A few men busied themselves attending, grooming or feeding them. One or two mucked out the stalls, sweeping the soiled grass and straw into piles.

"Sir, sir!" Mardes came running out of the stall. "There's a horse in there, sir. It's a magnificent sorrel stallion in there and they want to kill it. He's not..."

"Slow down. Explain yourself."

"Yes sir. The stallion is lame. At first they thought it might just be a sprain or something, but it's not. Now they don't know what's wrong, so they're going to slaughter him. Stop them! I know what's wrong. I can cure him." Mardes hopped up and down with excitement.

Nikometros turned to Partaxes. "Did you understand that?"

"Not all of it. He thinks stallion may not be lame?" He started for the stall, the other two following. Idanthes stepped out, talking so fast and animatedly Nikometros could not follow the conversation. Partaxes pointed at Mardes and said a few words in reply. Idanthes threw up his hands, a disgusted look on his face. Partaxes spoke again, drawing a reluctant nod from the other man. "He thinks it a waste of time but will let your man tend the horse. It is a favourite of

69

Spargises and Idanthes will gain much favour if your man can cure it."

"Are you sure you can cure the horse, Mardes?"

"I think so, sir. Someone fed him too much grain, perhaps because he's the chief's horse. The rich diet enlarged the blood flow in his hoof, making him lame. With rest and the proper attention, I'm sure he'll improve."

"Do your best then. It may be important. If you need anything, get word to me and I'll try to arrange it."

"Thank you sir."

The joy on Mardes' face brought a smile to Nikometros' face. He watched as the others disappeared into the stall again, and then turned and walked on until he came to the end of the double line of stalls. The rough path continued along the outside of the earthworks. Nikometros turned to Partaxes as he wandered up.

"I am surprised your men would not know how to cure a lame horse," observed Nikometros. "I thought Scythians lived with horses so much they knew everything about them."

Partaxes grinned and tapped the side of his nose. "Oh, we do, Nikomayros, we do." He chuckled. "The Persian tries so hard to be helpful we allowed him to find something we...er, missed. Now we know he is truly knowledgeable and can be allowed to treat any horse."

Nikometros stared at him for a few moments before allowing a smile to cross his face. He grinned and shook his head. "What other animals have the People? Cattle?"

"The People have great herds of horses, cattle, and goats. Some sheep too. Men look after the horses and cattle far away. Boys look after the sheep and goats near Urul. When we move north, they will move with us." Partaxes moved off down the path. The wind shifted, bringing the scent of blood. "We slaughter the animals over there," he said, pointing ahead. "The People have big appetites," he laughed. "Tell me, Nikomayros, do your people herd horses too?"

"We have horses, yes. Fine horses, bigger than Scythian ones. War horses like my golden stallion. Perhaps not as many. My family owns large farm, not wander with herds."

"You are farmers?" A horrified look came over Partaxes' face. "Here only the weak farm. Those who cannot be warriors. The People are warriors; we herd the wild horses. Do you come from a weak people, Nikomayros?"

"Not weak. Macedon is land very...I not know word. Land up and down. Hills and rivers. No plains for herds. Most people live in cities."

"Cities? Like Urul?"

"Bigger. Many, many people live together in one place. All of Urul would be only small part." Nikometros stopped, thinking hard. "It is difficult to explain. I not have many words to tell. I must learn words."

The two men continued down the path toward the slaughter area. The stench of blood and ordure filled their nostrils, and the buzzing of the ever-present flies became louder. A small herd of lowing cattle milled about in a rough wooden pen. As they watched, two men hauled a protesting cow from the pen and held it while another man dispatched it with a blow from a large bronze hammer. At once, another group of men dragged it away. They hauled it up on a frame and started butchering it. Blood soaked the ground. Ni-

71

kometros and Partaxes picked their way through piles of meat and offal, disturbing black swarms of flies. Some haunches of meat off to one side caught Nikometros' eye.

"Partaxes, do the People eat horse? I know horses must be killed if they are injured badly but I thought People hold horse in too much honour to eat."

"That is true. We hold them in high honour. For us the horse means life. He carries our men into battle and he carries our women and children in peace. We milk the mares so they provide sustenance. When a chief dies, his horses are sacrificed to aid him in the afterlife. Horses are wealth but when they grow old, or are injured badly, we kill and eat them. Nothing goes to waste; we use the meat, hides, and sinews."

A steady stream of young boys moved among the steaming piles of meat. Each boy picked up a large piece and carried it back to town. Curious, Nikometros followed them. Inside the earthworks, the meat cooked over large smoky fires. Several women tended the fires. They watched him discreetly as he approached. Nikometros noticed younger children at play nearby. "Partaxes, do children not go to...to place to learn?"

"Children learn all the time. Even when they play, they learn. Watch them. See? Some play with bows or sticks, learning to fight. Others learn how to look after horses and cattle or help slaughter and carry meat. Even girls learn. They cook and mend clothes like their mothers."

"Does no one learn from books or scrolls? What about writing, public speaking?"

"Nikomayros, you are a strange man," laughed Partaxes. "Why should a warrior need to write? Will it help him fight? Can a scroll feed a man or carry him into battle? We can all speak, even the women, especially the women." Shaking his head, he went on. "You must ask the Chief about our Priestess if you like writing. She has many scrolls I think."

"I do that Partaxes. I think it good to learn talk your tongue better. Where chief is now, know you?"

"I do not know. He may be in the place of the..., we shall go and see." Partaxes used another word Nikometros did not understand. He followed, hoping to find out the meaning of the word from their destination.

They moved back into the town, deeper into the warren of lanes and alleyways. The wooden huts huddled closer, as if sharing a secret and the stench of humans living close together assailed their nostrils. Crowds of people thronged the streets, talking and arguing. Most fell silent and turned to look as they passed. He noticed quite a few unfriendly looks. Merchants and sellers plied their trades along the edges of the streets, even inside the houses. Others bought goods, led livestock, showing off crafts, arguing, bartering and jostling good-naturedly.

"Ah, there is someone who will know where Spargises is today," said Partaxes, touching his arm. "Ho, Areipithes! We would talk with you." He waved vigorously at a small group of men passing by on the other side of the street.

Areipithes stopped and looked around. He walked slowly over to Nikometros and Partaxes. The crowd fell silent, watching warily. The men with Areipithes spread out on both sides of him, hands resting on their swords. They stared at Nikometros coldly. Areipithes looked Nikometros up and down, scowling then turned to Partaxes.

73

"Playing nursemaid to the barbarian, Partaxes? I thought when he butchered your cousin that you'd demand his life. It seems I misjudged your sense of honour. Perhaps you should be left behind with the farmers when we move north. Honour and the company of warriors obviously does not suit you."

Partaxes paled and stepped forward. "Areipithes, you dare to speak to me of honour? You know as I do, Araxes met an honourable death. He went to the Goddess as a warrior. If you think I am a coward then let us settle the matter now."

Areipithes smiled thinly. His men stepped forward, half drawing their swords. Areipithes waved them back. "Another time, Partaxes. I have pressing business." He turned to Nikometros, his face blank. "So it seems my father now calls you brother. Enjoy the honour while you can, barbarian. My father and my sister use you for their own purpose. When they have finished with you, I will kill you."

Nikometros responded to the threat without thinking, drawing himself up straight and moving close to the chief's son. Areipithes stepped back then checked himself. The men with him shifted again, drawing closer to their master, their eyes locking onto Nikometros' face. With an effort, Nikometros controlled his anger. He thought for a moment, searching his memory for the right phrases. "I hold your father in high regard, Areipithes, as I do everyone deserving of honour," he said slowly.

"Pah! What does a barbarian know of honour? You dishonour the People with your every word. Chatter in your own barbarian tongue and keep company with the women and townsmen. You do not belong with the People." He spun on his heel and stalked off, the crowd of onlookers scattering in front of him as his bodyguard pushed their way through.

I shall have to be very careful with this man, Nikometros thought. The silent mass of men and women around him started to remember their own business and moved away, conversation starting up again. Both Nikometros and Partaxes glared at the retreating back of Areipithes.

Pent-up rage suffused the Scythian's features, his eyes glittered with hate and his fists clenched by his sides. "He will insult me once too often," he growled. "One of these days I will avenge those words."

"He is dangerous man, I think. How is the son of your chief regarded by the People?"

"The People are divided on this. Spargises is a great warrior and leads us well but he has changed. When his wife died two years ago, he ceased to lead in war. The honour fell to Areipithes. Many now would follow him and abandon the father. I would not. He holds his own desires above the needs of his people." Partaxes cleared his throat and spat. "Come, we will find Spargises."

A few minutes questioning passers-by revealed the information that the chief was in the street of the armourers. Nikometros followed as Partaxes led the way down the street. They turned the corner into another, narrower street, where the rickety houses and huts leaned closer together. The crowds of people thinned out, but those that remained moved with a purposeful air. At the end of the street, strong stone buildings replaced the weaker wooden ones and the clanging of metal on metal assaulted their ears as they drew near. Nikometros stared into the open rooms of the buildings. Small boys knelt with leather bellows, directing streams of air into small stone furnaces.

Soot-blackened men bent low over the fierce fires. They drew forth glowing metal and beat it upon iron anvils, then plunged the hot blades into tubs of stale urine. The stench was almost intolerable and Nikometros felt deafened by the clamour. Even at a distance, sweat burst out on his face and arms from the waves of heated air.

Partaxes tugged on his sleeve and pointed. Nikometros saw Spargises and another man in close conversation near one of the forges. Spargises looked up as they approached, his mouth moving but the noise around them drowned out his words. Nikometros pointed to his ears and shook his head. Spargises leaned closer to the metalworker's head and shouted. The man nodded and turned away. Spargises beckoned to Partaxes and Nikometros, leading them out into the street.

"Nikomayros, my brother." Spargises grasped Nikometros by his forearms then stepped back. "Is Partaxes showing you our ways?"

"Thank you, yes." Nikometros nodded. "But I have problem with words. Need someone teach me language of People right. Also must have my horse. Is possible?"

Spargises nodded. "I think you are right, blood brother. Sometimes you are hard to understand. I will ask my daughter to teach you. She has much learning." He smiled. "You will also have to ask her about your horse. She claimed it as spoils of war." Turning to Partaxes, he said "Bring him to the priestess' hut this evening."

"Spargises...brother. I need ask two other things. I need water to wash." Nikometros lifted his arm, sniffed and grimaced. "I smell like goat."

Spargises laughed. "Washing! We do not use our water for washing, not unless we are near a river." He wiped his eyes with the back of his hand. "Partaxes will bring you some cleansing ointment and instruct you in its use." He laughed again at the expression on Nikometros' face. "We do not have enough water to waste in washing but our way is good, blood brother. Try it. And the other thing?"

"My man Timon is metalsmith, armourer. He like to work here making weapons, instead of with horses. I say to him I ask you."

Spargises waved his hand dismissively. "I will have a man see to it." He moved back to the forge and took up his shouted conversation with the ironsmith.

Nikometros shrugged and looked inquiringly at Partaxes. Together they walked back up the street. *Well, I have my teacher*, he thought. For some reason, his heart beat faster as he thought about seeing Tomyra again.

Chapter Six

Nikometros peered into the shiny copper plate. An indistinct face gazed back at him. He ran his fingers through an unruly shock of blond hair, trying to put it into some order. His face felt raw where his knife had scraped, but the golden bristles had disappeared. *At least I feel clean*, he thought. The cleansing ointment left his skin tingling and smelling sweet, but he felt sticky despite this and wished he had enough water for a proper wash. He brushed ruefully at his tunic. *Now if I can find some way to clean this...*A cough from the doorway interrupted his thoughts. Nikometros looked up.

Partaxes stood there with a smile on his face. "If I didn't know you for a fighter I'd wonder about you with that hairless face."

Nikometros grinned. "Where I come from, trousers considered soft and effeminate. I've learned better here." He walked over and clapped Partaxes on the shoulder. "So, have you come to insult me or fetch me to my lessons?"

"The priestess awaits you, Nikomayros." Partaxes gave an exaggerated bow, sweeping his hand towards the doorway. The smile dropped from his face. "A word of caution though. Have a care how you address her. The person of the priestess is considered inviolate. An insult or even a hand laid on her may carry the death penalty."

"I will take care, Partaxes. Know that I hold the priestess of the Great Goddess in the highest honour," replied Nikometros seriously. "Shall we go?"

Their breath plumed the cold night air. Nikometros looked up to where the inky night sky was liberally strewn with stars and a milky band of light spanned the heavens. He drew in a deep breath and exhaled slowly, watching his breath drifting to merge with the stars. "They take me back to my boyhood. I remember my tutor telling me about the fixed stars and the wanderers. He told me, that band of light..." He swept his hand across the sky. "...was the path to the palace of Zeus, the king of the gods. It always used to point to my grandfather's farm and I thought for years he was really Zeus."

Partaxes laughed. "Here we call it the milk of the Goddess. Our children are told how she streams it across the sky each night to guide her People."

"It's as good a story as any. Who but the gods can say what the stars really are?"

They resumed walking. The chill air bit into Nikometros' bare arms and legs. *It's getting cold. I'm going to need a cloak before long.* He swung his arms briskly and picked up the pace. In a few minutes, they came to a large hut with a welcoming flood of yellow light pouring through the doorway. A guard stood outside and challenged them as they approached.

"It's alright, Lyartes," Partaxes said. "Nikomayros is here for a language lesson."

Lyartes examined Nikometros suspiciously in the light from a burning torch. "Wait here. I will announce you." He ducked inside and was out again a few moments later. "Proceed."

Partaxes led the way inside. "Priestess. Nikomayros the Greek is here," he called.

Nikometros looked around the hut. Rich drapes hung on the walls, hides and carpets covered the floors and a number of wooden boxes and chests lined the walls between the draperies. Cushions were arranged around a clear space in the middle of the hut. Two iron braziers filled with glowing coals sat on opposite sides of the clear space, and several pottery lamps shed a warm buttery glow over the scene. An old woman stood near the back of the tent, regarding the newcomers attentively.

Drapes moved in one corner of the hut. Tomyra emerged from behind them, walking slowly out into the open space in the middle of the hut. The old woman sat down on a cushion near one of the braziers, eyes bright in a wrinkled brown face as she looked at Nikometros with an expression of intense curiosity. Tomyra advanced a few steps further and stood quietly looking at the two men. Partaxes put a knuckle to his forehead and bowed his head briefly. Tomyra tilted her head a fraction in acknowledgement. "You have leave to go. I will send for you when you are needed." Partaxes glanced at Nikometros then turned and left the hut, dropping the curtains back across the doorway as he did so.

Nikometros felt her eyes on him. Without thinking he straightened his back, threw back his shoulders and struck a pose. Then he realised what he was doing and a small smile flitted across his lips. Looking up, he saw an amused expression on Tomyra's face.

"Welcome, Nikomayros son of Leonnatos." Tomyra sat gracefully on an embroidered cushion. "Will you be seated?" She indicated another cushion near her.

Nikometros crossed to her side and sat cross-legged on the cushion. He remembered he was with a woman and hurriedly tugged his tunic down between his thighs. "Thank you...I am sorry, my lady. I do not know how I should address a priestess."

"I have many titles among the People. On ceremonial occasions, I am known as 'Voice of the Goddess' or 'Chosen One'. Less formally, I am called 'Priestess' or 'My Lady'. My father calls me 'daughter' or by my name when others are not around. In private, when we are alone, you may call me Tomyra." Nikometros glanced at the other woman when she said this. She caught his look and added, "Take no notice of my old nurse, Stagora, she is nearly deaf. She has served in my family all her life. Her presence is required for propriety. The Great Goddess is a virgin, as are all her servants. Just being alone in the same hut with a man who is not a close relative would compromise my position."

"Thank you, my lady...Tomyra." Nikometros felt his breath catch in his throat. Her nearness overwhelmed him, setting his heart beating faster. His senses sharpened and he gazed at the deep green eyes opposite him, framed in a pale oval face by raven locks. Though unadorned by gold or jewelry, her regal bearing told him he was in the presence of true royalty. A fragrance of cedar and cypress, mixed with other more exotic perfumes drifted in the still air. Faintly rhythmic sounds came to his notice. Dragging his attention away from Tomyra, he saw the nurse, Stagora, embroidering a small piece of cloth. As she worked, her tongue clicked softly against her teeth. She looked up at Nikometros and gave him a gummy smile. Her eyes twinkled in her wrinkled face.

"My father told me you were to be taught to speak our language properly," said Tomyra. "You already speak it very well for a foreigner. Where did you learn the People's tongue?"

"When our army came north and east into Bactria,...do you know Bactria?" Nikometros paused then as Tomyra nodded, went on. "We followed on the trail of the satrap, the ruler, of the province, Bessos. When our king, Alexander, conquered Bactria, he left behind officers to manage the area. I was wounded and left behind at one of these outposts. I found having knowledge of the people and the languages made my life easier. When Scythians started raiding I learnt their languages as well as I could from captives." Nikometros smiled wryly. "Though if I'd had a better understanding of the guide's dialect, I'd never have been captured."

"You must have a gift for speech. You mispronounce many words and put together some words strangely but I can understand most of what you say."

"Thank you. When I a child I learned speech of other peoples who visited my family at home. In the army I learned some Persian and a little Egyptian."

"I know some Persian and a little Greek too, so that will help us. My mother lived near a Greek colony on the shores of the Great Sea. She was a Sauromantian princess, a priestess of the Goddess. From her, I learned my mother's tongue and a few Greek words." Tomyra paused for a moment, thinking hard. Her lips moved as she rehearsed a sentence. "Ho, barbarian. Put down thy arms. Thou art here without the consent of our queen." She giggled and blushed. "Are you impressed that I can speak Greek?"

Nikometros struggled to keep a straight face but failed. "It is an ancient form, my lady. I have only heard it spoken thus in old plays during the festivals."

Tomyra clapped her hands delightedly. Stagora looked up from her sewing. She saw nothing amiss and bent over her work again.

"Tell me of these plays. I have some old scrolls given to me by my mother. They are in Greek and I can read them but I don't understand all that they mean."

"May I see them, Tomyra? Perhaps I could help you to learn Greek as you help me learn People's speech."

Tomyra leaned across and tapped Stagora on her knee. She gave her a sharp command, with gestures.

Stagora climbed slowly to her feet, grumbling under her breath. The old woman tottered off to a wooden chest across the room. After rummaging around in it she returned clutching an old papyrus scroll in one scrawny fist. She handed it to Tomyra and slowly reseated herself, muttering about old bones and young girls.

Tomyra smiled indulgently and opened the scroll. "She thinks I am still a little girl." She unrolled the papyrus and scanned part of it. "Yes, this is part of it." She traced her finger along the lines of writing as she read from it. "It says '...then rose up the fighting son of Atreus, lord of the wide domains, Agamemnon, furious, his dark heart filled to the brim, blazing with anger, with searing eyes of fire...'" Tomyra wrinkled her brow again. "This man is very angry, but who is he and why is he angry?"

"May I see the scroll, Tomyra?" Nikometros reached out and gently took the papyrus. He looked at it intently for a few moments, unrolling more of it. His lips moved slightly while he read. He looked up with excitement in his eyes. "This is Homer! A very old copy too. The writing uses old letters and phrases, but this is the Homer I had drilled into me as a boy." He dropped the scroll and leapt to his feet, striding back and forth, arms gesturing. "...then Patroklus giving cry to Automedon's team did sally forth to Ilium and to Lycia, blinded in his fatal frenzy — doomed warrior. Had he but heeded Achilles' strict command, yet might he have escaped his doom, and that stark night of death..." Nikometros' voice tailed off and he sat down again, looking bemused. "I am sorry Tomyra. The beauty of Homer and the old poets still rouse a passion in me, although it's been years since I learned it. Seeing it again brought it all back."

"It is beautiful. The words fill me with a joy and a desire to perform great deeds. What do the words mean though? Where is this Ilium? What battle was fought there?"

"It is a story of a war that happened long ago, time out of mind as some say, before my people came to Macedonia. The city of Ilium, the 'topless towers of Ilium', was on the shores of the Euxine Sea. A Greek king waged a war for ten years against it. Homer was a great poet who wrote about this war and what happened to the warriors, the kings and the gods."

"Tell it to me Nikomayros."

"It is a long story. Many nights would pass in its telling. I will tell you about the piece you read out if you like."

"Very well, but first let us have some refreshment." She turned to her nurse again. "Stagora, fetch some food and drink for our guest." The old woman got to her feet again and wandered off behind the drapes. "You may tell me about this piece now but I shall want to hear more of this story another night. Talking to me and explaining it in my language will make you learn too." She looked up when her old nurse returned. "Put it down here, please Stagora."

The old woman bent down and placed two wooden cups and a pottery jug in front of them. She straightened with an effort and wandered off again, muttering.

Tomyra poured a stream of a brownish liquid into the cups and offered one to Nikometros. He sniffed cautiously at his cup. A sour, slightly cheesy odour rose from the liquid. He coughed and drew back. "Gods!" he muttered. He raised the cup again and sipped. The drink tasted alcoholic and tart with a rancid cheese flavor. "What is this?"

"It is called 'koumiss'. We ferment mare's milk and honey." She laughed at Nikometros' expression. "Come, it is a pleasing drink, is it not?"

"It's different." He sipped again. "I suppose one could get used to it." Grimacing, he put the cup down. "I was brought up on wine. Even children drink watered wine in Macedon."

"We seldom drink wine, except in ceremonies and at feasts. The grape does not grow in our lands and it is costly to bring it from the south." She looked around, calling loudly. "Stagora, where are you? We must have some food."

A grumbling voice drifted out from behind the drapes. "I am coming, young mistress. I am old and cannot move fast enough to please you any more. Soon I shall pass on to my ancestors and you will forget old Stagora..."

Tomyra smiled. "She grumbles a lot but I love her as a mother." A shadow crossed her face and her voice faltered. She looked across at Nikometros, her eyes glistening moistly. Taking a deep breath, she exhaled slowly, calming herself.

"Now come, Nikomayros, tell me of this Agamemnon and why he is angry."

"First I must set the scene. Imagine, the war has lasted for nine years and the Greek army, led by Agamemnon, is no nearer capturing the city than when they started. Feeding such an army is a problem and they raid and pillage the surrounding countryside."

"Oh yes! Did they have a great many men, Niko-mayros? How many men?"

"As many as the stars on a clear night. They raided a small town and the daughter of the priest of Apollo, Chryseis was her name..."

"Who is Apollo? Is he a god of the Greeks? What is he a god of?"

"He is the god of light and the sun. He is an archer who strikes down foes with swift arrows."

"It is Oetosyrus! That is our god of the sun. Apollo is just your name for him." Tomyra clapped her hands together. Stagora limped across and put a small dish of pine nuts between them. "Oh, thank you Stagora."

Nikometros smiled and nodded at the old woman before continuing. "Chryseis was captured and taken back to the Greek camp. Her father came to plead for her release, offering a great ransom. Agamemnon re-fused. The girl's father, a priest of Apollo, prayed for vengeance and Apollo struck down the Greeks with sickness."

"How did this king dare to deny the priest of Oe-tosyrus? Surely, he must have known it was folly? If any man of the People dared such a thing, even a king, he would be killed at once!"

"Agamemnon ruled the Greeks, and no man dared do anything. Except an old seer called Calchas who could read the future in the flight of birds. He told the king that Apollo was angry with him and would kill all the Greeks unless he relented." Nikometros shook his head. He reached out and took a few pine nuts from the dish. He chewed on them slowly. "It is a wonder-ful story, Tomyra, but a king stands for his people before the gods. He is answerable to the gods. Aga-memnon should never have forgotten his duty."

Nikometros bent his head to the scrolls and read from them. Every now and then he would set them aside and speak earnestly to the young priestess, explaining the nuances, the customs of Greeks and Trojans. At last he sat back and stifled a yawn with the back of his hand.

Tomyra sat quietly, her eyes focused on some far scene of warfare. "It is a fierce tale," she said finally. "A warrior's story, one to stir the hearts of men. Yet this king was only a War leader, not a true father of his people. It makes me sad to hear it." She sighed gently. "I must hear more of this tale another time, Nikomayros. However, you must not be seen to stay long with me at night. You must leave me now." Tomyra rose and extended her hand.

Nikometros scrambled to his feet. He reached out and touched her hand for a moment. Her cool touch sent hot blood rushing to his face. "M...My lady," he stuttered, "I will take my leave of you. I thank you for your hospitality." He paused, unsure whether to say anything more.

"Until tomorrow then, Nikomayros."

He bowed and strode to the door. Pulling the curtain aside, he walked into the cold night air. Nikometros stood still, letting the cold air drain the heat from his face. He smiled ruefully. *Come, Nikometros. You have never been so affected by a woman. By the gods though, she is beautiful!* He allowed himself a few moments of dreaming what might happen. *Get a grip on your thoughts, Nikometros. She is a virgin priestess, consecrated to the Mother Goddess and to touch her is death. Be very careful...* He looked around him and realised he stood alone in almost total darkness. Even the guard Lyartes had disappeared. Buildings and tents loomed nearby, and as his eyes slowly adjusted to the starlight, he could make out a path leading between the darkened dwellings. He walked slowly down the path towards where he thought his own tent lay.

Within fifty paces, he lost his bearings. The shadows in the street formed inky pools and the buildings obscured the distant lights. Nikometros stumbled and almost fell. He swore violently when he struck his shin on a wooden water trough. Rubbing his leg, he looked about him. Every direction looked the same. Nikometros thought hard, trying to remember the way he arrived with Partaxes earlier in the evening. *The path of Zeus!* he thought. *The milk of the Goddess that guides her People.* Looking upward, he saw the familiar glowing band stretched across the sky. Allowing for the time he spent with Tomyra, Nikometros calculated how far the path had swung around the sky. *My hut should be over there.* He set off, slowly feeling his way along the darkened streets.

Blackness detached itself from the shadows behind him. A few moments later a second shape followed. They closed on Nikometros and metal flashed dimly in the starlight as one form flung itself forward. A whisper of movement caught Nikometros' ears and he half turned. The man cannoned into him, his blade sweeping past his intended victim's face. Nikometros fell, the man sprawling on top of him, his assailant's nauseating breath stinking of onions and rotted milk. The man cursed, trying to bring his knife up, but Nikometros brought his knee up into the man's side, knocking him off balance. Following up his advantage, his fist lashed out, hitting the man in the face. The man's head snapped back and Nikometros rose to his knees, his opponent groveling in front of him. Spotting the knife on the ground, Nikometros reached for it.

A foot thudded into him as the other man attacked. Nikometros grunted from the impact and fell onto the first man, the knife skittering into the shadows. The second attacker threw himself onto Nikometros, a pair of callused hands fumbling for his throat. Nikometros gripped the man by his wrists, straining. The man below him wriggled violently, trying to grasp Nikometros' arms from behind, so he let go of one wrist and slammed his elbow back. It connected with the nose of the first attacker and the man screamed.

Hands tightened on Nikometros' throat, and flashes of light swam in front of his eyes. Nikometros let go of the man's wrists and jabbed his fingers up into his assailant's face. He dug his fingers into an eye and clenched. The pressure on his throat disappeared when the man hurled himself backwards, screaming with pain. Nikometros gasped, drawing long painful breaths and struggled to his feet. Shouts echoed off the houses and lights appeared. His assailants scrambled away, disappearing into the shadows.

Light splashed in a golden flood from a door thrust open and a torch held high. Nikometros turned and raised his arms to meet this new threat. In the flickering light of the torch, he saw three men, one naked, the other two wearing breechcloths. *Thank the gods. No threat here*, he thought, lowering his arms. Nikometros cleared his throat painfully. "I am Nikometros the Macedonian, blood brother of Spargises. I ask your help."

The men rushed forward to steady him. "What is he talking about? Who is he?"

"The barbarian who bested the Goddess' champion."

"I heard about him. What is he doing here?"

"He has been fighting. Thyrses, go fetch the night watch. Hurry."

The man called Thyrses ducked into a hut and grabbed his clothes and a torch then ran off. The others helped Nikometros into the hut and sat him down. A woman appeared, looking apprehensive. She bent down, briefly examined his throat then left. In a few moments, she returned with a cloth she applied to Nikometros' throat. "Keep your hand on this," she said. "The herbs will help the swelling." She turned to one of the men. "Who is he? He is not one of the People."

"The barbarian who is in the chief's favour."

"Him?" The woman looked at him again, noting his blonde hair, clean-shaven face and linen tunic. "I have never seen anyone like this. Why does he dress like a woman? Is he a gelding?"

"Hush woman. He can understand you."

Nikometros nodded painfully. "I thank you, lady, for your help," he croaked.

The woman flushed. She bobbed her head and left. The man poured some water from a jar into a wooden cup and thrust it into Nikometros' hands. "Here, drink this."

Footsteps sounded on the street outside and an armed man shouldered his way into the hut. He turned to one of Nikometros' rescuers. "What is happening? Thyrses came running up with some story about a barbarian attack. Is this one of them?"

"Yes, but he was the one attacked. He is the barbarian Spargises took and made a blood brother. Don't ask me his name. He said it but it is some outlandish barbarian name. Some men set upon him in the street."

The armed man looked at Nikometros curiously. "I heard he was made one of the People." He squatted down and took a deep breath. "Barbarian," he bellowed. "Can...you...understand...me?"

Nikometros smiled. "I can indeed. I thank you for your concern. My name is Nikometros."

The man rocked back on his heels, gaping. "By the dust demon's hairy testicles," he muttered. "He speaks the tongue — after a fashion." He rose to his feet. "Well, I'd better take him to the chief. He'll know what to do."

A commotion outside drew everyone's attention. Partaxes burst in. "Nikomayros," he cried. "Are you hurt? I heard there was a fight with barbarians. It could only be you." He looked at the compress on Nikometros' throat. "Let's get you back to your hut and attended to." He turned to the watchman. "I will take responsibility for this man. Spargises put him in my care."

"Seems to me you need to watch over him more closely then," the man grumbled. "Very well, but I shall report this business." He turned and left the hut.

Nikometros put his hand out to his rescuers. "I thank you for your help, and that of the lady," he said hoarsely. They touched hands briefly. He and Partaxes exited into the now-busy street. The cold air stabbed Nikometros painfully as he breathed.

Partaxes picked up a torch. "Come then. We had best get your throat seen to or you won't be able to talk tomorrow." He strode off down the street.

Nikometros followed slowly, deep in thought. *Who would attack me? Was it planned? It seemed as though they were waiting for me.*

Chapter Seven

Clouds of dust rose into the heavens, carried on gentle breezes. As far as the eye could see, bobbing horse heads, seemingly disembodied, floated above the dust kicked up by thousands of hooves. Nikometros unwrapped the cloth from around his face and knocked it against his thigh. Caked dust flew up. He re-tied it and ran his hands through his hair, dislodging more dust. He reached down and patted the neck of his once-golden stallion. *It's good to have you back, Diomede old friend.*

Turning his horse, he kicked it into a trot across the herd, heading into the wind. The tribe traveled in wagons several stadia to windward. They traveled slowly, at walking speed, limited by the slowest wagon. The herds ranged out on all sides of them, the nearest downwind. Further out, cattle herds and flocks of goats lumbered along. Small brindle dogs ran snapping and snarling between the wheels of the wagons, as placid oxen plodded slowly along, the wagons groaning and bumping in their wake. Most families owned several wagons – the richer and more prominent Scythians owned many more. Nikometros traveled in one of Spargises' hundred or so wagons, his few belongings tucked into one corner. At night, he unrolled blankets and slept beneath the wagon, and often, during the cold nights, he would wake to find one or more dogs curled up with him.

Nikometros had to rethink what he knew about Scythians, for the moving mass of people, wagons and herds comprised only a part of the town of Urul. When the tribe set out, Nikometros found large numbers of craftsmen, and all the farmers, stayed behind. The Scythian horsemen did not consider the townspeople true tribesmen, merely a convenience for the winter months. The warriors and their families migrated, together with most of the herds, ranging far over the grassy plains for most of the year. The huts came down, the poles folded and the hides of the walls formed the upper part of the wagons. Most of these came off when the tribe made camp each night and were reconstituted into living quarters, while other wagons remained intact, acting as storage units.

When Nikometros came alongside the wagon he used, the driver greeted him. "Ho Nikomayros. You look thirsty. Have a drink?" Agarus threw a skin bag to him. Nikometros reached out and snatched it out of the air. Agarus was a goldsmith, crafting gold into cunningly worked brooches and necklaces. One arm, twisted since birth, denied him the life of a warrior, but instead, he showed himself skilled in metalwork, and a conscientious driver.

Nikometros unstopped the skin bag and sniffed. The now-familiar rank odour of koumiss met his nostrils. He grimaced and drank. "Thanks, Agarus." *At least it washes the dust from my throat.* He rode closer and tossed the skin back. "Have you seen Spargises? Or the priestess?"

"Our chief does what he always does when we travel. You will find him somewhere in the column, seeing to our people's needs. Up ahead somewhere, I think. As for the priestess, I have not seen her."

Nikometros nodded and kicked his horse into a trot once more. He moved slowly up the line of wagons, noting the variety of responses from the people. Many just looked at him or ignored him, while others nodded in his direction, and a few even gave him friendly greetings. He returned these with a wave, a comment, and always a warm smile.

He saw Timon in one of the uncovered wagons, locked in earnest conversation with a small group of metalworkers. Nikometros nudged his stallion with his knee, moving over to the wagon. One of the metalworkers looked up when he approached, smiling warmly.

"Greetings Nikomayros. Dusty work riding with the herds, isn't it?" The other men in the group looked around and nodded at Nikometros, before turning back to their conversation. Timon saluted then resumed his explanations, waving his arms around as he made his points.

"Indeed it is...Ixathres. It must be pleasant riding back here in the wagons in the clean air." Nikometros smiled. "It seems Timon has a lot to say."

"Timon has a great knowledge of metals. Now that he can speak our tongue passably, we are learning a lot."

Nikometros smiled again and waved, turning his horse away with a gentle pressure. Riding easily on Diomede, feeling the stallion's muscles ripple beneath him, the wind cool in his face, he felt like singing. Despite his comments, the thought of riding in a wagon paled beside the joy of riding a powerful horse on a bright spring day, with the whole of Scythia open before him.

Several stadia further on, Nikometros caught sight of Spargises riding off to one side of the column. He turned his horse in that direction and galloped across. When Nikometros rode up Spargises turned away from a man in heated conversation with him. "Greetings, Spargises." He looked at the other men, recognizing two of the chief's advisers, and the chief's son. He smiled at them, receiving curt nods in return.

Areipithes glared at him. Nikometros nodded at him pleasantly but Areipithes sat silently astride his horse.

"Ho, brother!" Spargises face creased in a warm smile. "I see my daughter returned your stallion. He is a fine animal – I shall want him to cover some of my mares."

"Willingly. I think Diomede is only too willing to perform such a service for you." Nikometros paused, glancing at Areipithes. "I would talk with you about something your daughter said during one of our lessons."

"Later, Nikomayros. We must deal with other things. First, I told you I would look into the attack on you three nights ago. Well, my son has investigated the attack. He can find no evidence of malice. He is sure it was merely some young men in high spirits."

Areipithes smiled sardonically. Nikometros refrained from argument, turning to him. "I thank you Areipithes, for your efforts on my behalf."

"There is also more urgent news," Spargises continued. "Scouts report a number of strangers to the north. It's possible they are merely passing by but they could also be part of a raiding party. I want you to go with my warriors. See how they fight. You must get used to fighting our way."

"Of course. It is an honour. I will need my weapons returned though as I cannot go into battle unarmed."

"Parasades will see to it. Ride with him now." Spargises gestured at one of the other riders, the younger of the two advisers.

The man called Parasades sidled his horse alongside Nikometros, reaching over to grasp his hand. "Well met, Nikomayros. In unarmed combat, you are a worthy fighter. I look forward to seeing you in armed battle." He grinned, showing a full set of white teeth. "I lost a horse on Araxes but I bear you no ill-will. Perhaps you will win me one in another fight. Now, let's ride." He squeezed his horse's sides with his thighs, sending it leaping forward.

Nikometros raised a hand in salute to Spargises, spurring his stallion in pursuit and soon pulled along-side, his mount's longer strides overhauling those of the smaller Scythian horse. They rode through the column of wagons, loud cheers of excitement follow-ing in their wake. To his right, Nikometros saw a large body of riders converging with them and called out to Parasades, pointing at the riders. "Who are they?"

"Ours," Parasades grunted, slowing his horse to look at the party approaching.

The body of men surrounded them, jostling and talking animatedly to Parasades. Several called out to Nikometros in greeting.

Partaxes rode up alongside. "Well, my friend. Per-haps we shall see some action. It has been far too qui-et of late."

"Quiet for you, maybe. Have you forgotten I saw some fighting just the other night?"

"No, I have not forgotten." He rode closer, lower-ing his voice to a murmur. "Word has it that a certain Palakes nursed an injured eye the day after. Now he cannot be found." Partaxes looked around and, seeing no one close by, continued. "Palakes does the bidding of someone closely related to our chief."

Nikometros looked at him sharply but said noth-ing.

"Good. You know the value of discretion and si-lence." He raised his voice when another rider ap-proached. "We will have to find your sword. In the meantime, use one of the spares." Turning to the approaching rider, Partaxes called, "Tirses, find a good sword for our new warrior."

Tirses saluted and galloped off. The mass of riders continued angling across the migration, passing herds of goats tended by small boys. The children called out excitedly to the men as they passed and one of the men broke off from the group, galloping over to the boys. He scooped one of them up onto his horse, talking to him for a few strides before letting him down again. Rejoining the group of riders, the man grinned at Nikometros. "My first-born. A good lad. He'll be riding with us before long."

They moved out beyond the last of the herds, into the silent rolling grasslands. The song of birds high in the azure sky came to them faintly above the muffled roll of hoof beats. The heat of the sun beat upon them, mingling the odour of sweaty men and horses with the dust and the scents of the limitless sea of grass.

Jostling through the riders, Tirses returned to hand a sword and belt to Nikometros. Nikometros took the sword out of its sheath, examining it closely, feeling the edge. Content with the quality of the blade, he re-sheathed it and buckled the belt around his waist.

Partaxes touched Nikometros' arm. "See, the scouts are coming." He pointed toward two distant horsemen. "Now we shall find out where the enemy cowers."

The scouts drew their lathered horses up sharply, pointing and jabbering. Nikometros strained to hear what they said. "What's happened?"

Partaxes turned to him. "Four sun's span to the northeast. Twenty riders of the Dahai. They are far from home."

Nikometros did a swift calculation. *About forty stadia at an easy pace.* His officer's training came to the fore. *It would not do to tire the horses unduly.* He looked to the northeast, assessing the route. *These rolling plains could hide whole companies of horse until you rode right into them.*

A decision reached, the scouts changed their tired horses. One rode off toward the distant wagons, while the other joined the riders. The horsemen moved off again at a trot, angling further to the right. Silent now, eager and expectant, the Massegetae warriors moved to the northeast, the land rising sharply in front of them. Parasades called a halt. He dismounted, walked forward to the top of the rise and peered over the top, while the horses blew and whickered softly. Nikometros' stallion edged closer to a gray mare, his nostrils flared. The mare shied away, lifting her heels. Nikometros pulled on his reins, patting the horse on the neck, talking to him softly. "Easy, Diomede, easy. Keep your mind on the job."

Parasades pulled back from the rise and rejoined the watching men. Nikometros pushed forward to listen. "Dahai. There are twenty men watering their horses at a stream, two hundred paces over the rise. Many have dismounted. The fools have not set guards." He swung up onto his horse and grinned. "Spread out. This will be great sport."

Nikometros coughed. Parasades looked up, an inquiring expression on his face. "Shouldn't we send a force to circle round behind them? What if they break in different directions?"

"We do not have the time. A sweep down the hill will overcome them rapidly." He turned away, stringing a bow. He fitted an arrow to it, testing the pull.

Around him, Nikometros saw others preparing, so he shrugged and checked his sword.

Parasades waved his arm and the riders fanned out on either side. Slowly they moved forward. The land dropped away in front of them. At the bottom of the slope, a small stream flowed gently between grassy banks. Men in leather clothing sat around on grass tussocks or stood in small groups while their horses drank. The line surged forward down the slope.

What manner of horseman lets his horse drink its fill in enemy territory? Nikometros shook his head. *They will be bloated and unable to run.* He tapped his heels and Diomede leaped forward. He drew his sword and leaned low over the galloping stallion's neck. The men below heard the drumming hooves and reacted instantly. Cries of alarm rang out. They swung up onto their horse's backs, frantically kicking them into action. Most turned their horses toward the slope, fumbling for weapons. A cloud of arrows overwhelmed them. Diomede collided with another horse, knocking its rider off balance. Nikometros then leaned over, judging his distance and swung his sword. The man fell, clutching his side, and Diomede, ears flattened and teeth bared, turned toward the enemy unbidden, using his front hooves to tear a path through the opposing horses. Nikometros stabbed and thrust; finally feeling his sword meet little resistance. The fighting faded, and the screams of wounded men stilled. He looked around, recognizing the milling horsemen.

Parasades supervised the stripping of the enemy corpses. Seventeen Dahai bodies and one of the People lay sprawled in and around the stream. He cursed; realizing three enemy horsemen had escaped. Parasades shrugged. "It happens. Strip the bodies. Check the horses for wounds and tie them up." He ran his eyes over the tribesmen, judging their condition. "Colaxes, Lycus, get back and report this to the chief, tell him three Dahai escaped." They saluted, remounted, and headed back. "Tirses, look to our fallen comrade. We shall take him back in honour." He turned to Nikometros, smiling. "I should have taken your advice. You fought well; I count three men dead by your hand. I shall not forget."

The tribesmen piled the Dahai bodies together, packing the clothing and weapons of the slain onto the captured horses. Nikometros dismounted and walked upstream looking for water, clear of mud and blood. He let Diomede drink, watching him carefully, not letting him drink too much. He dashed some water over his face, and washed his mouth out, and rinsed some of the spattered blood of the Dahai off his arms. Nikometros stood to remount, when he heard a groan from the long grass across the stream. He drew his sword and stepped across. Lying supine in the grass, a Dahai warrior struggled to rise. Nikometros stood looking at him for a few moments and then called downstream. "Parasades! There is a live Dahai here." The warrior rolled over, revealing an arrow in his shoulder. His white face stared up at Nikometros, filled with fear and pain.

Parasades ran up with other warriors close behind. He looked briefly at the fallen warrior. "Kill him."

Nikometros stood still, gazing into the Dahai warrior's face. He took in the clean-shaven face and small build. *He's only a youth!* Turning to Parasades, he shook his head. "No. I choose to let him live."

Parasades looked at him curiously. "It would be better to kill him now." When Nikometros just looked at him, Parasades shrugged. "Very well. We shall take him back." He turned and spoke to the man behind him. "Put him on a horse and guard him well."

They rode back slowly. When they neared the wagons, Spargises galloped up with Tomyra and several warriors. Nikometros' heart gave a leap when he caught sight of her. He smiled, hoping to see an answering smile, but was disappointed. The body of warriors rode on, taking the prisoner and the dead man back to the wagons. Parasades stopped near Spargises and spoke in a low voice, turning to glance at Nikometros between sentences.

Spargises nodded and called over to him. "Nikomayros. I hear you are a great warrior. Three Dahai are dead by your hand and one taken captive. Their horses are yours." He laughed and beckoned to Tomyra. "Daughter, I think our problem is answered. Would the Great Goddess accept Nikomayros as her champion?"

Tomyra nodded, her face serious. "Yes father. The Goddess accepts this man as her chosen instrument and protector of her priestess."

Spargises turned back to Nikometros. "Do you accept this high honour, Nikomayros? Will you protect the person of the priestess with your life, and carry out the duties that go with the position?"

Nikometros grinned and then quickly replaced it with a serious expression. "I do accept this honour." Turning to Tomyra, he put his hand on his heart then onto the hilt of his sword. "I will honour the priestess of the Goddess, my lady. I will protect her with my life."

Tomyra nodded. "Thank you Nikomayros. I shall consecrate you this evening when we camp for th night."

Nikometros watched Spargises and Tomyra ride away feeling very pleased with himself. *I will be able to see her whenever I want!* He glanced at Parasades and grinned. "Let's see how fast your horse can return to the wagons." Nikometros touched his heels to Diomede's sides. The stallion bunched his muscles and leaped forward, Nikometros leaning over the great stallion's neck. Behind him, Parasades yelled. Nikometros concentrated on urging Diomede still faster. The two horsemen swept past Spargises and Tomyra into the column of wagons. Nikometros brought his stallion to a halt in a cloud of dust by his wagon, a few moments ahead of Parasades. He leapt to the ground and stood laughing, hands on hips, as Parasades skidded his horse to a halt beside him.

Parasades dismounted and stepped up to Nikometros. "By the swollen paps of Apia, your stallion could race the wind!" He laughed and grasped Nikometros by his arm. "I must have him service my mares. What say you? Half shall be yours."

"Agreed. As long as I have first choice of the foals."

Parasades clapped him on the shoulder. "Done. I shall see you tonight." He grasped his horse's mane and vaulted onto its back. Waving, he trotted away.

* * *

A large fire crackled in the open space between the wagons that lay in a rough circle about two hundred paces across. Smaller cooking fires ringed the circle, nearer the wagons, wood smoke and sweat mingling with the scents of roasting meats. Groups of people moved about in the gathering dusk, performing the simple tasks of camp life. Several hide and pole huts ᵼtted the open area, and a small space in front of ʳgises' hut was roped off.

Nikometros adjusted his new tunic. At the chief's bidding, the women of his household had sewed linen cloth into a fair imitation of a military tunic. Water for washing was scarce, as usual, but Nikometros managed a bucketful and now, clean, shaved and brushed down, Nikometros felt half civilised again. He walked slowly toward Spargises' hut, mingling with the gathering crowd. A number of men greeted him, many nodding at him and smiling. News of the skirmish had spread rapidly through the camp, and the men were eager to talk to him about it, while several young women gave him bold looks as he passed.

Guards pulled the hide flaps of the hut aside as Spargises emerged and looked around the gathering crowd. Seeing Nikometros, he beckoned to him. "Go with my guards, Nikomayros. Your armour is in my hut. You will need it for the ceremony."

Nikometros bowed and entered the hut, accompanied by the guards. In a neat pile lay his armour and sword, polished and gleaming, the horse-head helmet freshly burnished, the crest brushed and re-tinted red. His sword lay in its sheath and he picked it up, feeling the familiar oiled leather. Drawing it out, he admired its sharp new edges. He picked up the pieces of armour one at a time, lovingly running his fingers over the lion's head design on the breastplate, noting the new leather straps.

The crowd muttered when Nikometros stepped outside. He strode over to the chief and bowed before him, the helmet crest bobbing, the fire throwing red and gold flashes across the burnished armour.

Tomyra stepped forward, a strangely shaped cup her hand, and addressed the assembled tribe. "F' O People of the Great Goddess. It is our cust the priestess of the Goddess to have a char warrior for her protection and dedicated to the Goddess herself. Araxes performed this duty well until the Goddess called him to her side and sent this warrior in his place. This is Nikomayros, chosen by the Goddess." A murmur ran through the crowd. "You have seen his worth in battle and know he is blood brother to chief Spargises." The murmur grew louder and a few angry shouts erupted. Tomyra held up one hand. She waited until all was quiet. "If any dispute the choice of the Goddess, let him stand forward."

Silence greeted her invitation. The front ranks of the crowd shuffled and looked away.

"I dispute this choice!" Areipithes pushed through the crowd and into the ring. He stalked up to Tomyra. "I do not believe the Goddess or our priestess have chosen. Instead, a foolish girl forgets her duty and chooses as her heart dictates." He turned to face the crowd. "Are we to allow our sacred customs to be polluted by foreigners and barbarians?" A few men pushed to the front, shouting agreement.

Tomyra flushed, looking quickly at her father before answering. "That is not so, Areipithes, son of Spargises. You forget yourself. You know, as does everyone here, that the priestess is consecrated to the Goddess and does the bidding of no man." She turned to face the crowd again, stepping toward them. "Nikomayros bears the sign of the Mother. He slew Araxes with his own blade. You have heard of his prowess in battle against the Dahai this very day." She walked back to Areipithes. "The Goddess selects this man. If you dispute it, you dispute the decision of the great Goddess herself. Will you risk her anger by facing him in battle, here and now, in front of the Peo-

104

Areipithes gazed about him angrily. His supporters in the ranks looked crest-fallen. One or two held their hands flat to the ground, muttering under their breath. Areipithes scowled and shouldered past Tomyra, disappearing into the crowd.

Tomyra took a deep breath before turning to face Nikometros. "Nikomayros, son of Leonnatos. The Great Goddess selects you to be her champion and protector of her holy priestess. In front of the assembled People, do you accept this honour?" She dropped her voice and spoke in a whisper. "Say, 'I accept this honour'."

Nikometros looked at her gravely. "I accept this honour." He hesitated a moment, looked at the solemn faces of the people and raised his voice. "I will defend the priestess with my life and honour her ways."

When his gaze returned to her, Tomyra nodded and lowered her eyes. She held the cup toward him. "Take the cup and drink from it."

Nikometros took the cup, his fingers lingering on hers. Suddenly, his hand jerked, spilling a few drops of wine on his hand. *The cup is a human skull.* He looked more closely and noticed it lacked a lower jaw. The bottom of the skull case was missing and beaten silver inlaid the cavity. Deep red wine pooled inside it, reminding Nikometros of blood. *They really are barbaric in some ways*, he thought. He gave a small shrug and lifted the cup to his lips, drinking deeply.

Tomyra took the cup from his hands. "Thus does the blessing of the Mother pass from her fallen champion to the next chosen one. Let all he acknowledge that Nikomayros drinks from the s of Araxes as custom dictates."

A low murmur of agreement came from the crowd.

Nikometros looked unbelievingly at the cup in Tomyra's hand. He felt slightly nauseated but forced his attention back to what Tomyra said.

"The People triumphed today over the Dahai. The Great Goddess filled our warriors with courage. It is fitting that we sacrifice the Dahai captured by our new champion. He will honour the Mother with his death." She beckoned and Parasades stepped into the circle, holding the young Dahai man by his arms. He shoved the man forward and forced him to his knees.

Parasades gave Nikometros a grim smile. "Better you had killed him in battle."

Nikometros looked at Parasades angrily. "I did not capture him to be sacrificed. He is but a youth, unarmed and defenceless." He turned to Tomyra. "It would be a dishonourable death for any man to die like this."

Her eyes hardened. "You are the champion. You must meet him in ritual battle. Slay him. You have no choice."

Nikometros grimaced, looking round at the expectant faces of the Scythian warriors. *I really have no choice.* "Parasades, cut his bonds and give me your sword."

Parasades drew his sword and cut the ropes. The young Dahai rubbed his cramped arms. Blood stained the shoulder of his leather tunic where his arrow wound bled. Parasades stepped forward and handed Nikometros his sword, hilt first. He accepted it and waited until Tomyra and Parasades stepped back out the way, and then looked at the young man still ...ing before him. The Dahai gazed back, shivering but holding his eyes steady. Nikometros

106

dropped the sword onto the ground in front of him and stepped back, drawing his own sword. The crowd muttered and fidgeted.

The young man picked up the sword and stood, looking around at the circle of eager and expectant faces. He licked his lips nervously. Hefting the sword in one hand he dropped into a crouch and edged toward Nikometros. His eyes widened slightly and he thrust the sword at Nikometros' chest.

Nikometros kept his eyes locked on the approaching man's eyes, ignoring the sword. *He is young. He doesn't know what he is doing.* The man's eyes widened again, signaling his intention. When the sword thrust at Nikometros' chest, he swept it aside easily. Before the man could recover, Nikometros thrust with his own sword, slipping the blade between the man's ribs. The man dropped the sword and fell soundlessly to the ground. The crowd erupted in cheers and shouts.

Nikometros bent, ripping a clump of grass from the ground. He wiped his blade carefully, slipping it back into its sheath. He looked at the young man, shaking his head regretfully. *A quick death at least. If I must kill then let it be quick. Let it be honourable.*

Areipithes stood in the shadows, his hooded eyes staring flatly at the men crowding around Nikometros. His hands clenched spasmodically at his sides in fury, and his lips drew back in a silent snarl as his father stepped forward, embracing Nikometros. Areipithes passed a hand over his face, muttering a curse to his gods; then turned and slipped silently away into the night.

Chapter Eight

Areipithes paced up and down, rage growing with each step. His face screwed into a grimace; he grasped his sword in one hand, his knuckles white against the ebony sheen of its hilt, and his mouth worked convulsively, muttering fierce imprecations beneath his breath. Areipithes glanced in the direction of the guard, standing ramrod straight, staring at the dirt at his feet. Areipithes dismissed him from his thoughts and glared around the hut, taking in the rich furnishings in a glance and a glowing brazier in one corner. His eyes stopped on an ornate copper basin intricately worked with human and animal figures around the rim. He locked his gaze onto it, his face suffusing with blood. "Greek work! May the gods curse all Greeks!" Raising his sword, he sprang across the room.

Areipithes' shriek of rage and the clang of metal on metal startled the guard. He dropped his spear then, nervously, ducked to recover it. Areipithes looked down at the dented vessel, breathing hard. He turned and glared at the guard. "Fetch Scolices, and take this piece of garbage with you!" Areipithes tossed the basin on the floor at the guard's feet. The man picked up the basin. Turning it in his hands and shuffling his feet, he hesitated. "Well? What are you waiting for? Get out!" The guard jumped, saluted hurriedly and left at a run.

Areipithes threw down his sword and resumed his pacing, his mind returning to his problem. *What do I do about this barbarian?* He refused to think of him by name. *Foreigners are less than human and do not deserve* _es. He should have been killed on the battlefield. If I had_ _here..._He ground his teeth at the thought. *Could I have done anything if I had been there? The tribe loves my dear sister, and will do anything she asks. That will change when I become chief.* The thought raised another problem in his mind. Leadership did not devolve by right to the son of a chief in the Massegetae. A man must prove himself in war first, and then be a successful war leader. Only then could he seek to be chief and only then if acclaimed by the whole tribe before acceptance. *I have led the war parties for the last two years. Now my father is showing interest in leading again. Ever since that god-cursed barbarian showed up!*

Approaching footsteps distracted him. The hangings swung aside and a thin, nervous-looking man slipped inside. The man bobbed his head. "You sent for me?" He stood quietly just inside the door, waiting for an order.

"Sit down." Areipithes growled. He waited while the man settled himself cross-legged on the floor cushions. "Well, Scolices, what have you to say for yourself?"

The man shifted uneasily. "About what? If you mean the barbarian, I've already told you, he took us by surprise."

"*He* took *you* by surprise? You attacked him at night, two on one, armed on unarmed, and he still bested you." Areipithes moved to stand over the man, his hands closed into rigid claws.

Scolices cringed, waiting, looking up at the flickering shadows from the brazier playing over Areipithes' face, turning his grin into a death rictus. He grinned nervously, displaying a mouth full of rotting teeth. A stench of decay rose from him.

Areipithes stepped back, a look of disgust on his face. His body relaxed and he flexed his aching fingers. "However, that is not what I want to talk to about." He moved over to the brazier, holding his hands over the warm coals. "What are people saying about the barbarian today?"

A look of relief flooded over Scolices. "He is more accepted tonight than last night. There were mutterings about the priestess making him champion, but they saw a good omen in his quick kill." He shrugged his shoulders. "The battle with the Dahai did not hurt his reputation as a fighter either."

Areipithes scowled. "It is unnatural to place a foreigner in such a position." He resumed his pacing, his brow furrowed with concentration. "The people must be made to see this. You will talk to all that will listen, plant seeds of doubt. Agree that he is a good fighter, even an asset to the tribe. Suggest instead that..." Areipithes stopped his pacing as an idea occurred to him. "Suggest that perhaps he is too friendly with our lovely priestess." He smiled. His eyes remained cold and hard. "Tell any who will listen that he thinks of her as a young woman, not a holy priestess of our Great Goddess."

Scolices looked puzzled but nodded slowly. Areipithes bent and picked up his sword. He examined its edge, slipping it back into its sheath. "Now, the other business. Where is Palakes? I don't want him where people can see him until his eye heals."

"He is camped about half a day's travel behind us. No one will think to look there." The man smiled, feeling the edge of Areipithes' anger slip aside. "He follows as we move. We can get him any time we want."

"Send someone trustworthy to travel with him." He thought for a moment. "Gnures will do. Tell him anyone discovers them, he is to kill Palakes imme-

110

diately and make his escape. I don't trust Palakes to keep his mouth shut."

Scolices nodded. "What about the barbarian? Do you want me to try to kill him again?"

Areipithes threw up his hands in disgust. "Kill the Goddess' champion by stealth? Are you mad? It would be seen as a cursed act. If anyone suspected me..." He held his hand flat to the earth for a moment to placate the Goddess. Areipithes paused and reflected. *Should I...?* He shook his head. *No, the Great Goddess would seek revenge. Perhaps it is better not to risk things, when there are surer methods.* "Accidents happen in battle. Even the best warrior can be struck down by a chance arrow." He smiled at the thought.

Scolices grinned. "Shall I see to it?"

"No, you fool. You had your chance with him. Now be quiet. I must think on this." Areipithes resumed his pacing, muttering in a low voice. "Talking to the tribesmen as I instructed you will sow mistrust but the barbarian is now close to my dear father and sister. I must separate them. But how?" He stopped and stared through Scolices, as if looking for inspiration in his thin features.

The man flushed and fidgeted under his scrutiny. He coughed. "Er...Lord?" He hesitated a moment. "Perhaps you could drive a wedge between them. If the barbarian did something dishonourable..."

Areipithes' cold stare continued. "How do you propose I persuade the barbarian to do this?" He turned away, his eyebrows drawing together in thought. "Perhaps there is a way..." He smiled slowly. "Not only does the barbarian think of her as a woman but my lovely half-sister foolishly returns his interest. She tries to conceal it but not well enough – she conceived an unnatural passion for this man pletely against custom. If he scorned her, or appeared to do so, her anger might provide the wedge." He clapped his hands together vigorously, turning back to Scolices. "I shall see to this myself. Go, see that Gnures has his instructions and start spreading your concerns."

Scolices leapt to his feet and hurriedly left the hut, anxious to get away. As he turned aside a fleeting look of fear and loathing crossed his face.

Areipithes rubbed his hands together. *Yes, this could destroy the barbarian's reputation in my sister's eyes. Show him to be nothing special and my father will tire of him. Then I will kill him myself.* He seated himself on a pile of ornately embroidered floor cushions and poured wine into a gold-plated skull cup. Sipping the wine, he contemplated the power that would be his when he became chief.

Chapter Nine

Nikometros sang softly to himself as he helped Agarus repack his wagon. Wood smoke hung in the still air. The bustling throng of men and women cast long shadows over the dewy grass in the early morning light. Brilliant motes of light reflected up from the myriad of droplets, making the campsite look as if the gods had scattered tiny jewels. *Today I start my new duties. To ride with and protect Tomyra. Ah, to be alone with her!* He flashed a broad smile at a passing warrior, who looked at him askance.

Agarus noticed Nikometros' demeanour and smiled. The camp buzzed with rumours and stories of this young man. The previous day's battle lost nothing in the retelling, and now came his elevation to the position of champion of the Great Goddess. 'It is unheard of to arm your foe before the sacrifice, and then such a swift victory! It must be an omen,' men said. Tales already circulated about the priestess' prophecy of the king of gold in Nikomayros' future. Agarus limped around to the front of the wagon, checking the harness of the oxen, tightening straps. He clambered awkwardly onto the driver's platform and cracked his whip. The oxen lumbered forward.

Nikometros walked over to where Diomede stood grazing patiently. The stallion lifted his head as he approached, thrusting his muzzle into Nikometros' face, blowing softly. Nikometros stroked the horse's nose fondly and patted his neck. He moved around to the stallion's side, grasping his mane, but before he could vault onto Diomede's back, a man's voice hailed him.

"Ho, Nikomayros! A word with you, my friend."

Nikometros looked round. The man approachi͡ him looked familiar, but he could not remembe͡

113

name - a small rotund middle-aged warrior with a broad smile on his face. Nikometros smiled uncertainly. "Greetings...er..." His voice trailed off.

"Menaraxes, my friend. You remember, we talked last night. I have someone who wants to meet you." He reached out and grasped Nikometros by the arm. "Come, this will take but a moment."

Nikometros drew his arm back. He looked around but could see no one else interested in them, no one watching. "Who is this person? Why does he want to see me?"

Menaraxes grinned, winking conspiratorially. "Come and see. You will not be disappointed." He reached out and tugged on Nikometros' arm again.

Nikometros shrugged, putting a pleasant smile on his face. *What can happen among the wagons in broad daylight?* "Very well then, Menaraxes. Let us see this person who is so eager to meet me." He grasped Diomede's reins and walked with Menaraxes towards a nearby wagon.

Alongside the wagon, which stood harnessed and ready to move, was a slim figure in loose voluminous robes. A brightly coloured linen cloth covered the figures' head. Menaraxes ran forward a few steps then turned smiling to Nikometros. "Nikomayros, my friend, may I present my daughter Roxana."

The figure slipped the linen cloth back, revealing a young girl's face framed by long raven hair. She smiled, white teeth flashing in her pale bronze face. Her brown eyes gazed levelly at Nikometros. For a moment the young woman's face took on a calculating look then she cast her eyes down demurely. "Greetings, Lord. Forgive a young girl's presumption. had to meet the hero everyone is talking about."

114

"The honour is mine, lady." Nikometros smiled and then glanced at Menaraxes who hopped excitedly from foot to foot, smiling broadly.

He bobbed his head as Nikometros looked at him. "I must attend to my wagons, my friend. I shall leave you two young people to get acquainted." Menaraxes turned and hurried off before Nikometros could protest.

Turning back to the girl, Nikometros found her looking up at him, a small, amused smile on her lips. She stepped closer to him and took his arm. "Are all Greek warriors as tall and handsome as you, my Lord?"

He smiled at her again, finding it extremely easy to smile at her. *Gods, remember this is a young unmarried girl. If I remember the custom here, I'm not supposed to even be alone with her. What is her father thinking?* "My people are not usually so tall, Roxana. I come from a tall family." He paused, seeking around for another subject. "Your name is familiar to me. One of the chiefs back in Sogdiana had a beautiful daughter called Roxane. Our king, Alexander, married her."

"I do not know of this woman, despite her having a similar name to mine. It means 'little star' in both our tongues. I have lived among the Massegetae all my life," she said with a small sigh. She gazed up at him, fluttering her eyelashes slightly. "It must be exciting to see far-off places. I wish I had a man who would take me away and show me such things."

"I am sure that some brave warrior will seek your hand, Roxana, and show you far-off wonders." Nikometros looked around, hoping to find other peopl close by. "We should not be alone. By the custom your people it is unseemly."

115

Roxana smiled and dropped her eyes. "Do you not think me beautiful, Nikomayros? Do you want to leave me already?"

Nikometros flushed. "By no means. You are indeed a beautiful girl, and I enjoy your company, but I cannot talk now. I have my duty." The tribe's wagons rumbled into motion around them, pulling into rough columns as they resumed their northward migration. "I must get you back to your father. Come." He took Roxana gently by the elbow and guided her towards her wagon.

The young girl laughed softly and took his hand, walking alongside him, swinging her hips provocatively. At the wagon, she called out. "Father...Nikomayros has brought me back."

Menaraxes' head popped out of the wagon coverings. "Ah, daughter, you have returned." He beamed at Nikometros. "You make a handsome young couple. It pleases me to see young people together."

"Father, may Nikomayros call on me tonight and tell me of his people and adventures?" Roxana turned to Nikometros with a warm smile. "Please say you will come, my Lord. I would be no trouble and would dearly love to hear of your exploits."

Nikometros hesitated. She was very beautiful but he felt uncomfortable talking to her. She was too forward in her behaviour for such a short acquaintance. He knew he must be careful not to break any customs or offend the tribes-people. "Of course I would be happy to talk to you and your father sometime. Now, if you will excuse me, I must attend to my duties." Nikometros nodded at Menaraxes, smiled at Roxana ⟶n vaulted up onto Diomede's back. The stallion ⟶ed and as he touched his heels gently to his sides, ⟶ off at a trot.

Roxana watched him go. The smile slipped from her lips and a hard gleam appeared in her eyes. She adjusted the linen cloth over her head again, and then climbed into the wagon. She leaned back against the supports, looking at the distant figure of Nikometros. "Menaraxes, you will invite the Greek over tonight after the evening meal. Now, get this wagon moving. I must rest."

Menaraxes nodded and cracked the whip, starting the oxen. He watched Roxana disappear into the back of the wagon and grimaced. *I wouldn't like to get on the wrong side of that one. At least I have done as I was told. Why in the name of all the gods was I picked to act as her father?* He shrugged and cracked his whip again, urging the oxen onward.

Nikometros guided his stallion through the throng of wagons, absently nudging his sides with a knee or heel. His thoughts returned to Roxana. Despite his sense of unease at the rapidly developing situation, he felt a small thrill of excitement at the thought of seeing her again that night. His body, used to long periods of hardship and abstinence, stirred with desire. He quashed the feeling with an effort, feeling vaguely guilty. He turned his thoughts to Tomyra. *She is the one I would love. Ah, but she is not for me, or any man. She is a virgin, consecrated to her Goddess.*

In the distance, he saw a small knot of riders and thankful for the distraction, he urged Diomede into a gallop and closed with them rapidly. Approaching, he recognised Spargises and Tomyra, together with a number of advisers. A larger group of armed horsemen trotted off to one side.

"Ah, Nikomayros, I was wondering where y were this morning." Spargises exclaimed. "I am a to send a patrol out with Tomyra and it is your duty to accompany her."

"My apologies, sir...my lady. I was detained." Nikometros smiled at Tomyra, feeling guilty about his recent thoughts. An image of Roxana flitted into his mind and his smile slipped. He looked down, flustered, as he collected his thoughts.

Tomyra looked at him quizzically, holding her mare to one side. "You are troubled, Nikomayros?"

"No, it is nothing, my lady."

"Then let us ride." She turned to her father. "I shall take the Western flank, father." Tomyra raised one hand above her head and gestured to her left. At once a group of about twenty riders broke off from the body of horsemen, wheeling left. Tomyra touched her heels to her red mare, setting off at a gallop. Nikometros saluted Spargises and urged Diomede in pursuit.

The horsemen rode at a slow gallop to the northwest, angling through the herds, kicking up clouds of dust. They broke through into clear air at last, continuing until the columns of dust rising to the heavens were dwarfed by the immensity of the plains.

At last, Tomyra raised a hand and the band of warriors slowed to a trot then to a walk. Twisting around, Tomyra scanned the wide spaces around them. She pointed ahead, and behind, and off to the side, rattling off names. Pairs of riders peeled off and trotted to their assigned positions. "Do you approve, Nikomayros? We are the eyes of the tribe. We must find danger in time to act against it."

Nikometros looked around and nodded in approv-

"You have an eye for tactics and guardianship."

"Every man learns these things when he is old enough to ride a horse. Sometimes women are allowed to ride with the men." She smiled. "I learnt because my mother was a horsewoman of the plains, trained to arms."

"You mentioned that before, my lady. You also said she was Sauromantian. How did she come to be with the Massegetae?"

"A moment." Tomyra turned to a nearby horseman. "Lycus, I will ride ahead with my champion. See that we are not disturbed unnecessarily." Lycus nodded and dropped back a few paces. "Come, Nikomayros. We will ride ahead."

Trotting ahead a stadium or two, the two slowed again to a walk. They rode in silence for a while. At length, Tomyra started talking in a low voice without turning her head. "My mother, Starissa, died two years ago. When she was a young woman, not much older than I am now, the Triboi captured her from her people on the shores of the Great Sea. Her people are known as the Sauromantians, Amazons some call them. My mother was a virgin priestess of the Great Goddess, consecrated and holy. She was a horsewoman, trained to arms in defence of her people and of her Goddess."

Nikometros could hear the pride and sorrow in her voice. He kept silent, waiting for her to continue.

"The Triboi descended on her people, took her by force then sold her as a slave. The Goddess did not forsake her though. Her curse stuck and the Triboi were destroyed years later when the earth shook." Tomyra's voice trembled slightly with emotion as she recounted the story. "My mother was sold to the Dahai. The Massegetae captured her in a raid and Spargises claimed her as a prize of war. She refused t give herself to him, though he greatly desired her he married her. I was born a year later." To turned toward Nikometros with tears in her eyes. "I was her only child. The Triboi had damaged her inside and she could have no others." She wiped her eyes with her sleeve. "I have never told anyone of this. Not even my father knows the reason. I trust you with this knowledge Nikomayros."

Nikometros cleared his throat. He felt his heart go out to this slim young woman touched by tragedy. "I am honoured by your trust, my lady. I will never betray that trust." He smiled reassuringly at Tomyra.

Tomyra returned his smile. "Thank you. It is a relief to tell someone. Already I feel as if I have known you for all my life. The Goddess told me we are connected but She does not always speak clearly."

"Did the Goddess tell you when you prophesied for your father and I?"

"Yes. The images are not always clear. I can see our lives running together but not the exact nature of this connection." Tomyra looked down as she talked, not meeting Nikometros' eyes. After a pause, she looked up. "There is great danger for you too. I should tell you about Areipithes."

Nikometros pursed his lips. "Your brother detests me enough to have made an attempt on my life already. I don't know why he hates me so virulently."

"He is my half-brother. When my father was a young man, he married a Scythian woman of good family, Pasagora. He was struggling to make a name for himself and it was a marriage of convenience. Their child was Areipithes. For a while everything went well then plague came. Pasagora died and Areipithes could not be consoled. He became a secretive child and a cruel one. When my father took my mother Starissa as wife, Areipithes hated her. Now she too is dead, he hates me for the love my fa-

120

ther gives." Tomyra turned to look at Nikometros. Her eyes searched his face. "Do not underestimate Areipithes. He is a skilled warrior and a good war leader. He wants to be chief after my father but he would not make a good chief. He thinks of no one but himself. Nikomayros, be warned. He regards you as a threat. He will try to remove that threat."

Nikometros rode on in silence for a while, digesting her words. "I will be careful, my lady. I cannot be other than true to myself though. I will not avoid him or seek to please him as others do."

"I would not want you to. My father needs a strong man beside him. He recognised that strength when he made you a blood brother." Tomyra sighed deeply. "Tell me more of yourself, Nikomayros. How is it that you have come to me?"

The sun rose higher in the azure sky, drying the morning dew as they talked. The still air carried no sounds to their ears except the slow muffled tread of their horses and occasional snatches of birdsong from high above them. Towards noon, a cool, gentle breeze sprang up from the north, carrying with it a feeling of dampness. Low clouds hung on the northern horizon.

Hoof beats came up fast behind Nikometros and he swung round on Diomede's back, his hand on his sword. Lycus galloped up and saluted Tomyra. "My lady, our relief approaches."

Tomyra nodded and scanned the horizon. A small dust cloud approaching from the direction of the wagons signaled the relief party. "Lycus, signal the scouts to return, and take the men back to the wagons. I will return later with Nikomayros." She turned to Nikometros as Lycus rode off. "I had not though the morning passed so quickly. I feel as if I h known you all my life. The Goddess spoke the when She said we are connected." She reached across and briefly touched Nikometros' arm, smiling. "And in private, Niko, you must call me Tomyra."

"Tomyra...it is a beautiful name. I think I have said that before. I shall use it as often as I can."

Tomyra laughed lightly. "Then I shall have to give you that opportunity." She tugged gently on her mare's reins, nudging its side with her knee as it turned. "Come, Niko, let us enjoy the rest of the day."

They set off for the distant wagons, almost alone under the great blue bowl of sky. On the horizon, they could just make out the dust columns kicked up by the migrating herds. Somewhere beyond them the wagons rolled steadily north, towards the black clouds building up in the distance. Away to their right, they saw Lycus and the patrols moving away, and twisting around, they saw the new patrols taking up their stations.

The hot sun threw small shadows on the ground. The long grass rippled and waved in the freshening northerly breezes, carrying the faint song of meadowlarks and the occasional thin cry of a hawk. The dry scent of the grass, overlain by a faint scent of distant rain, and the odour of sweating horses, pervaded the air.

Nikometros took in great lungfuls of air, exhaling noisily. "I love the open spaces, Tomyra. Macedon is a small land, ringed by mountains and I remember even as a lad I would climb the hills to feel free. Riding on these great plains gives me that same feeling. I wish I could ride forever on a good horse, with you by my side, carving out a kingdom for my sons..." Nikometros' voice trailed off and he looked flustered.

"͏y apologies, Tomyra...my lady. I did not mean to
'v...you are a priestess. I spoke without thought."

Tomyra kept a neutral look on her face. "No offence is taken, Niko. We are all in the hands of the Mother." She took a deep breath of air. "I have often felt the same freedom out here. Why do you think I ride out so often? I, too, wish to ride forever and see the world. Perhaps one day I shall." Tomyra glanced at Nikometros out of the corner of her eye. "Today, though, I shall content myself with racing you home!" She leaned low over her mare's neck and touched her flanks lightly with her heels. The mare leaped forward.

Nikometros sat astride Diomede for a long moment, as the stallion fidgeted impatiently, waiting for his rider's command. He watched the slim figure of Tomyra clinging effortlessly to her horse's back, admiring her skill, and then he urged his stallion in pursuit.

The two riders swept into the wagon column and beyond, before slowing and doubling back. Both horses were breathing hard from the exertion, so they walked them slowly toward Tomyra's wagon.

"I must attend to my other duties now Niko. As priestess, I have oversight of the women of the tribe. I must arbitrate disputes that do not warrant the attention of my father." Tomyra sighed. "It is necessary, but tiring. Now you can see why I ride out on patrol when I can."

Nikometros nodded. "May I see you later, Tomyra? Perhaps after the evening meal?"

"Yes, that would be pleasant, Niko. We should continue our lessons anyway. You speak our language very well now, but sometimes your pronunciation..." she grinned.

"Until tonight then." Nikometros raised his hand in salute and rode off slowly.

Tomyra watched him go and giggled to herself. *I really will have to get him into some decent clothes. That short tunic does not cover much and the sight from behind, as he rides his horse....!"*

Chapter Ten

Nikometros hummed a chorus from the 'Myrmidons' as he strode through the camp, the overcast sky and the first few drops of rain doing little to dampen his spirits. All around him lay cooking fires and the bustle of women clearing away the remnants of the evening meal, of men relaxing with a pot of koumiss. He thought with satisfaction on the day's events, and he eagerly anticipated an evening spent with Tomyra. Nearing the chief's hut, he saw Parasades and others of the chief's retinue engaged in conversation – Parasades called out a greeting to him as he passed. Nikometros replied with a wave of his hand and turned toward Tomyra's hut.

"Nikomayros, my friend. Have you forgotten your promise?" A voice came out of the shadows, startling Nikometros. Two shadows detached themselves and sauntered toward him.

Nikometros turned sharply, his hand moving swiftly to his sword. He recognised one of the figures and relaxed, trying to remember his name. "Greetings...Menaraxes. Of what promise do you speak?"

"Surely you cannot have forgotten you promised my daughter Roxana you would visit her this evening? She awaits your arrival most eagerly."

Nikometros looked embarrassed. "I thought she spoke in a general way, not meaning tonight. I cannot come now, Menaraxes. The priestess expects me."

"Ah, you will bring such pain to my daughter. She has talked of nothing else today, even telling her friends of your promise. She will be shamed before them if you do not come."

Nikometros cursed softly under his breath then nodded at Menaraxes. "Very well then, I shall come, but only for a few minutes." He turned toward To-myra's tent. "I must first tell the priestess that I will be delayed a short while."

"Come, my friend," Menaraxes said softly. "The sooner away the sooner you will return. My friend here will tell the priestess of your short delay in coming to her. You will be back almost before she knows you are gone." He waved vaguely at the other figure that bowed, and backed away.

Nikometros hesitated then shrugged his shoulders. "Lead on then, Menaraxes."

* * *

The other man watched them leave, disappearing between the wagons. He turned and walked away in the opposite direction, bypassing Tomyra's hut. As he passed into the shadows, another figure fell into step with him. The man flinched, glancing sidelong at the figure as the light from a nearby fire revealing his features. "My lord Areipithes. The trap is set."

Areipithes clapped him on the shoulder. "Good. Now disappear for a few days. Another shall spring the trap." He smiled to himself as the man hurried off.

* * *

Nikometros felt a few twinges of concern as he followed Menaraxes through the camp. He stopped and called out. "Menaraxes, this is taking longer than I planned, just to get to your wagon. Perhaps I should visit your daughter another time."

"No, no, my friend, we are almost there. See," he pointed. "There are the lights of my wagon." Menaraxes ran up to the wagon and tapped on the frame. "Daughter...Roxana. Here is Nikomayros. He has come as he promised."

The hide curtains were drawn aside, a flood of buttery-yellow light pouring out. Roxana, dressed in colourful and richly embroidered skirts and bodice, smiled in the entrance and beckoned to Nikometros. "My lord, you honour us with your presence. Please enter our humble dwelling." She held the curtains aside as Nikometros climbed up into the wagon.

Nikometros moved past the slim figure of Roxana into the body of the wagon, stepping lightly over piles of cushions strewn over the carpeted floor. Oil lamps hung from the roof casting a rich golden glow over everything, and a small pot of scented oil was heating gently over a small flame, wafting a heavy perfume through the enclosed space. Nikometros could feel his eyes watering. He turned as Roxana touched him lightly on the arm. "Where has your father gone, Roxana? We should not be alone unchaperoned."

Roxana laughed pleasantly. "I know I am safe in your company, my lord. My father has gone to fetch my friends." She smiled and gestured at the cushions beside her as she sat, adjusting her voluminous skirts. "I hoped you would not mind, my lord. I told a few of my friends of the honour you promised me and they desired very much to meet you. They will be here presently."

Nikometros carefully sat on the cushions across from Roxana. "I do not mind at all. It is best that we talk in company anyway, as I would not want you gossiped about unfairly."

Roxana smiled at him. "You are thoughtful my lord, as well as brave and handsome. Will you have some refreshment while we wait?" She gestured towards a skin container.

Nikometros grimaced slightly at the thought of more koumiss, but nodded his acceptance. Roxana arose gracefully and picked up the container and two pottery cups. She sat down beside him and poured a rich red wine into the cups. Nikometros grinned and sniffed the wine. "By the gods, it is good to drink wine again instead of koumiss." He flushed then went on. "Forgive me, Roxana. I did not mean to imply that your people's ways are not pleasing to me. It is just that I was raised on wine."

"I am not offended, my lord. I prefer wine my-self." Roxana laughed again, raising her cup. "Please drink, my lord. Tell me if it is to your taste." She sipped from her own cup then put the cup down carefully. Nikometros drank deeply, holding the wine in his mouth for a few moments before swallowing. He drank again. "It is a good, rich wine. It has a faint taste of something I cannot quite place." He looked enquiringly at Roxana.

"It will probably be one of our spices. We drink it so often we no longer notice, but it is new to you." Roxana reached out and refilled his cup. "Tell me my lord, of your land and your people."

Nikometros drank again, passing the back of his hand across his brow. The air felt oppressive in the wagon, the heavy cloying scent making his head hurt. "My people? Yes, I can tell you of them." His throat felt dry and he drank again. He collected his thoughts as she refilled his cup. "Macedon is a small land, filled with mountains. The people there have always had..." Nikometros stopped and looked about him. "Where is your father and your friends? I should be getting back."

"He will be here in a little while to lead you back, my lord. Come, drink your wine and tell me of your battles." Roxana lay back on her cushions, watching as Nikometros drank again then pressed a palm to his forehead. She saw him close his eyes and sway slightly.

Nikometros raised his cup again. "Battles? I will tell...what was I saying?" His vision blurred. He put the cup down carefully, not noticing as he knocked it over, the red liquid rapidly soaking into the carpet. "I must go...I feel..." He struggled to rise then fell headlong onto the floor and lay still.

* * *

Roxana smiled and reached across, lifting one of Nikometros' eyelids and looking carefully at his eye. She listened to his breathing for a moment, nodding in satisfaction before rising and lifting the entrance curtain. "Menaraxes...Where are you? Menaraxes, you can come in now."

Menaraxes got up from his seat against the wagon wheel and climbed up. He saw Nikometros lying sprawled over the cushions, breathing hard. "He is asleep? How long will he remain so?"

"Several hours. He drank more of the wine than I thought he would. Now undress him and make him comfortable. I will return shortly." Roxana turned and left the wagon.

Menaraxes moved over to the wineskin and picked it up, sniffing gently, his nose wrinkling at the faint scent underlying the wine. He stoppered the flask carefully and put it away, before turning to the motionless body and looking down on it dispassionately. *So, my fine young barbarian, it was easier than I thought to compromise you.* Menaraxes squatted down beside him and started removing Nikometros' tunic.

Chapter Eleven

"Wake up, my lady. Wake up!" Stagora's old quavering voice cut through the remnants of Tomyra's dream. She opened her eyes in early morning light to see her old nurse standing above her, wringing her hands in excitement. "My lady, arise. There are rumours flying through the camp."

Tomyra stretched and sat up. "There are always rumours. Why should these ones excite you?" She got up, and moved behind the screens at the far end of her hut. Adjusting her shift, she squatted over the pottery urn to relieve herself, listening to Stagora babbling on.

"It is the barbarian again, my lady. Anyone can see he is a real man so perhaps it is not surprising..." Stagora stopped abruptly, a smile wrinkling her old face. "Ah, yes. Such a man...I remember when I was a young girl I had a lover like him, many lovers. You would not think it, to look at my old face now but I was once..."

"Stagora. Stop babbling, and tell me what is happening." Tomyra came out from behind the screens and stood staring at her nurse. "What is this about Nikomayros?"

"He has taken himself a lover, mistress. It is all over the camp."

Tomyra felt her heart cramp within her breast, and she sat down abruptly, staring at the ground blankly for a few moments as Stagora's words sank in. She looked up at her nurse with a stricken look on her face. "What do you mean?" she whispered.

"It seems that Thyrsus, son of Lyces came back from patrol early this morning to find the barbarian in bed with his betrothed. He was exceedingly angry and had to be restrained from killing him as he lay naked with her." Stagora prattled on; unaware of the effect her words were having on Tomyra. "They have all been taken to your father, my lady, for judgment."

Tomyra drew a shuddering breath and calmed herself. "Fetch my travelling robes, Stagora, and hold your tongue. You talk too much about things that do not concern you." Her nurse gave her a startled look then turned to find the robes, muttering beneath her breath. Tomyra rose and stripped off her night shift. She anointed herself with perfume from a small flask then held her arms above her head for Stagora to slip her robes on. She took a sip of wine from a cup sitting on a low table, holding it in her mouth for a few moments, before spitting it into a bowl. Taking a few dried leaves from a pouch at her waist, she sniffed them tentatively then transferred them to her mouth. She chewed them, feeling the fresh herbal taste cleanse her mouth.

I should not feel like this. I am a virgin priestess of the Mother. Why then do I feel betrayed by his actions? Tomyra sighed and turned to Stagora. "I will go to my father. Have the hut packed by the time I return."

Tomyra walked through a camp buzzing with activity. The normal routines of breaking camp were being carried out in a desultory fashion. Groups of men stood around in earnest conversation and women whispered to each other, falling silent as she passed. The crowd of men around her father's hut parted to let her through, the guards on the door holding it open for her. Inside, her father stood talking to Areipithes and Parasades. To one side, Thyrsus, a tall tattooed warrior, stood glowering at Nikometros across the hut. She paused, shaking her head when Nikometros opened his mouth to speak.

131

Her father looked up as she approached. "Daughter, we have need of your advice." He nodded in the direction of Nikometros. "You have heard?"

"Only that there is a disagreement over some girl, father. I do not see why everyone is so interested."

"Nor I, sister." Areipithes turned toward her with a smile on his face. "The barbarian is a man after all, it seems. He is only doing what a man must do, taking pleasure where he can find it. He has been without a woman in his bed for too long." He looked searchingly at Tomyra as he spoke. Satisfied with what he saw, he gave a small laugh. "Perhaps we should marry him off to this girl?"

Parasades broke in. "With respect, my lord. The situation is not that simple. The girl is apparently formally betrothed to Thyrsus and cannot marry Nikomayros." He turned to Nikometros and nodded to him, smiling as he did so. "I can understand his need for a woman from time to time. Indeed, we have been remiss in not finding one for him. He cannot, however, come between two betrothed people. It goes against custom and decency."

"What is your interest in this matter?" asked Areipithes.

Parasades looked at him levelly. "As you are well aware, my lord, it is my duty to advise your father on any issue that disturbs the peace of the People. Furthermore, Thyrsus has recently been transferred to my patrol. His interests are therefore my interests."

"I agree with Parasades, my son. We cannot come between Thyrsus and his betrothed. We must concentrate on settling this matter without resorting to actions that would bring division." Spargises beckoned to Thyrsus and Nikometros. "Come, we have some questions for you."

132

Tomyra watched as the two men moved forward warily. Nikometros looked embarrassed and a bit bemused by the events of the morning. He glanced sidelong at Tomyra who met his eyes briefly with a stony stare then looked away. *Why did you break your promise to me last night and go to this girl instead?*

Thyrsus still looked angry. His hands hung clenched by his sides and he scowled at Nikometros, his teeth grinding audibly.

Spargises nodded at him. "Thyrsus, tell us why you accuse Nikomayros."

"He has dishonoured me. I demand his death or compensation." Thyrsus turned to Nikometros and spat at his feet. Nikometros paled, his hand jerking to his sword.

"Thyrsus, attention!" Parasades stepped forward, barking his order at the furious man. "You forget yourself, man. Tell us just what happened."

"Yes, sir." Thyrsus stood for a moment collecting his thoughts and visibly controlling his temper. "I was on night patrol, sir. I came back to camp at first light and went to see my woman. I found this man..." He swung his arm in Nikometros' direction, "...in bed with her."

Parasades nodded and stepped back. "Nikomayros. Is this true?"

Nikometros stood silently, looking down. Spargises spoke gently. "Nikomayros, as blood brother you must speak the truth to me. Is there any truth to this accusation?"

Nikometros looked round at the circle of faces then locked eyes with Spargises. "I went to her hut last night. I was invited. We talked and drank wine – that much I remember. This morning I awoke to find

133

myself in bed with her, but I do not remember anything about last night."

Areipithes snorted loudly. "So drunk he cannot even remember bedding the girl. He is a worthy warrior, but his head is not as hard as it looks."

"My betrothed would not invite a man to her bed." A note of outrage crept into Thyrsus' voice. "This man has forced her, and must pay the penalty."

Spargises held up his hands and shook his head. "There is no reason, as yet, to speak of forcing." He turned to Nikometros. "You say you were invited. Can you prove that this girl..." he turned to Parasades. "What is her name?"

"Roxana."

Spargises gave Parasades a searching look then resumed talking to Nikometros. "...that Roxana invited you to her wagon?"

"Yes, I can. It was her father who invited me there."

"Her father? Darses? She is a townswoman of Urul; her parents still live there. How can her father have invited you?"

A look of puzzled consternation crossed Nikometros' face. "But Menaraxes is her father. He invited me to her wagon to talk to her."

"Menaraxes is not her father." Spargises replied in a flat voice. He swung round at Areipithes. "Menaraxes is in your patrol. Why is he representing himself falsely?"

"I doubt he is. The barbarian just misunderstood him. Obviously his command of our language is not as good as he thought." Areipithes turned his eyes on Tomyra. "Despite the long and arduous efforts of my beloved sister in the privacy of her tent." He made a small mocking bow in her direction, an amused smile

134

on his lips. "However, even if he was invited to her wagon, I am sure he wasn't invited into the maiden's bed."

"Maiden!" Tomyra snorted derisively. "I am sorry Thyrsus, but Roxana is not noted for modesty. She has a reputation in Urul that follows her here it seems. Just when did you and she become betrothed?"

Thyrsus fidgeted and looked down at the ground. His anger of a few moments before had vanished. He cleared his throat then spoke hesitantly. "Priestess, with respect, you malign her. She is young and no doubt foolish, as young girls are, but she is promised to me and would not willingly go with another man."

"My daughter has raised a good point though. This Roxana has a reputation and I have not heard that she is betrothed to you before now." Spargises' voice lowered and took on a silky smoothness. "No announcement has been made. The Goddess' blessing has not been invoked. Why is this?"

Thyrsus looked more uncomfortable. He shot a quick look at Areipithes. "It was arranged just before we departed. We have not had time to announce it."

"In over two weeks?" Spargises raised an eyebrow. "I am not convinced that you are properly betrothed. Should I send for her father to confirm the matter?" He watched as the man flushed and fidgeted, not meeting his eye. "Do you still accuse Nikomayros of bedding your betrothed?" He spoke softly but Tomyra caught the steel in his voice.

"No, lord. I admit that Roxana is not formally betrothed to me, though she is promised to me, and I have a claim on her."

"If she is not betrothed, then by custom she is free to bed whoever she wants." Parasades pointed out.

135

"She is mine," Thyrsus muttered. He stood slumped sullenly before his chief, his bearded face pale.

"A man who would falsely accuse another is no longer honourable. You are relieved of your duties and will confine yourself to your wagons until I can investigate this matter. Now get out." Spargises dismissed him with a flick of his hand and watched as the man backed out of the tent. The chief turned to his son. "This man has recently come from your patrol. Find out why he accused Nikomayros falsely. Another member of your patrol, Menaraxes, is implicated in this affair also."

Areipithes smiled and nodded pleasantly. "I am sure it is merely a misunderstanding but I shall look into the matter fully. Young men's blood runs hot." He looked at Nikometros with a smirk. "Well, barbarian, it seems you are free to enjoy the girl's favours without hindrance."

Nikometros shook his head. "I cannot remember anything of last night. I have no intentions toward her."

"A pity, barbarian. She is quite beautiful I am told. Maybe another time?"

"There will be no other time. I was lured to her wagon to talk to her and the person I thought was her father. I remember drinking and talking to her then waking up with Thyrsus shouting at me." Nikometros shook his head and glanced towards Tomyra's stony face. "I am sure I did not act dishonourably. I would not."

"Then perhaps another girl," Areipithes said. "As you said, father, we have been remiss in not finding him a bed companion. A man needs a woman from time to time."

Spargises nodded sagely. "We must provide for all my blood brother's needs."

"I do not need a woman," Nikometros said. "And if I did I am capable of finding one for myself."

"As long as you obey our customs, barbarian."

"And do not trouble any married or betrothed women," Parasades added.

Spargises grinned at Nikometros. "Well, no great harm done, brother. You are free to take your pleasure with any unattached girl who is willing. Just make sure first. It will save us all a lot of trouble." He clapped Nikometros on the shoulder and started walking towards the door. "Areipithes, Parasades, walk with me. We need to discuss today's patrols."

The three men left the tent. Nikometros looked at Tomyra standing silently across the tent from him. He smiled tentatively. "I really cannot think what happened to me. My head feels as if a Titan is hammering on it."

Tomyra looked at him coldly. "Perhaps you should drink less." She gathered up her robes and started walking for the door.

Nikometros fell into step with her. "I can usually handle my wine." He shook his head gingerly. "I will let the air clear my head today."

Outside, the camp was a bustle of activity. Nikometros could see wagons already starting to move. Men moved in behind him, packing up the chief's tent into wagons. "It will take me but a few moments to mount up, my lady. I will meet you outside your tent."

"Do not concern yourself with that today. I am sure you can find other duties, more pleasant than accompanying me. You are dismissed."

Nikometros stopped in his tracks and looked at her in dismay. "My lady? Tomyra..." He hesitated then as Tomyra continued on her way, turned and trudged off, his head low.

Tomyra continued on her way, anger and sorrow tugging at her heart. *He is just another man after all, governed by his appetites. Why did I think and hope he was more than that?* She turned her head and saw Nikometros disappear between the wagons. A tear glistened at the corner of one eye. She angrily wiped it away with the back of her hand and kept walking. The bright new morning already seemed less appealing.

Chapter Twelve

Nikometros sat astride his stallion on a low hillock watching the great herds moving slowly northward. In the distance, through the gray sheets of rain, he could just make out the straggling line of wagons, while groups of armed riders rode slowly back and forth on the outskirts of the moving mass of people and beasts, keeping a watchful eye out for hostile tribesmen. He wrapped his cloak tighter about him, as another cold gust blew a mist of rain across him, and the small group of men huddled at the foot of the hill. The colder conditions and wet weather had depressed him further these last few weeks.

A low cough behind him made him turn. Mardes guided his horse carefully up the muddy slope to Nikometros' side. "Sir? Have you orders for us?"

Nikometros scowled at Mardes sitting comfortably astride his roan gelding in his thick tunic and trousers. The rain beaded and ran off the greased leather. He looked warm and dry under his hood. *He looks comfortable in those clothes but I will be dead before I will wear such effeminate-looking things.* He shivered again when a rivulet of water found its way down his back. "We will resume our patrol. The priestess cannot be far from here. We will rejoin her." He sat and looked out over the plains again, seeking Tomyra's patrol. The presence of his old comrade lifted his spirits. "Mardes, I am gladdened that you are by my side again. Sometimes the days weigh heavily on me among these people."

Mardes grinned. "It is perhaps for the best, sir. One of these days we'll be returning to our own people. I wouldn't want to be too much a Scythian when that happens."

139

Nikometros looked around quickly then turned, and gave him a searching look. "You still think of escape? I thought you were happy here with your horses."

"Oh, I like it well enough but these aren't my people. I hope to return to my family one day. I know Timon thirsts for it too."

Nikometros grunted. "I thought Timon contented as a metal worker. I never see him these days."

"His skills are much in demand but I talk to him most evenings. He only waits for your lead, as do I, sir. Give us the word, and we'll escape with you."

"Every day takes us further away from Alexander's empire, and only the gods know where Alexander himself is now. We wouldn't stand a chance negotiating these open plains with every man's hand against us. Be patient. My understanding is that these people will return to Urul by next winter. We'll find an opportunity then." Nikometros brushed the water off his face. "I need Timon to be with us though. I will request his services from Spargises."

He looked around at his other men waiting patiently at the foot of the hill. He beckoned to Partaxes, who immediately kicked his horse into motion. When he came alongside, he looked up enquiringly at Nikometros from his small wiry horse.

"We ride to rejoin the priestess' patrol." He gazed to the north again, forcing his voice into a lighter tone. "The rain is clearing at last. It will be good to dry out."

"Indeed, Nikomayros. The rain is good for the pastures, but it dampens men's spirits." He gave a broad grin from underneath his leather hood. "We all look forward to the sun."

Nikometros turned his horse, and rode slowly down the muddy slope, guiding his stallion carefully. Mardes followed as Partaxes turned, and waved the other horsemen into motion. They joined up at the foot of the slope, splashing through sheets of water that glinted in the first rays of sunshine breaking through the clouds. Nikometros waved his patrol onward, watching them as they rode past, noting how they sat their horses. *Gods, that takes me back. Less than two months and I'm watching another patrol ride past me.*

Nikometros examined their riding stance and equipment critically. The Scythian horsemen rode in a much more relaxed manner, moving with their horses, not trying to dominate them as his Greek soldiers had done. *They are better riders,* he thought wryly. *Possibly better in battle too, though disorganised. Could that be remedied?* He urged Diomede forward, catching up with the riders easily. He moved closer to Mardes. "The men are coming along well. I thought they would be too independent, but you have trained them well."

"They want to learn, sir. These men have all volunteered to be in your patrol. They see it as a great honour and already think of themselves as elite horsemen."

Nikometros reflected on the past few weeks. He still felt a deep pain and confusion when he thought of Tomyra's continued lack of interest in him. She refrained from riding out on patrol most days leaving Nikometros to find other duties. Parasades gave him five youngsters, as the nucleus of a new patrol group, and others came in by one's and two's. He now led a group of nearly thirty men. When Mardes came to him asking to be allowed to ride with him, he made him his lieutenant, putting him in charge of instructing the men in basic cavalry techniques and manoe vres. Long days of grueling instruction followed, the men at first balking at the intense discipline. Within days, though, they could see the differences between themselves and the other Scythians and applied themselves more willingly to their lessons. Already they rode as a single body of men rather than the usual Scythian way as thirty individual riders. They learned the meaning of signals raised on a lance, and the value of looking after their fellows. As a mark of respect, they called themselves 'Lions' after Nikometros' family crest – that of Leonnatos.

Nikometros caught sight of a body of riders far off to his left and shaded his eyes against the glare from the westering sun. *Yes, it is Tomyra.* He galloped up to the front of the patrol and raised his lance above his head twice then pointed to the left. He glanced back to see the horsemen react immediately, angling to the left. *They move like a flock of birds, wheeling in the sky.* He grinned with satisfaction.

The other horsemen caught sight of the Lions and raised a shout. A few broke ranks and galloped out to meet them. Nikometros ignored them, watching his riders closely. He raised his lance again, stabbing to left and right. The riders split into two groups and swept around Tomyra's patrol to left and right, before slowing and falling into step alongside them.

Nikometros edged his horse close to Tomyra. "My lady. The eastern flanks are clear. Allow me to accompany you back to the wagons."

Tomyra had been watching Nikometros' patrol with interest as it closed with hers. She nodded her approval of the discipline evident in the riders. As Nikometros spoke however, she stared straight ahead, refusing to look at him. "Very well. You may lead our combined patrols back."

Nikometros sighed gently then saluted and dropped back. Raising his lance once more, with its fluttering pennant at the tip he pointed it forward and to the left, calling out, "Lion patrol, lead out, double line."

The Lions immediately broke into a trot, moving out ahead of the other patrol, wheeling to the left as they did so. Several other horsemen followed them whooping and shouting. Nikometros noted with approval how his men studiously ignored them for the most part. A few sneered openly at the other patrol's lack of discipline. *They are developing a pride in themselves*, he thought.

Nikometros signaled to Mardes then dropped back to ride with Tomyra. He rode in silence, feeling the strained tension between them. At last, he could bear it no longer. "My lady, why do you turn me away? I seek only to be with you, protecting you as is my duty."

Tomyra turned toward him. "Why should I need your protection when I am surrounded by my own people?" She looked forward again, adding coldly, "As for turning you away, I am sure that can be no real hardship. There must be many young women eager for your attentions."

"My lady...Tomyra, there is no one I would rather be with. I seek the company of no other women. How can I prove to you that I care only for you?"

"That is no concern of mine. Like all men, you will find other distractions in time." She touched her heels to her mare and galloped away.

Nikometros followed at a distance until she reached the column of wagons. Already the sun was low in the sky and the wagons were being pulled into large circles. Dry firewood and dried dung were u~

loaded from the wagons and fires lit. Nikometros found his wagon deserted. He looked around for Agarus then decided he must be off feeding the oxen. He slid down from Diomede's back and stretched tiredly.

Mardes trotted up and saluted. "Any orders, sir?"

Nikometros tossed his head in negation then remembered that Persians often misunderstood that gesture and shook his head in the eastern fashion. "No. Get a hot meal into you, and a good rest. Meet me back here at daybreak."

Mardes saluted again, and gathering Diomede's reins trotted off again. Nikometros watched him go, a small smile on his face. *He loves that horse as much as I do. He counts it a privilege to groom and feed him.* He turned and climbed into his wagon. Although the rain had stopped, the air was still humid and the felt coverings were soaking. A musty odour filled his nostrils. *I hope that it will be fine tomorrow and things will dry out.*

Nikometros stripped off and dug out a clean tunic. The chill evening air made him shiver so he picked out a warm woolen cloak. He cast a speculative eye at a leather jacket and leggings left in the corner then tossed his head again. *I will not wear those trousers!* He pulled on a dry pair of sandals and climbed out of the wagon. The gathering dusk was laden with billows of wood smoke as the cooking fires glowed sullenly on the sodden ground. Agarus squatted by the nearest one, fussing over an iron pot. Nikometros' feet squelched in the wet grass and mud as he walked over.

Agarus looked up as he approached and smiled. "Won't be long, Nikomayros. A fine mutton stew." He bent over the fire again, stirring the pot with a long dagger. "Oh, by the way, Taxicus was here earlier looking for you. He said he would return after the meal."

"Taxicus? Ah, yes, I remember him, one of the chief's advisers. Did he say what he wanted?"

Agarus shook his head. "He didn't say; I didn't ask." He got up and limped over to the wagon, picking up a couple of battered bronze plates and a large spoon. He squatted down by the fire again and ladled stew onto the plates.

Nikometros felt his mouth start to fill with saliva, as he smelt the rich meaty odours, seasoned with spices. He took a plate from Agarus and drew his dagger, stabbing steaming chunks of meat. The gravy ran down over his chin, scalding him, as the hot meat filled him and warmed his belly. He tipped his plate, mopping up the last of the juices with a hunk of coarse bread. He swallowed, belched gently and grinned at Agarus. "By the Gods, that was a meal worth serving a king."

Agarus looked pleased as he gathered up the plates. "A drink? I have a nice flask of wine."

Nikometros hesitated then shook his head. "Scythian wine does not agree with me. I will just have water."

Agarus looked around quickly and lowered his voice. "I don't think you need to worry about our wine, Nikomayros. Just what is put in it."

"What do you mean?"

"I've never heard of a man passing out from a few cups of wine. Some people say there must have been something else in it. Poppy maybe."

"There was no poppy, I would know the taste."

Agarus made an impatient gesture. "Something else then."

145

Nikometros squatted down beside Agarus. "What I don't understand is why someone went to all this trouble then stopped short of finishing it. If I were to be lured into a trap then why not into a trap with a married woman. The husband could then demand my death for adultery, or even kill me in a fit of anger. As it is, they failed."

"Did they, Nikomayros? Your death could not be sought without facing you in battle and few men would risk that. Maybe even fighting the chief too. You are blood brothers, remember. Few warriors would willingly meet Spargises in single combat. Besides, most men regard you with affection and many women too. You have lost the affection and respect of our priestess though. In the long run, this may be more important."

Nikometros remained silent, thinking. At last, he spoke in a low voice. "Who benefits by the priestess losing respect for me?"

"Do you need to ask?" Agarus scowled at the fire as the wood crackled. Smoke gusted toward him in the fitful breeze, making him cough. "Spargises gained a strong ally in you, just when his influence over the tribe was slipping. A warrior, chosen by the Goddess herself. His other support comes from the priestess who stands steadfastly by him always. Two pillars to support his leadership. Now his strong pillars are at odds." Agarus grunted and spat into the coals. "A certain man will seek to take advantage of this."

"Depose or kill his father? Such actions are god-cursed. Even Areipithes would balk at that."

"Hush, name no names. And who said anything about killing?" Agarus glanced around nervously, and dropped his voice to a murmur. "A chief is elected by acclamation of the people. Let a man prove himself

146

more worthy in battle and the leadership may pass to his shoulders. A certain man was on the verge of doing this when you arrived. Now he is not so sure of his support."

Nikometros plucked a grass stem and chewed on it moodily. "Then I must regain the priestess' favour. But how do I do this when she talks to me with ice in her voice?"

"Keep close to her, my friend. Show her that you are a man to be trusted, a man that her father can rely on. She is a woman, as well as a priestess..." Agarus broke off, holding his hand palm down over the mud. He muttered something under his breath. "The Goddess knows I meant no disrespect. Show yourself a true friend of the People, and she will forgive you in time."

The sucking and squelching of footsteps warned Nikometros of the approach of a group of men. He got to his feet quickly and turned to meet them. He relaxed a little when he recognised Taxicus.

"Greetings Nikomayros." Taxicus raised a hand as he approached. "I would have a word with you." The two men with him moved over to the fire and warmed themselves, talking to Agarus in a low voice. Taxicus put his arm casually over Nikometros' shoulders and drew him to one side. "I have been talking to Spargises and Parasades. They are impressed with the handling of your patrol. I would not have believed you could persuade Scythian riders to be so disciplined." He laughed loudly, the men at the fire quieting and turning toward them. "We of the Massegetae are an independent people. I would be interested in knowing how you achieved it."

147

"They take a pride in themselves. They can see already that they can do something that others cannot. It makes them feel special."

Taxicus nodded soberly. "Can they fight as well? Or is it just pretty riding?"

"Find some more foes for us, and you will see." Nikometros grinned.

"Very well. We are about to cross the disputed borders of the Jartai people. Bring your patrol to the van tomorrow. We'll find you your foes." Taxicus signaled his men with a gesture. They moved away from the fire, standing alert and ready.

Nikometros hesitated a moment. "I would like my old comrade Timon back in my patrol. He is a good cavalry officer, and would be invaluable in a battle. Will you ask Spargises if he can be released from his duties?"

"I will instruct the metal workers' guild to release him for a few days. If he proves himself in battle he will be released permanently. A good fighter is worth many artisans." Taxicus nodded at his men and walked away into the darkened camp.

Nikometros stood and smiled to himself. *Reunited with my men and maybe even a battle tomorrow. We must acquit ourselves well.* He beckoned Agarus. "Seek out the Lions. Tell them we are in action tomorrow. I will inspect them at dawn."

Agarus grinned broadly and saluted, limping off into the shadows. Nikometros turned back to his wagon feeling in a better mood than he had for weeks. *I will show Tomyra that my Lions are a strong pillar of support for her father. She will come to trust me again.*

Chapter Thirteen

Diomede stamped his hooves on the rain-softened earth and blew hard, the great golden stallion rolling his eyes at every horse that came galloping up to the little group of men on the low rise. Nikometros sat impatiently astride his mount, as he stared out across the small shallow valley at the hundreds of opposing Jartai tribesmen. His iron and bronze armour gleamed, throwing dazzling glints in the strong morning light, his tunic was freshly laundered and the horsehair crest of his helmet shone red as arterial blood. Timon sat on a black gelding a few paces behind him, his eyes fixed on his commander. He too, fidgeted impatiently, waiting for a decision to be made.

Nikometros noticed a similar grouping of horsemen on a low hillock among the Jartai. He squinted into the sun, shading his eyes. At this distance the enemy tribesmen looked indistinguishable from the Massegetae. Dressed in felt and leather trousers and armed with bows and lances they could have mingled unnoticed in any company of Scythian horsemen.

Spargises and Areipithes stood huddled together with their advisers discussing the scene before them. Every few moments, one or other of them would raise his voice or gesticulate violently, but there seemed to be no real decisions being made. Parasades strode up and down in front of the chief pointing animatedly at his company of men sitting patiently to one side. At length Areipithes nodded and joined Parasades in his argument. Spargises kept shaking his head then at last threw up his hands and nodded.

Parasades saluted and leapt onto his horse, urging it toward his company, yelling and shouting. As he reached his men, he swerved towards the massed Jartai tribesmen, his men spurring their horses after him. The company swept in a loose rabble along the front of the enemy, loosing off a barrage of arrows that fell, for the most part, harmlessly among them. Parasades and his men reached the end of the enemy line and turned, galloping back in the opposite direction. Tribesmen on both sides shouted and jeered, firing off stray arrows that fell between the armies.

The company raced back to their former positions, the horses blowing hard, and their riders grinning broadly. Parasades trotted toward the chief, receiving smiles and the occasional pat on his back. Spargises pointed out across the valley to where company of Jartai horsemen separated from their army and swept along the valley in an identical movement, firing arrows and yelling at the top of their voices.

Nikometros edged his stallion closer to the group and tapped Parasades on the arm. When he turned, he looked at Parasades expectantly. "What is happening, my friend? Why do we not charge the enemy?"

Parasades scowled. "We are not here to fight a battle, my fierce friend. The Wolf will exact a tribute from us and allow us to pass. We posture merely out of bravado."

"I do not understand. Who is this Wolf?"

Parasades pointed toward the Jartai leaders on the small hillock across the valley. "See the man in the centre? The one with a wolf's head cap? His name is Jurtes. A few years ago he was one of many advisers to the then Jartai chief – I forget his name. Then Jurtes slew him and took his place. He killed all who opposed him, and now leads his tribe conquering and slaying all the smaller and weaker tribes."

"Our People are a strong tribe though. Why does our chief fear this Jurtes?"

"Strong in numbers, yes." Parasades lowered his voice. "But for the last two years, since his beloved wife Starissa died, our chief has avoided conflict. He would rather pay the Wolf off than risk all in a battle."

"You do not believe Spargises should pay a tribute to the Wolf?"

"No, and neither do most of his advisers. For all his failings, Areipithes would at least fight for the honour of our People. As it is, the payment to the Wolf increases each year. A thousand horses last year and an equal number of cattle, perhaps more this year. He bleeds us of our strength until we are weak enough to swallow whole." Parasades leaned to one side and clearing his throat, spat on the ground.

Areipithes waved an arm above his head and another company of riders set off at a gallop. These rode straight towards the enemy, pulling up fifty paces from the opposing riders and loosing a torrent of arrows before turning tail and fleeing back to their own lines. At once, a section of the Jartai repeated the manoeuver.

Nikometros looked puzzled. "If we are to pay this tribute then why do we pretend to oppose them?"

"We are still too strong to be swallowed up. Spargises hopes that by putting on a show of force, he may get better terms."

"He may get even better terms if he really attacked, rather than just galloping up and down, firing off a few arrows."

"You may be right, my friend. But you see both armies arrayed before you. How would you attack to our advantage?"

Nikometros thought for a moment, surveying the opposing lines. "A cavalry charge with lances. If we carried our charge home, we would roll right through their line. A determined charge on that hillock could reach their leaders and end this conflict at once."

Parasades shook his head. "That may be how your people fight, but here we hit the enemy hard when they don't expect it and ride away before they can retaliate. Our warriors are not trained to fight in your way. The Jartai army stands before us, armed and ready. We cannot charge them, and we cannot surprise them."

"My Lions could," murmured Nikometros, "had we some loyal support."

Shouting erupted from the far end of the line. A small group of Massegetae tribesmen broke away from their companies and raced out into the gap between the armies. Ahead of them a small form jinked and swerved. Spargises and his advisers pointed and shouted with laughter as the horsemen galloped after the hare fleeing toward the Jartai army. At the last moment, it saw the waiting riders and doubled back. A group of young Jartai riders whooped and spurred forward in pursuit. The two groups of horsemen merged and milled around in confusion at the bottom of the valley, the hare streaking for cover in the long grass by the stream.

Nikometros gestured at the rabble in the valley. "Even now they do not fight."

"Our tribes have always been friendly, Nikomayros. It is only since the coming of the Wolf that fear and hatred has arisen. Left to themselves, the young men would rather feast than fight. The Wolf has tainted their minds."

With a great deal of laughter and taunting, the riders separated and returned to their respective tribes. There was a lull as the two armies stood under the hot sun, waiting for their chiefs to make the next move. Nikometros edged Diomede closer to Spargises who was arguing with Areipithes again.

"...send someone to parley with them now. We have shown our strength. With a little luck he will agree to let us pay only a few hundred head of horses, a thousand at most like last year, and we can be on our way."

Areipithes spat on the ground. "A few hundred head? It is a waste of good horseflesh. Let us spill some blood first at least. We are warriors, not merchants to buy our way out of trouble."

"And if we attack and lose? We could end up paying far more in compensation."

"We will not lose." Areipithes looked around and saw Nikometros listening. "Even our brave barbarian is prepared for battle. Let him show his worth," he sneered. "If nothing else, his company of performing horses can provide us with some entertainment."

Nikometros pushed forward alongside Spargises. "Let me attack with my company, brother. I know that I can break their line."

Spargises looked at him doubtfully. "Brother, I thank you but it is not necessary. We can parley successfully for our passage. We can afford the price."

"Let me try at least. If I fail, your position will be no weaker. And if I win through..." Nikometros let his voice trail off.

Spargises thought about it for a few moments, scrutinising the opposing army. "If you fail, we may well be weaker..."

"Then I must not fail," Nikometros declared.

Spargises sighed and then nodded his agreement. "Very well, brother. If you can make the Wolf move back from his hill, that will be enough. We can use it as a good bargaining tool."

"Allow me to accompany Nikomayros." Parasades pushed forward. "His ways are strange but exciting. He had good ideas when we attacked the Dahai patrols."

"I, too," said Taxicus. "A show of strength is needed."

Areipithes scowled but said nothing. Spargises nodded. "May the gods favour you then. Bloody their noses for me and I will extract favourable terms in parley."

Nikometros saluted and turned his horse back toward Timon. "Come Timon," he said, his voice shaking with pent-up excitement. "We have a battle at last."

The two men swiftly rode down the front of the line towards the waiting Lions. Parasades and Taxicus followed them, listening as Nikometros quickly outlined his plan. Saluting, the two warriors grinned fiercely and galloped back to their own men. Nikometros conferred briefly with Mardes then turned to the Lions and addressed them. "We ride into battle under the eye of our chief, and for the glory of all our people. Today we hunt the Wolf. Remember your training, and watch for the signals."

The men raised their lances and shouted "Nikomayros! Lions!" A murmur rippled through the massed tribesmen around them at the cries. The Jartai sat up straighter and looked across the valley with interest.

Nikometros smiled and turned to Timon and Mardes. "Lead them out slowly, straight ahead. Watch

154

for my sign." He nudged Diomede into a walk then after a few paces into a trot. The Lions spread out on either side of him in a ragged line, Timon and Mardes snapping at them tersely. Nikometros looked off to his left and saw with satisfaction that Parasades was leading his company out at a trot, followed a few moments later by Taxicus and his men.

Nikometros reached down and patted Diomede's neck, talking to him in a low voice. The stallion's muscles were bunched tensely, eager to engage the enemy and Nikometros restrained him with an effort. His horse splashed through the stream at the bottom of the shallow valley, the line of warriors following an instant later, and started up the gentle incline. A pressure with his thighs and Diomede increased his pace to a canter. Ahead he could see the Jartai horsemen excitedly pointing and chattering. Nikometros glanced back and saw Parasades' company sweep round behind them, filling out their ranks. He drew his sword, pointing to the left and his company swung about, heading directly at the opposing chief of the Jartai on his little hillock.

A few arrows started to fall among them as the Jartai realised the attack would be pressed home, one hit Nikometros' breastplate a glancing blow. Timon and Mardes raised their spears and the company pivoted, pulling into a narrow arrowhead formation as they broke into a full gallop. Like an arrow loosed by a hunter at a snarling wolf, the company thundered up the rise, Nikometros in his burnished armour gleaming like fire at its tip. In the instant before they met, Nikometros filled his lungs and shouted the chilling battle paean of his ancestors. A hundred throats behind him picked up the cry and hurled it at the enemy, the thundering hooves of their mounts only seconds behind their war cry.

Even before the two armies met, the Jartai were falling back in disarray, suddenly unsure of themselves at this very un-Scythian tactic. Uncertainty turned to panic as Diomede crashed into the line, kicking and biting. An ecstasy overcame Nikometros as he forged ahead, every eye drawn to his shining form. Jartai horsemen shrank from his flashing sword, fleeing or falling beneath it. His men strove to keep up with the golden stallion, carrying all before them. The fury of their charge carried the Lions deep into the enemy line, cutting and slashing. Around them rose the cries of wounded men and screaming horses, impaled on the lances and swords of the Massegetae tribesmen.

Nikometros' headlong rush slowed. He dimly heard a distant shouting and felt the earth tremble as the waiting Massegetae warriors roared their approbation, breaking ranks and surging across the valley toward them. The struggle of fighting men around Nikometros paused, appalled at the sight. The whole Jartai army started to draw back as hundreds of screaming Massegetae warriors raced onward. A yelling mass of horsemen broke on the Jartai lines and overwhelmed them. The main body of Massegetae, still waiting on the low ridge, now yelled and raced forward, throwing their weight into the ruptured Jartai line. Fighting became general, the moving mass of men and horses shoving and pushing back and forth. Even Nikometros' Lions lost cohesion and their concerted attack dissipated into individual hand-to-hand fights.

A tremor ran through the struggling mass – standards dipped and the Jartai wavered and started to fall back in disarray. Nikometros caught sight of the Wolf as he turned to flee, and urged Diomede after him. He broke free of the confusion, and roared a challenge. The Wolf turned in his direction, snarling, his wolf's head cap hanging awry, and Nikometros saw the man's eyes widen as the great golden stallion, streaked with blood and foam, carrying a gleaming figure with upraised sword, bore down on him. The Wolf half-turned away again, his heels drumming into his horse's sides in panic, as he forced the horse through his advisers. Diomede cannoned into the horse's flank and Nikometros' sword descended in an arc as the horse fell. The Wolf screamed and disappeared into the dust and milling hooves. Loud cries of dismay went up, cut off abruptly as Timon and other riders caught up with him.

The noise of warfare grew more distant. The battle fury seeped from Nikometros' mind, as he became aware, once more, of those around him. He looked about to see the Jartai streaming away across the plains in confusion, the Massegetae harassing them as they fled. Timon gave rapid orders to the Lions around him, setting up a defensive ring around Nikometros and the fallen Jartai chief. Several of his advisers sat dejectedly on the ground; their hands bound behind their backs, with the fallen battle standards.

Hooves thudded behind him and Nikometros whirled, sword in hand, ready to meet this new threat. He stared hard for a moment then passed a hand wearily across his face, lowering his sword. He saw Spargises and Areipithes, together with several other men, push into the circle around the Jartai standards.

"By all the gods and goddesses of this and other worlds," breathed Spargises. "What demon possessed you to attack their whole army? I thought you were just going to probe his line a little." He looked around in amazement, shaking his head. He stood regarding the body of the Jartai chief and the totality of the victory started seeping into his consciousness. "The whole army..." he muttered. Spargises laughed suddenly then raised his arms above his head and screamed aloud to the heavens, "The whole Jartai people is mine!" He dropped his arms and turned slowly to Nikometros. His broad smile slipped as he saw the blood-slimed figure standing wearily in front of him. "Nikomayros, my brother, you are hurt?"

Nikometros eased his head back. "I am unhurt but others are wounded. I must see to my men."

"Even as we speak our healers move among them, helping those that will live, sending those beyond our help to the Goddess in mercy." Spargises walked up to Nikometros and embraced him. "My brother, you have won me a great victory today. Tonight we shall feast, and tomorrow we divide the spoils of a whole tribe." He rubbed his hands together cheerfully, calling to his bodyguards for wine.

Areipithes stood quietly off to one side, a sour expression on his face. He watched as a small herd of captured horses trotted by, guarded by several smiling men. Abruptly, he turned and strode through the circle of guards to his horse. He galloped off in the direction of the Massegetae army now starting to wander back.

Timon nudged a warrior beside him. "Where is he off to in such a hurry I wonder?"

The warrior laughed. "Off to make sure of his share of the plunder I expect. Areipithes is never far away when there are spoils to be had."

Spargises lowered his wineskin and belched loudly. He looked around and caught sight of Parasades riding up with his company. "Ah, there you are Para-

sades. A marvelous day's work is it not? Take charge
of these prisoners and the body of their chief." Parasades saluted, and at once, started his preparations.
Spargises turned to Taxicus who was squatting nearby, stripping jewelry from a corpse. "Nikomayros and
I will advance on the Jartai village immediately." He
called to his bodyguards to bring his horse. "Taxicus,
sound a recall. We must gather our army together and
strike hard at their camp before they have a chance to
regroup." He pushed the wine flask into Nikometros'
hands and swung up onto his horse.

Nikometros rinsed his mouth out and spat to remove the grime and blood stink. He drank thirstily
then tossed the empty flask to Taxicus. He turned to
Timon. "How many of our Lions have fallen?" He
listened as Timon recounted a short list of names
then nodded. "Have their bodies seen to in honour.
Gather the others. I will talk to them before we move
off." He smiled and reached across, grasping Timon's
forearm. "You fought well, my friend. As did all of
our company." Nikometros watched as Timon
mounted his horse and rode off, waving his lance and
shouting commands. He returned to where Parasades
supervised the removal of the chief's body.

Parasades looked up and smiled, the fallen chief's
headdress in hand. "Here, my friend. Until we can
prepare the Wolf's head, you may have this wolf's
head." He threw back his head and roared with laughter, his men joining in, slapping their thighs. "That
was nobly done, Macedonian. Perhaps those who see
you as a future leader are not wrong after all."

Nikometros smiled briefly, accepting the bloodied
pelt. "What happens to these men?" He waved at the
sullen prisoners around him.

159

Parasades shrugged. "No doubt they will soon join their ancestors. They have preyed on their own people long enough."

Nikometros looked out to the north, where the Massegetae warriors were reforming. "And the rest of the Jartai?"

"Their fate is in their own hands. It is usual where one tribe falls to another, to offer the warriors the choice of brotherhood or death. Most will choose life."

"And the women?"

"Theirs is the fate of women everywhere. Those whose husbands fell will gain new husbands and make the best of their situation." Parasades cleared his throat before continuing. "That charge by your company was amazing, my friend. I did not think our riders could carry it through. You must teach me your methods."

"Gladly, but now I must rejoin our chief. We must secure the Jartai village before they think to oppose us once more." Nikometros put his fingers to his mouth and whistled softly. Diomede whinnied in reply and trotted over to his side. He vaulted onto the stallion's back, briefly saluted his friend, and galloped off toward the head of the gathering army.

Chapter Fourteen

The Jartai village nestled between the confluence of two small streams. The women and old people were hastily throwing up a rough earthwork as the first of the defeated tribesmen streamed back in disarray. As the full measure of the defeat sank in however, they downed tools and stood around disconsolately in family groups. Women wept for their fallen men and children screamed. The surviving leaders hastily conferred with much gesticulating and raised voices. A murmur rippled through the throng as the Massegetae army came into sight, armed and alert for the least sign of trouble. The murmuring changed to cries of surprise and wonder at the tall figure of Nikometros, in bloodstained bronze, riding proudly on a great golden stallion near the front of the column. Several men made warding signs against the demons as the gleaming figure drew near.

Spargises drew rein and sat looking down on the huddled remnants of the Jartai army. Though defeated, they still outnumbered the Massegetae. He signaled and his warriors spread out on either side, the riders at the front of his army fitting arrows to their bows. Keeping the arrows pointed at the ground, they stared intently at the Jartai. The mass of people drew back slightly, and bowed their heads.

An old man dressed in richly coloured felt and leather pushed through the crowd, and crossed the open space in front of Spargises. He held out his bow in front of him in his left hand and a knife in his right. The old man sighed deeply then swept the blade across the bowstring, the string parting with a high-pitched twang. In the silence that followed, the old man gave a sob and let the bow and knife fall to the ground.

Spargises looked up at the armed Jartai warriors. He raised his arm and hundreds of bows raised in answer, menacing the warriors before him. "How say you? Are you of like mind? Choose your fate now."

There was a pause lasting for several breaths. At last, a bow was thrown down, followed by another then many more. Spargises relaxed, gesturing with his arm before lowering it slowly. He turned to Nikometros and Areipithes with a smile. "So, they have decided to live. My son, organise a formal meeting with the surviving leaders and army commanders. We must bind the Jartai with bonds of friendship and blood."

Areipithes nodded and turned, shouting orders to his men as he trotted off. Spargises started issuing rapid orders to Parasades and Taxicus. Steady streams of riders were dispatched carrying instructions to various army commanders. Gradually the mass of people in front of them moved away, and a semblance of order was restored. Spargises at last turned to Nikometros. "You would normally be required to perform many sacrifices to the Goddess tonight, in your capacity as Her champion. However, I wish the Jartai to show their good faith. They shall perform the sacrifices."

Nikometros bowed. "As you wish, blood-brother." He smiled inwardly in relief. It was one thing to kill in the heat of battle – any soldier was required to do that – but to kill prisoners in cold blood, for no better reason than that they had won, was distasteful. He did not enjoy his sacrificial duties but neither would he shirk them. Nikometros saluted the chief and rode off, seeking his patrol.

Great bonfires blazed that night on the plain out-side the Jartai village. Throngs of tribesmen gathered round them, drinking and eating. Whole oxen and sheep, from the Jartai herds, hung above the cooking trenches, gouts of smoke billowing upward as fat dripped into the hot embers. Swarms of children ran everywhere, and Jartai women chattered in groups around the fires. Some faces showed signs of grief, but most appeared resigned. None of the Massegetae womenfolk were present, and the warriors of the People walked around fully armed.

Nikometros and Timon moved slowly through the crowds, greeting friends and getting stares from strangers. "I'm amazed, Timon." Nikometros looked around him. "A few hours ago we fought a battle with this tribe, and now they feast together with our men."

Timon shrugged. "I'm told it's usual if there is no great enmity between the tribes. These two tribes have traditionally been quite close, at least until the Wolf arrived on the scene. Now he's dead it's as if he never lived."

Nikometros smiled. "You seem to have a good knowledge of the history of the tribe. You are learn-ing a lot of useful information I see."

A Jartai man, singing at the top of his voice, lurched out from the shadows and collided with Ti-mon. The man stumbled and almost fell, grasping Timon's arm for support. He muttered something in a slurred voice then peered up at Timon and Ni-kometros with an inane grin. His face froze in horror as he recognised the pair, his eyes darting swiftly back and forth between them. He stumbled backward, holding his arms out in front of him as if trying to ward off an attack. On the edge of the shadows he stopped and lowered his arms. Muttering and shaking his head he turned and wandered off, pushing his way into the swirling mass of people.

Timon brushed his arm where the man had gripped him. "What was that all about, Niko? I thought he was another drunk, but he seemed to know us. Or you at any rate."

"He was Jartai, perhaps he saw us in the battle. It's not important. Come on, I want to see the ceremonies that bind this tribe."

Nikometros pushed through the throng with Timon beside him. The bonfires gave way to smaller fires and a large open area ringed with smoky torches. Away from the heat of the fires, Nikometros drew his cloak about him, the golden lion's-head emblem on it flashing as he did so. Groups of men huddled together talking, and Nikometros caught sight of Spargises, talking animatedly to one of these groups, his breath white in the frosty air. As he watched, he saw the chief clap his hands loudly and call to his guards. Horns sounded a long plaintive call into the cold night air then again. As Nikometros looked around, he saw people streaming into the open area, jostling each other as they formed a large circle around the figures of Spargises and his advisers. The crowd fell silent, watching expectantly.

Spargises walked into the middle of the ring of tribesmen and turned slowly in a complete circle then once more, searching the faces of the people lit by the flickering torches. He put his hands on his hips and threw out his chest, his powerful voice sweeping over them. "Men of the Jartai, you have a choice to make. Your chief lies slain and his advisers shall follow him into death shortly. Do you choose to elect one of your own to lead you, or do you choose to live in brotherhood with the Massegetae?"

Complete silence followed. After a space, quiet mutterings started and gathered in volume, leaping from man to man. Spargises waited then as the noise died away lifted his arms and called out again. "Let the leaders of the companies stand forth."

The murmuring started again, and men pushed through the crowd, walking out into the open space. Nikometros counted sixteen men in all, most standing impassively, hands on sword hilts, others fidgeting and looking around. Spargises walked forward and looked searchingly at each man, completing the circle slowly. He resumed his place in the centre. "What say you? Do you speak for your companies?"

A ragged chorus from the leaders raised itself in affirmation. A short man with a long dark beard stepped forward. "I will answer for my people."

"What is your name, man of Jartai?"

"I am Lugartes, son of Perisces, son of Martes of the Eastern Jartai people. My father and grandfather were chief of this tribe, before Jurtes, known to you as the Wolf enslaved us."

"And what say you, Lugartes, son of Perisces? Will you lead your tribe as chief or join with the Massegetae as one people in brotherhood?"

Lugartes looked around at the encircling crowd, his eyes resting on some briefly. He caught sight of Nikometros and Timon standing quietly just inside the circle. He gazed for a long moment at them before turning back to Spargises.

"What terms do the Massegetae offer?"

"Only that which is honourable. If you choose to be chief of the Eastern Jartai then you must swear an oath of friendship with the Massegetae and allow us free access to the Mother-waters each year. You must live in peace with the tribes around you as far as you

165

are able, only defending yourselves, never attacking others."

"And if I choose to join? Do you speak in truth of common brotherhood?"

"Our two peoples shall be as one, united under one chief. No man of the Jartai shall serve the Massegetae. He will be welcome at our fires and at our counsels as a brother. The bonds will be forged with blood."

Lugartes paused, obviously thinking hard about his decision. He turned and pointed at Nikometros. "I see one among you who is not of your people. He avenged my father by slaying the Wolf, for which action he has my thanks." Lugartes inclined his head toward Nikometros. "I would know his name, and whether he is, in truth, as many of my people believe, a fire demon. He led your armies like a thunderbolt, a lion of fire blazing into the heart of my people."

Spargises smiled broadly. "He is a man but one loved by the Goddess, wearing her sign upon his arm. He is also my brother. Bonds of blood brotherhood bind me to him. Our priestess sees a glorious and golden future for him." He gestured to Nikometros. "Let my brother speak his own name."

Nikometros stepped forward into the circle, throwing back his cloak. His eyes locked with Lugartes' as he spoke in a clear voice, pitched to carry to the whole crowd. "I am Nikometros, son of Leonnatos of the Macedonian people. I am also known as Nikomayros, blood-brother to Spargises, warrior of the Massegetae."

The crowd stirred and a confused babble arose. Lugartes bowed his head toward Nikometros in acknowledgement. "A worthy warrior indeed. I see you wear a lion's head upon your cloak. You fought indeed, as the great Scythian lion today." Lugartes stepped closer to Nikometros, looking intently into his eyes. "You are Macedonian, a soldier of the Great King, Alexander?" When Nikometros nodded, he sighed deeply, muttering, "So, it was true..." He paused for a moment then looked back at Nikometros. "There is someone in this tribe you should meet. An Egyptian slave with a gift of prophecy it seems. I will introduce him to you."

Lugartes turned back to Spargises. "Your priestess speaks the truth, I think. This Macedonian lion of yours is a powerful weapon." He paused briefly before continuing. "The Jartai will become one tribe in common brotherhood with the Massegetae, under your leadership."

Spargises clapped his hands with delight. "Excellent. You will not regret the decision." He gestured to his guards and once more, the mournful notes of the horns disturbed the night air. "First though, there is the matter of the Wolf's henchmen."

A group of a dozen bound figures were hustled roughly into the circle. The crowd moaned and drew back, and one or two women uttered screams of grief. Lugartes leaned over and spoke quietly to Spargises. "Not all of these are the Wolf's men. I know Lascus there...and Scyces. Both are good men who followed unwillingly."

"You would vouch for them?"

"I would," replied Lugartes.

Spargises spoke to a guard, and the two men were released. They stumbled toward Lugartes, white-faced and shaking, rubbing the circulation back into their wrists. They fell at his feet, Scyces gabbling in a high-pitched voice. "Thanks be to the gods, Lugartes, that you were here. Assure him," he gestured at Spargises, "that we are innocent, we were led by the Wolf, we could not refuse, we..."

Lugartes held up a hand, cutting off the trembling voice. "Thank Spargises here. He has spared you. Now rise, and conduct yourselves like men."

Spargises gestured once more, and the remaining ten prisoners were brought forward and thrown on their faces in front of the chief and Lugartes. Spargises walked down the row of prostrate men, nudging one or two with his toe. "You are accused of aiding the Wolf in his depredations of other tribes, of feeding off your own tribe and ravaging your own people. How say you?"

One of the men struggled up onto his knees. He looked around him, staring at Lugartes. "Then why is he standing in judgment over us? We only followed the Wolf in fear for our lives and the lives of our families, as did Lugartes here. Are we to be condemned for that?"

Lugartes scowled and spat in the man's face. "You lie, Coscus. How many men have died, falsely accused by you? How many young girls have you torn from their families to satisfy your unnatural lusts? How many families live in poverty because of your greed? I will kill you myself." He turned and held out a hand to Spargises. "My lord, I beg to be allowed to remove this vermin."

Spargises turned to the surrounding crowd of people. "Who among you also accuses this man of the crimes Lugartes, son of Perisces, accuses him of?" After a brief hesitation, several hands rose, and a ragged chorus of voices, growing in strength, called for the death of Coscus.

Spargises turned back to Lugartes and nodded. Lugartes drew his sword and stepped forward, raising

168

it high. Coscus screamed and threw himself backward as the blade flashed in the torchlight, burying itself in the man's chest. His scream cut off abruptly, followed by a bubbling moan then silence. Lugartes withdrew his sword and wiped it on the dead man's clothes. He stepped back, and sheathed his sword.

Spargises turned back to the crowd again. "And what of these others?"

"Death! Kill them!"

The Massegetae chief smiled grimly, gesturing to the other Jartai company leaders, still standing nearby. "Follow the example of your spokesman, rid us of these jackals that oppressed your tribe so long."

The Jartai leaders hesitated a moment then stepped forward grimly, drawing their swords as the prisoners started calling out to their erstwhile colleagues, begging for mercy. In a few moments, ten corpses lay bloodily on the grass.

Spargises nodded in satisfaction, beckoning to his guards. "Remove this filth. Bring the wine and the large vessels, we shall take the oaths of fealty and commonality." Areipithes leaned over and whispered in his ear. Spargises looked baffled then turned to Lugartes. "We have a problem. Our priestess is still at our encampment. We cannot invoke the Goddess without her."

Lugartes thought for a moment then snapped his fingers. "We can use our own priestess." He turned to the crowd. "Where is Lynna? Send for her immediately." He turned back to Spargises. "She is very young, but she was consecrated by our old priestess before she died."

The crowd parted as a young girl stepped through into the circle. She was robed in green felt and linen, with several pieces of gold jewelry pinned to it. Thick black hair fell in shimmering waves around her shoulders as she walked slowly up to the group of men. She held herself taut, stepping precisely with head held high. Her nervousness betrayed itself by the stiffness of her shoulders, and the rapid blinking of her deep brown eyes.

Nikometros felt his breath catch in his throat as he watched her approach. *She is a child*, he thought. *A beautiful girl but a child nonetheless. Can she be a true priestess?* He felt a brief moment of desire stab him then quickly extinguished. Following hard on the heels of this thought came an anguished ache for the other priestess, his Tomyra. He closed his eyes and conjured Tomyra's face before him, imagined her smiling at him.

Lugartes put his hand to his forehead when she stood before them. "My lord," he said, addressing Spargises, "This is Lynna, priestess of the Great Goddess."

Spargises inclined his head and smiled. "You are welcome, my lady." He waved his hands around at the assembled crowd. "Our two tribes are to become one. We need you to pray to the Goddess for us, and to conduct the oath-taking ceremonies."

Lynna glanced toward Lugartes. When he nodded, she turned back to Spargises. "Surely your own priestess...?"

"She is not here. She will join us tomorrow but the ceremony must take place now. You can do it? You know the forms?"

Lynna nodded. "I have been fully instructed." She looked around. "We will need wine and a suitable vessel."

"It will be here shortly."

"And what form of oath do you require, my lord? Blood Brotherhood, common brotherhood, or an oath of fealty?"

"An oath of fealty to their new chief, myself. One of friendship between men, an oath of common brotherhood between two peoples." He turned to Lugartes. "All your company leaders must take the oath, as will those of the Massegetae, including my Macedonian brother." He gestured towards Parasades as he led the rest of the Massegetae leaders into the ring.

Lugartes looked at Nikometros gravely. "It is fitting. I shall count it an honour to be a brother of the Scythian lion." He bowed in his direction.

Two guards ran up to the chief, carrying a large wineskin and a large copper vessel. They waited as Lugartes took the wineskin and splashed a generous amount into the vessel. He set it carefully on the ground and stepped back. Lynna removed a small ceremonial dagger from her robes and, holding it high above her head in both hands, turned to the north and intoned indistinct but sonorous phrases. She repeated the actions to the west, the east and the south, invoking the gods and goddesses each time.

Turning at last to Spargises, she took his large callused hand in her tiny one, holding his hand over the copper vessel. Swiftly she nicked the ball of his thumb. Dark blood welled out and ran over his hand, dripping into the wine. After a moment, she released his hand and reached out to Nikometros.

He shivered as their hands met, a feeling of dread lifting the hairs on his arms. He shook himself and stepped forward, staring into her eyes. She gazed back at him boldly, a small smile on her face. The knife flashed and Nikometros felt his blood oozing forth, heard it splashing into the vessel. She released him

171

and moved on, around the circle of men. Blood spattered the sides of the vessel and the grass around it before she finished.

Nikometros looked around the circle, recognizing Areipithes, Parasades, Taxicus and the other leaders of companies he now knew well. Other faces were strangers, looking back at him blankly, or with curiosity. Lugartes flashed a smile at him, as he caught his eye. Nikometros smiled and nodded back before turning his attention to the priestess again as she continued the ceremony.

Lynna mixed the blood and wine with the dagger. "...gracious Mother, bind these men as brothers, no longer as Jartai and Massegetae, but as one people." She looked up at the ring of men. "Let each man swear allegiance to Spargises as elected chief of his people and to his elected heirs, as is the custom." She bent and lifted the brimming vessel with some difficulty, blood and wine slopping over the sides onto her robes. She turned to the ring of men again. "Swear by the Mother who hears all."

The circle of leaders put their hands on their swords and in a ragged chorus, swore allegiance to Spargises. Lynna held the vessel up and called out in a clear voice. "Let the Great Goddess and gods of air and water witness your oath. Take the vessel and drink. Let all who drink be as brothers." She turned and gave the heavy vessel to Spargises who lifted it and drank deeply. Nikometros took the vessel from him and sipped the bloody wine, feeling slightly nauseous but being careful not to show it. He passed it on to a man of the Jartai who beamed and drank thirstily.

Spargises leaned over to Nikometros and whispered. "Do you see the difference between this oath and the one we took?"

Nikometros thought for a moment then nodded. "We drank from the cup together and swore to hold each other's life and honour dear. Here we drink separately and swear allegiance to you as our chief."

"You have it," nodded Spargises. "We are not full brothers to these men, as we two are. Remember that, my friend. And while you have sworn allegiance to me as your chief," he grinned, "We are still brothers."

The vessel passed around the circle of men, each drinking deeply of the blood and wine. They stepped back, wiping their mouths on their sleeves. Lugartes put his fist on his sword hilt and stepped into the open space in front of the crowd. "You have heard and you have seen. Our peoples are joined now by oaths of friendship and brotherhood. Let all enmity vanish." He stood silently as the crowd of men, women and children slowly dispersed, moving into the night in quiet discussion. Turning back to Spargises, he saluted. "What are your orders, my lord?"

"For tonight, we feast. Tomorrow we start to bring our two peoples together. Our herds and womenfolk will be here then. We shall encamp for five days."

"And then, my lord?"

"Then we complete our journey to the Mother Sea. We are no more than forty days travel from our summer pastures." Spargises smiled and waved dismissively at the group. "Go now, see to your men."

The group saluted and separated into small knots of men, drifting off towards the cooking fires. Presently Spargises was alone with Nikometros. He looked at the Greek gravely. "A good day's work, my brother. But I fear our problems are not yet over. We

173

must form these two peoples into one...and quickly." Spargises started pacing up and down. "I am convinced that you must train other companies to fight as you do...how did Lugartes put it? Like thunderbolts, like fiery lions." He stopped in front of Nikometros and gripped his arm firmly, looking up into his eyes. "Can you do that, my Lion of Macedon? Can you form me a great thunderbolt to be led by my Lion of Scythia?"

Chapter Fifteen

Nikometros sat alone on the slope of a hill in the bright afternoon sunshine, hugging his knees, and watching the ebb and flow of the armed men below him. Tiny blue butterflies, their iridescent wings reflecting the azure sky above, danced over the turf, while Diomede quietly cropped the grass a few paces from him, looking up from time to time to check he was not needed. Every now and then, the gentle breeze died down, and a distant curse floated up to Nikometros. He grinned to himself as he imagined Timon's face, purple with rage and the effort of making himself understood, shouting at the new recruits. *He has done well this last month. They are unused to discipline but they are eager to learn.*

The smile faded from his lips as a mass of riders emblazoned with the insignia of the Bulls formed into a ragged arrow formation, and charged the Eagles led by Taxicus. The Eagles waited patiently until the whooping riders were almost upon them then wheeled and split, ripping into the lines of attackers, unhorsing them with swift blows of their staves. Roars of laughter drifted up to Nikometros as he tossed his head in disgust.

His eyes swept across the plain, automatically noting the banners and distinctive colours of the horses and their trappings. His own Lions now rode golden horses similar to Diomede. Other companies copied their lead, Parasades' company all rode black horses now, and Taxicus' rode brown. They had adopted insignia too. As well as the Eagles, Parasades led the Leopards and Lugartes' men were the Foxes. Even Areipithes had adopted the Wolverine as his standard. Nikometros grimaced. *Even in this, he displays his greed and lust for power.* Shading his eyes, Nikometros could just make out the altered insignia his Lions had adopted since the battle. The lion's head of his family now grasped a Scythian arrow in its jaws.

Far to the left, the raw recruits worked under the vigilant eye of Mardes. Unconcerned with the finer points of tactics, he strove to instill in the unruly tribesmen the first semblance of discipline. Riders lined up abreast, each man gripping the staff of the rider to each side of him. Using the staffs as a guide, the horsemen maintained a rough formation. At a command, they started forward, the men striving to maintain the proper distance and bearing of their line. Within moments the line disintegrated into chaos. Patiently, Mardes rounded up the recruits and set them to the task once more. A company of riders broke off to watch the recruits, jeering and laughing at their efforts.

Below him, Nikometros saw Timon galloping about waving a white banner, emblazoned with a lion's head, trying to whip the laughing men into some semblance of order. Gradually they quieted then on an unheard command, each company trotted out in line abreast. *Good,* thought Nikometros, *this will test their control and discipline.*

The lines trotted across the plain keeping in rough lines. Nikometros grinned as he caught sight of the Lions, rigidly controlled, bringing up the rear. *Time and patience pays off. Timon and Mardes have worked themselves to exhaustion getting them into shape and it shows!* The first line came abreast of a cairn of rocks topped by a lance and wheeled to the right. Instantly the formation fell into confusion, the riders bunching up and losing coherence. Their company leader rode up and down furiously, his distant shouts causing Diomede to lift his head.

The second line passed the cairn and the difference was obvious. Parasades maintained an iron control over his men, drilling them continuously. They rode past the disarray of the first line then wheeled again in sections, forming into a square of riders ten abreast and eight ranks deep. They broke into a slow gallop curving around to the starting point. Nikometros applauded them, slapping his thighs. Diomede walked over to him and nuzzled his face, puzzled by the sudden noise.

One by one, the lines of horsemen went through their maneuvers, with varying success. The Lions brought up the rear, at a furious pace, showing off their newfound skills for their commander. Nikometros stood up, dusting himself off and waved his arm above his head. Below him, Timon rode out of the formation, and galloped across to the hill, and up to his commander.

He slid off his horse and saluted, grinning. "A rare company of riders we have there, sir. They insisted on doing everything at a gallop, just for you."

"They are good men and fine riders. Unfortunately, not all of our companies are as skilled."

Timon grimaced. "They can all ride well...they are reared on horses after all, but they don't like the discipline of an army." He put a finger to his nose and blew, wiping it on a sleeve. "They'll learn. Our old Massegetae groups are doing best, but some of the new Jartai companies such as Lugartes' Foxes and Tymus' Elks are improving fast."

Nikometros nodded. "They have done well in the last month. I'm just hoping they will be trained enough if we find real opposition. We reach the

Mother-waters in a few days and the gods alone know what we will find there."

Shouting from the plain below distracted Nikometros. He shaded his eyes, straining to make out what was happening. A mass of horsemen milled around a knot of men on the ground. Timon swore. "It's those Wolverines again. They stir up trouble wherever they go. They think themselves above discipline because Areipithes leads them."

Nikometros turned and let loose a piercing two-tone whistle. Diomede's head came up at once and he hurled himself forward toward his master. Nikometros stepped to one side as the stallion plunged down the hill past him, gripped the tossing mane in strong hands and let the force of the galloping horse swing him up onto Diomede's back. They were at the bottom of the hill and racing toward the army before Timon could remount his own horse.

The mob of riders parted as he approached and slowed. The group of men in the centre drew back. Nikometros leaped down from his horse and strode into their midst, his hand on his sword. He looked around at the circle of faces. The anger in them cooled and several started to look away, shuffling their feet. "What is happening here?" he rasped. Nikometros recognised one of his men. "You, Tirses. Report."

Tirses snapped to attention and saluted. "Sir. These men slandered you and your parentage. We were only defending your honour, sir."

"Do you not think I am capable of defending my own honour?" Nikometros spoke quietly, calming the situation. He looked Tirses full in the eye, noting a flush of guilt in his face. "What else has happened?"

The young man's shoulders sagged. "It was an accident, sir. We did not mean for blood to be shed." The young man's voice trailed away and he stood looking down at his feet.

"Whose blood has been shed?" Noises behind him made Nikometros swing round, half drawing his sword.

Parasades shoved through the jostling men, a grim look on his face. Timon followed on his heels. "Menaraxes has been slain, one of Areipithes' men."

"Menaraxes!" Nikometros looked troubled. "Who killed him?"

"Colaxes, one of your Lions." Parasades leaned closer, lowering his voice to a whisper. "There may be trouble, my friend. Already there are whispers that you ordered his death over the Roxana business. We must settle this openly and quickly."

"I agree." Nikometros raised his voice, addressing the crowd. "This matter will be investigated fully before the chief. Let all who have reason to speak on this matter hold themselves in readiness." He glanced to where Timon waited. "Timon, take Colaxes into custody and Tirses, see to the body of Menaraxes." He looked around at the faces of the crowd, some angry and muttering, others worried, most eager with anticipation. "Parasades will take the names of the witnesses now. Our chief will rule on this matter in open assembly." He turned, and with the Lions at his heels, walked through the crowd to where his horse waited, held by Mardes.

Nikometros thanked Mardes absently and mounted his stallion, turning toward the wagons. His mind already working on the news, he failed to see Mardes, together with a cadre of Lions, fall in behind him. *So Menaraxes is dead. There will be those that think I had some-*

179

thing to do with it. Especially since one of my men did it. His right hand rubbed his armband steadily. *Curse the man! How can I possibly prove my innocence to Tomyra if Menaraxes is dead?*

Nikometros' thoughts were interrupted by Lugartes trotting over to him, a small group of his men in escort. "Greetings, Brother Lion." The broad smile on Lugartes' face made Nikometros smile in spite of his worry. "Soon our chief will have a whole pride of lions for his battles."

"Yes, I am content with the progress of some of the companies, my friend. Others need a lot more work."

Lugartes laughed. "Your man Timon could train hares to run in lines. How he manages to make our wild Scythian horsemen bend to discipline amazes me. I would not have believed it possible." He rode alongside chuckling to himself. After a time, he turned to Nikometros with a serious expression. "Do you have some time to spare, brother?"

Nikometros cocked his head on one side. "It will take Parasades a span or two to get the assembly organised, I think. Why?"

"You have been so busy this last month, I did not like to call on you. I would have you meet that Egyptian slave I told you about. I think you would find the meeting of interest."

Nikometros thought a moment then nodded. "Why not? I could do with a break before the assembly. Where is he?"

"He is in the Jartai encampment, close to our priestess. He's a scribe and finds pleasure in books and scrolls rather than manly pursuits." Lugartes smiled. "He is a slave after all."

The small group of men rode through the crowded Jartai encampment. Although the two tribes were now one, the unity was more in name than in reality. The two groups kept to each other for the most part, traveling separately. The Jartai had fewer wagons and now, perforce, traveled on foot. At least the main wagon columns moved no faster than walking pace. The warriors formed their own fighting units under their own leaders and mingled freely with the other Scythian warriors. A friendly rivalry had grown up between the warriors of the two tribes, most now eager to learn the new battle methods of the Scythian Lion.

They halted at a patched tent near the middle of the camp. Lugartes slid off his horse calling out to his men. "Ho, Jaxes. Send for wine and food. Sopartos, fetch the Egyptian, hurry!" He turned to the riders. "Come, brother, I offer you the meagre comforts of my tent. My men will see to the needs of yours." Lugartes beckoned to Nikometros as he vaulted to the ground.

The inside of the tent matched the run-down exterior. The carpets were worn and threadbare, and the furnishings Spartan. The sides of the tent had been drawn up and tied back to let in the cool breezes, the setting sun throwing long shadows across the floor. Lugartes unbuckled his sword belt and tossed it into a corner. Picking up a pitcher he shook it and, satisfied with the gurgling sound poured koumiss into two cups. He handed one to Nikometros. "Be seated my friend. The Egyptian slave will be here presently. He is an old man and cannot be hurried."

Nikometros took a long drink and wiped his mouth with the back of his hand. He squatted down on the rug facing Lugartes. "It is strange that an

Egyptian would be found so far from his home. How did he come to be here?"

"You can ask him yourself. Who knows, you may even get some sense out of him." Lugartes lowered himself to the floor and leaned toward Nikometros. "He is a strange man, perhaps touched by the gods. Certainly his mind is going. He rambles on about everyday things most of the time then just when you feel like striking him for wasting your time, he says something strange." Lugartes snorted and poured them another drink. "He talked of you, you know."

Nikometros looked at the other man, his cup raised. "What do you mean? When? After the battle?"

"No. It was some days before, when our scouts had just revealed the presence of the Massegetae. He was in the priestess' tent tending to the scrolls when apparently he stopped his usual mutterings and said very clearly 'The Greek comes like a lion of fire. Scythia will not be the same again.' No one could make sense of it at the time. Some thought he referred to Alexander, but he had already passed eastward." Lugartes grinned. "Until we all saw you in action."

Nikometros lowered his cup and frowned. "You believe he prophesied my arrival? I am no king, or general of armies to warrant the attention of the gods."

"You think not? I have heard stories of the Great Mother's love for you. Perhaps She spoke to this Egyptian about you." Lugartes shrugged. "Anyway, ask him yourself. Here he is."

Shadows crossed the floor ahead of Sopartos and two other men. One was a young man in servant's clothing, clutching a large willow-stick basket. The small, bent figure between them drew Nikometros' attention. He saw a very old man clothed in worn linen robes showing the stains and patches of much use. A gnarled face topped by a wrinkled hairless scalp seemed lifeless but for two rheumy black eyes and thin lips in constant motion. His hands were curved claws that hung in front of him, stroking each other spasmodically. A thread of spittle hung from a corner of his mouth.

Lugartes motioned to his man who seated the old slave before them, withdrawing in silence. The young servant deposited the basket beside the old man, bowed and followed the warrior. Lugartes smiled at Nikometros. "Well my friend, this is the old slave. He has some unpronounceable name but call him Ket, he answers to it...sometimes."

Nikometros studied the old man sitting in front of him. "Greetings...Ket. My name is Nikometros son of Leonnatos. I am a Macedonian soldier in King Alexander's army and a warrior of the Massegetae. I am told you foresaw my coming."

The old man raised his eyes and peered at Nikometros. "Where is my Bubis?" He looked around the tent, his hands fluttering in agitation. "Bubis. Where are you my little one? Come to me, Bubis."

Nikometros turned to Lugartes, raising an eyebrow. Lugartes sighed and picked up the wicker basket. He put it in front of the old man and removed the lid. A small black furry head raised itself hesitantly over the rim, looking round at the seated men. Large green eyes surveyed the room carefully then the eyelids slowly drooped. A deep rumbling noise emerged from the basket.

The old man gave a cry of delight, lifting the cat in his hands and clutching it in his lap. He rocked back and forth, a contented smile on his face. "Bubis. My

183

Bubis. Ah, sweet one, you were hiding from me again. You are always so naughty, worrying me like that but I forgive you. I always do, you know." He stroked the cat with gentle motions, his attention so obviously on the cat that his next words took Nikometros by surprise. "She spoke to me of your coming, Greek."

Nikometros gaped. "The cat spoke?"

The old man looked up and laughed. "Do cats speak in Macedon? I must go there." He turned once more to the cat, deep rumbling noises still emerging from its throat. "The Goddess of course. Bubis is a male. Aren't you my sweet? My great royal king of cats." He cocked his head to one side and looked up at Nikometros again. "Cats are holy. Did you know that? The goddess Bubastis takes the form of a cat. We are all her children." He tittered, scratching the cat behind the ears. "Some more than others, perhaps...I am Ketherennoferptah, scribe and least of the priests of Ammon-Ra at Siwah. I saw you there, you know. You were with the pharaoh."

Nikometros stirred and looked searchingly at Ket. "I went to Siwah, though I do not remember you. I was among the Companions of the King when my lord Alexander consulted the oracle but who is this pharaoh you speak of?"

"He who was ordained by his father Ammon-Ra to free our land from the yoke of slavery and raise it up once more." Ket looked deep into Nikometros' eyes. "Alexander, who men call son of Philip." He laughed. "Philip could no more sire that one than he could sire the sun itself. The pharaoh Alexander was born of the gods to fulfill their purpose." The old man sighed. "I don't suppose you have any fish? Bubis does so love fish but it is hard to get here on these awful plains."

Nikometros stared at Ket, trying to remember whether he had seen him that day at Siwah. So many years had passed; he had been a young man awed by the presence of his king and the importance of his duties. "No, I have no fish...how did you know I would be here, old man?"

"The priests at Siwah introduced Alexander to his father in the holy sanctuary in private. His face glowed with an unearthly radiance after the audience." Ket put the cat on the floor and watched, smiling, as Bubis stretched, rump in the air. "He is old now and doesn't get out much. He likes to remain close by me, don't you my sweet? You thought you were unseen and unnoticed among the young men. 'Three royals at the same time', the priests said. It was unprecedented. Many people knew of the king's earthly half-brother Ptolemy but you were a surprise."

"I? What do you mean?"

Ket cackled and rolled Bubis over onto his back, rubbing the cat's belly. The cat bit his hand lightly, spurring its back legs in a desultory fashion. "Not a son of Leonnatos, but rather of Ptolemy. Nephew to the great king himself." Bubis rolled away from the old man and crouched, twitching its tail in mock anger. "Ah, my sweet, do not take offence. Since then, I have often wondered how it must feel to be related to a god." Ket looked at Nikometros again. "I saw you at Siwah with kings, and I see you with kings again in Egypt." He sighed. "I am getting old and sometimes I think I shall not see my beloved country again with these eyes."

Nikometros shifted and leaned forward. "Old man – Ket – how do you know of my true father? How can you know my future?"

Ket leapt to his feet with surprising agility. Bubis jumped back with a hiss, his ears laid flat. The old man's eyes stared unfocussed into the last rays of the setting sun, his voice deep and commanding. "Hear me Nikometros, son of Ptolemy of the house of Philip of Macedon. The gods of Egypt call out to you. You will bring the Great King back to his father's land in a house of gold. Lion of the plains, Lion of Scythia, much death will accompany you before you accomplish your task." The old man stumbled and almost fell. Lugartes reached out and steadied him then lowered him gently to the floor again.

Ket looked around vacantly. "Bubis? Where are you my sweet?"

Lugartes stared at Nikometros. "Do his words make sense? He spoke with power then, I swear it."

Nikometros drew a deep breath. "He knew things no man could possibly know about my family. It was a closely guarded secret."

"He named you a lion of the plains, of Scythia." Lugartes held his hand low over the ground. "He foretold your coming." He licked his lips nervously and glanced toward the door. "He spoke of much death."

Nikometros shrugged and looked at Ket. The old man was again clutching his cat tightly, rocking back and forth and crooning to it in a low voice. Whatever spark had fired his spirit had gone, leaving the old man alone in the gathering shadows. Nikometros shook himself, feeling the hairs on his arms prickling. A shadow moved and Nikometros whirled about then relaxed as he recognised Mardes standing in the doorway.

Mardes cleared his throat. "A messenger from the camp, sir. All is in readiness."

186

Nikometros turned back to Lugartes. "I thank you for this meeting. It has been...instructive. I must get back however. Our chief will decide on the death of Menaraxes. My man was responsible. I must be there." He turned and strode from the tent, calling for his horse.

Chapter Sixteen

The chief's tent seethed with motion and excitement when Nikometros entered. He glanced about, noting the way the men stood in groups, isolating themselves from their fellows, glowering at each other. Smoky torches lit the interior, sending flickering shadows over the emotion-wracked faces. He saw Spargises at the far side, seated on a stool, talking to Areipithes and Parasades. He walked over and saluted Spargises, nodding pleasantly to the other men.

"Greetings, brother." Spargises nodded in reply, motioning to Nikometros to stand beside him. "This matter must be dealt with quickly. An incident like this could damage the unity of our tribe."

Areipithes frowned. "It is interesting that once again it is the Greek at the centre of the trouble. His presence damages the unity of our People."

"That's nonsense." Parasades stepped in front of the chief's son. "Nikomayros has unified all, except those that feel threatened by his presence."

Areipithes bristled and flushed, his hand creeping to his sword hilt.

"Enough." Spargises spoke quietly, but forcefully. "This serves no useful purpose." He rose to his feet and called out. "Bring the prisoner."

There was a stir around the entrance as Colaxes was ushered in. His face was drawn and pale. He crossed the tent accompanied by two guards with drawn swords, and stood in front of the chief. The young man's eyes darted around the room, resting on the group of men around the chief. Nikometros met his eyes, seeing the pleading look in them.

Spargises raised a hand for silence. "Colaxes, you are accused of the murder of Menaraxes, son of Mennales. Do you admit to this murder or deny it?"

Colaxes cleared his throat. "My lord, I admit I killed him but I plead..."

"He admits his guilt, put him to death!" Areipithes turned to his father with a shout. "You have heard..." he quieted as Spargises gestured for silence again.

"Let him speak, man. There were reasons for his action." Parasades spoke quietly into the expectant hush.

Areipithes flushed with anger. "One of my own men, a valued warrior, was murdered by this man. He admits it freely. What need have we to hear his excuses?"

Spargises raised his hand. "Even so, I would hear him." He looked straight at Colaxes. "Why did you kill Menaraxes?"

"My lord, there was an argument over precedence at the water casks during the manoeuvres. The Wolverines – Areipithes' company," he nodded hesitantly at the chief's son. "Pushed into the line, claiming precedence. We thrust them back as was our right." Colaxes licked his lips, hesitating. "We are the Lions."

"Go on, Colaxes." Nikometros smiled at him encouragingly. "What happened then?"

"My lord, they insulted you." Colaxes turned back to the chief. "They said Nikomayros was plotting to take over the tribe, that he lusted after other men's womenfolk, and even the sacred priestess. It was lies, my lord! Then Menaraxes boasted how he had seen the girl Roxana sleeping with him. He blackened my commander's name. I accused him of lying, and when he would not withdraw, I drew my sword and cut him down." He faltered and looked down.

189

Spargises cursed softly. "This matter of the girl again. I will get to the bottom of this." He raised his voice. "Are there any witnesses? Let them stand before the accused."

Several men pushed forward into the middle of the tent. Parasades formed them into a line, and then called the first one out. "Scolices, of the Wolverines, sir."

Scolices glanced at Areipithes then smirked at Colaxes. "It happened much as he said. Words were exchanged, though Menaraxes only said what is common talk in the camp. He did not even have time to draw his sword before this man attacked him."

Spargises nodded. "You would swear to this by the Great Goddess?"

Scolices hesitated only a moment. "I would. It is the truth. These other men will bear me out." He gestured at the waiting men, three of whom nodded, the rest looking uncertain and shuffling their feet.

"Does anyone say differently? Come, one of you others."

Another man stepped forward and saluted. "Tirses, my lord. I am in my lord Nikomayros' command. Colaxes was provoked sir, beyond all bearing. Any of us would have done the same."

"You would murder?" asked Areipithes. "A man who had committed no crime?" He turned to his father with a triumphant expression on his face. "You see the influence the Greek has on honest men? He is divisive and will bring harm to our People."

"My lord, no!" Colaxes dropped to his knees. "I was hot-headed I admit but the man was guilty of a crime. As he lay dying he admitted falsely accusing my lord Nikomayros."

190

Spargises strode over to the man and gripped his tunic, staring into his face. "What did he say?"

Colaxes' hands scrabbled ineffectually at the chief. "Menaraxes said he plotted to discredit our commander," he gasped, "that he accused him falsely of seducing another man's woman."

Nikometros sucked in his breath sharply. "Did he say why he did this...or say who was behind it?"

"This is all nonsense," broke in Areipithes. "Why are we even listening to this man's excuses and lies?"

Parasades put his hand gently on Areipithes' arm, restraining him. "Let him speak, the truth will hurt no one here, surely." He nodded at Colaxes. "Well, did he name names?"

"No, my lord. He prayed to the Mother for a moment then died."

Areipithes raised his voice angrily. "I say again, this is all nonsense. Are we to take the word of this self-confessed murderer? He is trying to justify his actions. I say he should be put to death immediately. It is our custom."

The crowd of men in the tent murmured and shuffled their feet, many of them nodding their heads. Spargises raised his hand again, and waited for the noise to die down. "Scolices, did you hear Menaraxes say this as he lay dying?"

Scolices looked down at his feet. "I was not near enough," he muttered. "He said something but I did not hear it."

"I did, my lord." A man at the end of the row spoke out. "Parmicus, of the Elk company." The man saluted. "I did not want to interfere in this quarrel, my lord, but the dying man spoke clearly to those near him. If this man," he gestured at Scolices, "did not hear him then he must be deaf, or chooses not to re-

191

member." Scolices shot a look of hatred at the man but kept silent. Parmicus thought for a moment then continued. "His exact words were 'Great Mother, I have lied...Forgive me...I accused the Greek falsely.' He muttered something else I didn't catch, then 'Roxana lied.'"

"You swear this on your life, before the Great Goddess?" When the man nodded, Spargises turned to his guards. "Fetch the woman Roxana." He hesitated then added, "Ask the lady Tomyra to attend upon us immediately too."

* * *

The crowd parted to admit Tomyra after a few minutes. She was dressed in her robes of office and accompanied by the young Jartai priestess, Lynna. They crossed to the group around the chief. "Greetings, father. What need have you of the Goddess?"

Spargises smiled and beckoned to her. "Come, daughter, stand beside me. You have heard of the events of today?"

Tomyra inclined her head in assent. "I have heard that Menaraxes has died in a fight with one of the Greek's men." Nikometros felt an ache in his heart at the indifferent tone in her voice, and the use of the word 'Greek'. He stared at her, willing her to turn and look at him.

"Indeed, daughter. But the interesting part is that before he died, Menaraxes confessed he lied about my blood-brother and that girl Roxana." Tomyra stiffened. Her neck flushed and she struggled to maintain her calm. Spargises went on, unaware of her confusion. "She has been sent for. We will question her again."

Tomyra turned to Lynna and dismissed her, crossing to stand beside her father and brother. She

192

glanced at Nikometros, and as swiftly, away to where the guards pushed the struggling form of Roxana. The girl stumbled and almost fell, recovering herself with an effort. She stood looking around at the hostile faces surrounding her, and shivered. She drew her robe around her, hugging her breasts.

"You have been brought here to answer a dying man's charge." Though Spargises spoke softly, every person in the tent could hear him clearly. "Menaraxes said that you lied about your involvement with my brother Nikomayros. What say you?"

Roxana looked at him as if she hadn't heard. She swayed on her feet and looked helplessly at Spargises then at Areipithes, her lips moving soundlessly.

"Do you deny the charge? I will have you swear before the Goddess on the sacred objects. I am determined to find the truth here."

"I...I..." Roxana started crying softly. "Menaraxes told me to do it, my lord. He said he had orders to discredit the barbarian."

Areipithes stirred and rasped out, "Whose orders? Be careful you do not slander your betters."

Roxana cowered, looking up at Areipithes, her eyes darting. "He...he did not tell me, my lord. Only that I must do it." The crowd started muttering and moved forward a few paces. Areipithes nodded slowly and stepped back from the girl.

Spargises raised his arm. "What were you told to do?"

"I was to encourage the barbarian to seduce me." She shrugged. "He had already said he would not, so I drugged his wine and made it look as if he had done so." There was a roar from the crowd and voices raised in argument.

"Silence!" roared the chief. "Go on, woman. Did Nikomayros dishonour you in any way?" When Roxana only shook her head, weeping, Spargises gestured to his guards. "Take her away. I will decide her fate tomorrow." He stepped into the middle of the circle and waited until all was quiet. "Let no man dispute this. Nikomayros, my brother, was falsely accused. He is proven innocent. Let this be an end to the matter."

Tomyra looked down at the ground, her mind whirling. As her father spoke, she looked up and into Nikometros' eyes. She blushed deeply then gave a tentative smile. "My lord," she murmured. "I have wronged you."

Nikometros smiled in return. He lifted his arms as if to embrace her and then remembered where he was, his hands falling to his sides. "No, my lady. You were not at fault. Others sought to bring this dispute between us." He glanced sideways at Areipithes, who scowled and looked away.

Spargises turned to where Colaxes stood silently, under guard. "However, this man is still guilty of murder. You all know the penalty for murder...it is death, unless his next of kin will accept compensation." He looked around slowly. "Menaraxes, though, has no living relatives. His commander must stand for him." He looked at Nikometros and said gently, "It is the law, my brother."

Areipithes grinned savagely. "I do not accept compensation," he barked. "I demand the death penalty for this willful murder."

Colaxes paled and he shook slightly before steadying himself. He raised his head and looked straight at Areipithes. "I accept your decision. It is the law." Turning to Tomyra, he asked softly, "Speak well for

194

me to the Goddess, my lady?" His voice trembled slightly and he looked away, clenching his jaw.

Nikometros grasped Spargises by the arm. "He is only a youth. He acted out of love for me. Brother, you cannot let him die."

Spargises glanced across at his son, noting the look of hatred and triumph in his eyes. He gazed compassionately at Nikometros. "It is out of my hands, my friend. It is the law. Only the next of kin, or in this case, the man's commander, can forego the death sentence." He lifted his hand to his son in supplication. "Son," he whispered, "Will you not reconsider?"

Areipithes smiled cruelly, staring at Nikometros. "I demand his death."

Spargises gestured to his guards. "Take Colaxes out. The sentence is to be carried out immediately."

The guards grasped Colaxes by the arms and started to drag him out of the tent. He wrestled an arm free and half-turned to Spargises. "My lord, I beg of you a favour. I have served the People well, hear me."

Spargises raised a hand and the guards stopped, holding their prisoner firmly. "Speak then. But swiftly."

"My lord, I accept my death. I ask only that I go to the Goddess by her chosen, rather than a common executioner. I have served you well as a warrior. Grant me this last wish."

Spargises looked at Areipithes. "What say you?"

Areipithes looked at Nikometros for a long moment then smiled. "Yes, why not? Let the chosen one send his friend to his death. It is fitting."

Nikometros stepped back. "No. I cannot do this. He is one of my men, not a captured enemy."

"Please, my lord. I beg you." Colaxes held out a hand toward Nikometros. "I swore to lay down my

195

life for you as my commander. Let me die with dignity."

Nikometros stepped close to Colaxes and grasped his arms. The youth looked into his eyes, fighting to control his tears. "Please, my lord," he repeated. "Do not let me shame myself."

Spargises moved up behind Nikometros. "It would be a kindness, my friend." He drew his dagger and slipped it into Nikometros' hand.

Nikometros grasped it firmly. He leaned close to Colaxes and murmured into his ear. "I will not forget you, my friend. You have been a loyal and brave soldier. I am proud to be your commander." As he said the last word, Nikometros rammed the blade upward under the young man's ribs. Colaxes eyes flew wide. A drop of spittle hit Nikometros in the face as the young man's breath rushed out. A look of agony crossed his face then his eyes rolled upward and he collapsed to the floor.

Nikometros knelt beside him and closed the youth's eyes tenderly. "Go to the Goddess," he breathed then straightened and stood. He looked up and locked eyes with Areipithes who was looking down at the body of Colaxes with a smile on his face.

Areipithes' smile slipped and he involuntarily took a step backward. He swallowed and pushed past the guards and out of the tent.

Nikometros watched him go. *I will remember this day, Areipithes. Be sure of it.*

Chapter Seventeen

The small body of horsemen rode under a low and threatening sky along the shores of an inland sea. A cold wind pushed small waves onto the rocky shore, throwing a fine spray into the air. The water sucked back noisily over the pebbles, clattering like the wooden spear hafts of nervous soldiers. Timon shivered despite the warmer felts and leathers he now wore instead of his tattered tunic. *Gods*, he thought, *it's been less than half a year but it seems like we've been riding these plains for a lifetime.* He shifted uncomfortably as his horse's hoof slipped on another moss-covered rock, throwing him off balance, and looked around at his companions, mostly riding in pairs and chattering away as if they hadn't a care in the world. *I should have insisted on bringing at least an honour guard of Lions. These Owls may ride their horses well but they are not warriors.*

Timon scowled fiercely at the nearest rider who smiled back at him before turning back to her companion. *Women should keep to their station*, he thought, *not try to be warriors with the men.* He hawked noisily and spat, ignoring disapproving looks. Timon pulled his horse aside and let the column pass him slowly, casting a practiced military eye over the young women.

At a distance, the riders could pass for men, although slight of build. They wore the same trouser and tunic outfits with a close fitting felt cap pulled down around their ears. Felt boots and in some cases, soft leather gloves, gave protection against the cold wind from the north, and the swarms of biting flies inhabiting the shoreline. The women carried short bows and each slung a quiver of arrows across her back. Linen cloths fell in brightly coloured swathes about the horses, flapping fitfully in the gusts. Each had a stylized owl emblem stitched into the fabric, and the women rode in pairs, talking animatedly, their faces as open and fresh as a youth's.

Timon smiled wryly in spite of his sour mood. *Up close, there is no mistaking them for men!* His glance passed appreciatively over one or two of the women. He looked up the length of the column then on to the pair of riders in the distance. Timon nudged his horse into a trot, passing the other riders and settling into his position at the head of the column. Up ahead he could see Nikometros and Tomyra, riding easily over the uneven turf. He resisted the temptation to close with them. *They deserve time apart but why do they have to take it in unknown territory and without a decent guard?* He scowled and spat again, resuming his search of the horizon, determined that no enemy would catch them off-guard.

* * *

Nikometros glanced back over his shoulder at the distant figure of Timon on his black gelding, plodding stolidly along at the head of his column of young women. He smiled at the thought of Timon as the leader of women and the expression he knew must be on the old soldier's face. Diomede fidgeted beneath Nikometros, restless at the slow pace they were setting. Tomyra rode beside him on her mare, talking animatedly about some involved anecdote of camp life, but despite his increased knowledge of the Scythian languages, the finer nuances still managed to escape him, though the tale was plainly humorous.

Nikometros brushed absentmindedly at the flies around his face and laughed at the way Tomyra mimicked her brother. A fly, bolder than the rest, bit him on the neck, and he swatted it with a curse. He looked down at his clothes and grimaced. Gone were the light tunic and sandals of his army life. Months on the plains had finally worn them out and Nikometros now wore a serviceable but in his eyes, completely barbaric leather coat and leggings. He grudgingly accepted that they were at least warm and gave good protection against the swarms of stinging and biting insects.

Nikometros laughed again as Tomyra finished her story, blushing. Her eyes sparkled and met his boldly and Nikometros felt a great surge of well-being. He looked up at the gray skies from whence a few drops of rain were starting to fall, and then at the sullen sea to his right. He took a deep breath, his nose wrinkling at the sodden smell of the air. "By all the gods, Tomyra, it feels good to be out riding, even on such a dull day. What say you we exercise our horses? I know Diomede could do with a run." He leaned over and patted the stallion's neck. Diomede tossed his head and whickered, sidestepping in eagerness.

Tomyra laughed. "I think your friend Timon would have something to say about that. He is nervous enough riding guard with my Owls. He would have a fit if we just galloped off."

Nikometros turned and looked back at the column. "He takes his duties seriously. He wanted to bring a column of Lions today, you know."

"Doesn't he think my Owls can guard us well enough? Women can fight as well as men with the bow, and I prefer to have some women around me." She smiled at Nikometros and lowered her eyes. "Of course, I also enjoy the company of some men." Tomyra giggled and reached over to Nikometros, touching his arm.

She squeezed his arm gently then straightened and they rode on in silence for a time. "I thought my brother was going to choke on his meat when I told him I was forming my own company of warrior women." She grinned. "There is a precedent though, so he could not prevent me."

"I have never seen any other women warriors among the people."

"No. The Massegetae women have seldom desired to go to war themselves. My mother's people, the Sauromantians do, though. Young women dedicate themselves to the Goddess and her priestess. They foreswear men and families and live a warrior's life. Other tribes have copied them from time to time, and in my great-grandfather's day even the Massegetae priestess had a few women companions, who bore arms in battle."

"I have heard of these fighting women. My people...Macedonians I mean," he amended when Tomyra frowned, "call them 'Amazons'. They are supposed to ride around with one breast bared and carry small axes as weapons." Nikometros glanced at Tomyra quizzically. "Is that true?"

Tomyra snorted in derision. "What nonsense! No free Scythian woman is going to bare her breasts in public. And we fight with the bow, from a distance." She shook her head. "Some people will believe anything."

Nikometros smiled. "Well, it was a tale told around winter fires. Stories from far away places. Since I have traveled to these places I find that little I was told is true. Even Xenophon, who has written much on far-off lands, is not always accurate."

"I do not know this Zen-o-phen, but I would like to travel to distant places." Tomyra looked wistful. "I hear the stories told by the merchants in Urul and now you tell me even stranger stories of the places

200

you have been. I would like to see for myself but the People will not allow their priestess to travel far from them."

"Only the gods know the future, Tomyra. You have your own company of warriors now; perhaps you will be allowed greater freedoms." Nikometros laughed aloud, pointing to a range of low hills inland from the sea. "Come on, I'll race you to the rise." He dug his heels into the stallion's side, leaning low over his neck. Diomede gathered his muscles and leapt forward.

Tomyra's mare responded to her touch, surging in pursuit. Nikometros glanced back at the young girl's excited face, catching a glimpse of the riders further back now hurrying to follow. He grinned and urged Diomede onward. The two riders raced over the uneven ground away from the water, splashing through small streams and marshy meadows, scattering flocks of water birds. The land rose in front of them, the grasslands giving way to patches of scrub and small, gnarled trees, and the horses slowed, forced to negotiate rocky outcrops and loose scree. Nikometros reined his stallion in, slowing to a walk when Tomyra came alongside. Below them, Timon and one of the young women riders started up the slope, the others strung out over the meadows.

Tomyra nudged her mare up to the crest of the hill and stared beyond. "Nikomayros, look!" She pointed down the other side.

Nikometros caught up and stared in the direction she pointed. The hills fell away to wide rolling plains streaked by silvery streams. Sheets of rain fell from dark clouds on the horizon and a low rumble of thunder came from the distant storm. He sat and stared at the plain for a few moments before slowly scanning the slopes below them. Abruptly, he grabbed her reins and turning, urged Diomede back down the slope.

"What is it? Let me go." Tomyra grabbed ineffectually at the reins.

Nikometros stopped and slid off Diomede's back, helping Tomyra to the ground. "Horsemen. We don't know who they are and we could be seen against the skyline." He gestured to Timon as he rode up and moved on foot back up to the crest of the hill. He lay carefully on the ground, raising his eyes enough to see over the rim. A few moments later Timon and Tomyra dropped down beside him. "There, see. To the left of that outcrop."

Timon grunted. "I see eight. They carry weapons but don't look as if they expect trouble."

The riders sat motionless facing down into the valley, away from the eyes observing them from the hill. Lances trailed in the dust and bows were slung over shoulders. The men appeared to be watching some activity further down the valley, out of sight of the watchers on the hill. The only movement came from the horses' tails as they flicked at the ever-present flies.

"What are they looking at so intently?" Tomyra peered over the edge. "We must find out all we can. It could be important."

Nikometros nodded. "Stay here, my lady. Timon, come with me." He dropped back a few paces and started moving to his right, negotiating the loose rock with care.

Tomyra scowled at his retreating back then turned to the girl tending the horses. "Bithyia," she hissed. "Follow me." She started after the men, scrambling to catch up.

Timon turned at the noise of gravel slithering over rock. He groaned softly. "Sir!" he whispered urgently.

Nikometros dropped to his knees beside a large rock on the crest. He looked over his shoulder when Timon whispered and a look of concern came over his face. "My lady, you should wait below. There may be danger."

Tomyra shook her head. "Nevertheless, I am coming with you." She dropped down beside the men and looked carefully down the slope in front of her. Bithyia sat alongside her, her young face glowing with excitement.

Nikometros nodded slowly and flashed a brief smile at Timon before turning his attention to the scene in front of him. Their changed vantage point now revealed not only the eight horsemen but also another smaller group below them. The valley sloped steeply at first, covered with dirt and loose rock then more gently down onto great grassy meadows where a small village ringed by an earthwork and wooden palisade dominated the plain. Between the horsemen and the village lay a large open space bereft of grass. Men swarmed over the area excavating a large pit. Flurries of rain crept slowly over the plains and the distant rumble of thunder lent the scene an ominous air.

Timon looked puzzled. "There are no fires in the village, despite it being near midday." He pointed carefully at the ramparts. "There are sections of their defences lying on the ground too. Have they been attacked, do you think?"

"There is no sign of fighting. Look, there, at the village. Men are taking more of the palisade down." Nikometros looked across at Tomyra and the woman warrior with her. "Do you know what is happening here?"

Tomyra shrugged. "They have extinguished all their fires. This is only done at the time of the re-birth of the sun, or at a time of great sorrow or calamity." She caught Nikometros' unspoken query. "The re-birth of the sun...at mid-winter. The fires are put out and lit again with great feasting." She frowned. "This is not mid-winter though." The girl pointed and whispered. Tomyra nodded. "They are digging. It looks like it is intended to be a grave. To douse the fires means an important person must have died."

There was a clatter of hooves behind them as the remaining Owls came up the slope. Nikometros frantically signaled for them to keep back, cursing their lack of discipline. One girl rode up to the crest before he could prevent her, dislodging a rock. Nikometros watched in horror as it tumbled down the slope, gathering speed, bouncing and leaping. The horsemen below turned and pointed, shouting. One man drummed his heels into his horse's sides, shouting as he rode down the valley, sliding on the loose rubble. The others raised their lances and urged their horses up the slope toward them.

Timon drew his sword, swearing. "Trouble." He turned to Nikometros. "Sir, you must protect the priestess. I will hold them as long as I can."

Nikometros reached out and held Timon's sword arm. "Put it away. Let us find out their intent, before we fight." He gestured to the young women to spread out along the crest, bows at the ready.

Tomyra shaded her eyes, staring down at the approaching horsemen, noting their ornaments and horse tassels. "They have the look of Dumae I think. If so, they have always been courteous neighbours here at the Mother Sea."

Nikometros touched her arm. "My lady, please stay back with your women. I will meet with these men." He glanced back at the riders, missing the flash of annoyance that crossed her face. "If the worst happens, you are to flee at once. Timon and I will hold them." He gestured to Bithyia. "Protect your mistress with your life."

The riders halted twenty paces away on a shallow ledge among the loose rock of the slope. Their leader looked up at the heads peering over the crest at him, noting the tips of bows beside them. "Who is it that hides like rabbits among the rocks?" he called.

Nikometros stood up and advanced to the edge, Timon beside him. The riders below stirred and murmured at the sight of Nikometros' fair hair. "I am Nikometros of the Massegetae. I do not hide from any man."

"You do not have the look of the Massegetae and your name is strange and uncouth. What is your purpose on our lands?"

"Nevertheless, the Massegetae are my people. They are not far behind us." Nikometros gestured towards the Sea. "We seek only peaceful passage through these lands."

"Why then, have you not come openly to our village, instead of skulking about here in the rocks?" The man turned to his nearest companion and whispered. He listened a moment before turning back to Nikometros. "Come down, now, if you come in peace. My men shall escort you to our village."

Tomyra stepped up alongside Nikometros and called down in a clear high voice. "I am Tomyra, daughter of Spargises, chief of the Massegetae and a priestess of the Great Goddess. You risk her anger by forcing us to your will, man of the Dumae."

The man looked up at her and smiled. "We all hold the Great Goddess and her servants in the utmost respect." He held his hand palm down over the ground as he spoke. "The Dumae know of the Massegetae and welcome you if you come in peace." The smile slipped from his face. "Our welcome would be great were not your arrival so ill-timed."

Tomyra turned to Nikometros. "We must go with them and find out what we can. We shall be in no danger."

"It seems we must. To refuse could give offence." He looked at Timon and spoke quietly. "Make sure some carry our news back to the camp. I would send you back yourself..." Nikometros held up a hand as Timon opened his mouth, "but I know you would disobey me in this."

Timon saluted and dropped back from the crest, shouting commands. Three women quietly started leading their mares back the way they had come. The other women mounted their horses and, following Timon rode them up over the crest toward the waiting riders. Nikometros pushed forward, alongside Tomyra. He watched the Dumae leader carefully but the man gave no sign he knew that not all the women warriors were present.

"What is your name?" Nikometros asked as their horses drew up beside them in the dusty rubble.

The man hesitated before replying. "Nemathres, son of...Serraces." A look of intense sorrow crossed his face and he turned away, urging his horse down the slope. The other Dumae tribesmen formed up on either side of Nikometros and Tomyra's riders as they followed Nemathres down the valley.

Several riders met the group as they emerged from the valley onto the plains. The newcomers were fully armed, with drawn swords or strung bows. They sat motionless across their path as dozens more hurried from the diggings. Nemathres held up his right hand and called out reassurances to the waiting men. They relaxed at his words, putting away their swords. A ripple of laughter ran through the men when they caught sight of the armed women riding behind their leader. Ribald remarks made Tomyra flush with anger.

"Is this how the Dumae greet their guests?" she ground out. "My women are warriors dedicated to the Mother."

Nemathres turned to Tomyra with a smile. "Apologies, mistress. Women seldom bear arms among the Dumae and the sight of so many beautiful young women has made them forget their manners." He raised his voice and shouted out over the crowd. "This lady is a priestess of the Goddess. Her companions are dedicated to her service."

The laughter and comments ceased abruptly. Several men squatted and held a hand low over the earth, though several still cast appraising eyes at the young women. The crowd parted to let the group of riders through. They rode past the excavations where women and children still toiled, toward the village.

Nikometros looked at the large pit with interest. "What is the pit for, Nemathres?"

"It is a grave," he replied curtly. "Our chief Serraces...my father, died two moons ago. We will send him to the Mother tomorrow."

Tomyra reached out to touch the young man on his arm. "All men are born of the Mother and all must return to Her. May the Mother take your father to her breast in peace."

Nemathres nodded. "My thanks, lady." He rode in through the dismantled gates of the village, followed by the other riders. He dismounted outside a plain hut, passing the reins of his horse to a waiting servant. "May I offer you meat and drink? We have no hot food of course but you are welcome to what we have."

"Thank you." Tomyra gestured towards her companions. "We would be honoured to accept your hospitality." She dismounted and followed Nemathres into the dim interior of the hut.

Nikometros signaled to Timon and the women to dismount. "Stay with the horses, Timon. I do not think there is treachery here, but be on guard."

Timon nodded. "I will, sir."

Nikometros turned and entered the hut. The light of the overcast day barely penetrated the gloom. Nemathres and Tomyra sat on cushions near the doorway. Nemathres gestured to one side. "Come, sit. I have sent for food and drink. The fires have been doused but I can offer you some hospitality."

Nikometros sat beside Tomyra then turned to the other man. "May I offer my condolences on the death of your father. It seems we came at an inauspicious time."

Nemathres inclined his head. "I thank you." He paused for a moment. "You are obviously..." he gestured at Nikometros' blond hair, "...not born of the Massegetae, though you hold rank with them. How is this?"

"My name is Nikometros. I am a Macedonian officer of Alexander's army but also a blood brother of Spargises, chief of the Massegetae."

"He is also held in high regard by the Great Goddess," broke in Tomyra. "She has made her will known very plainly. Nikomayros is a great warrior and war leader."

"There have been rumours, even here by the Mother Sea. Spargises we know of as a chief of some note, but lately the talk was of a new war leader. I assumed it was his son." Nemathres looked up as a shadow fell across them. He beckoned a woman in carrying a flask of koumiss and a plate of bread and cold meat. "Thank you, Ranna. Just put it down here."

The woman put the plate and flask down then leaned forward and whispered to Nemathres. He nodded, whereupon the woman dipped her body briefly and left. Nemathres rummaged in a sack behind him and took out three plain cups. He poured koumiss into two of them and passed them to his guests. He filled the third one and sipped from it, watching Nikometros' face. "A body of riders approaches swiftly from the east. They bear pennants with a lion's head and arrow. They are your men?"

Nikometros nodded. "They are my own company."

Nemathres briefly smiled. "You sent back riders at once, of course. I expected that. I would do so myself." He rose to his feet. "My people seek only friendship, Nikomayros, my lady. Will you ride out with me to meet your company?"

Nikometros and Tomyra got up and followed him out of the hut. Nikometros turned to Timon standing patiently with the horses. "The Lions are on their way to rescue us, my friend. We must meet them and prevent bloodshed."

Timon saluted and started shouting orders. The women of the Owls swung up onto their mares. Nikometros helped Tomyra up then vaulted onto Diomede's back. He urged his head around toward the gate as Nemathres, and five of his men, joined him.

Together the party of horsemen galloped out of the village, heading east towards the hills.

In the distance appeared two riders moving fast towards them over the plain. They slowed as they neared, pointing back the way they came, shouting to Nemathres, "Horsemen, my lord. Over a hundred."

Nemathres slowed his horse to a walk. "Nikomay-ros,...my lady. Tomorrow the Dumae send their chief to the Mother. I would deem it an honour if you would attend the ceremonies."

Tomyra smiled. "We thank you, son of Serraces. It would be a privilege to attend." She turned to Nikometros. "My lord, we should ride on to meet your men alone. We do not wish to risk a misunderstanding."

Nemathres turned his horse, raising a hand in salute. "Until tomorrow then." He signaled to his men, and they urged their horses back toward the village.

Nikometros pointed toward the hills. Pouring through a small gap came a flood of riders, pennants waving. He grinned, and waved his hand forward. The Owls, with Nikometros, Tomyra and Timon at their head, rode to meet the forerunners of the Massegetae army.

Chapter Eighteen

A sombre air hung over the waiting crowd of mourners slowly swaying back and forth under the lowering clouds. The keening cries of women and children made the hair on Nikometros' arms bristle, a sense of despair and the damp chill of the water-logged plain made him think of the open tomb scarring the low mound over to his left. Around him, his Massegetae bodyguard jostled and talked in subdued tones, waiting for the arrival of the Dumae chief's body. Only when it arrived and was greeted by its kin, could the burial ceremonies begin. In the meantime, the hundreds of men, women and children of the Dumae, and the score or so visiting Massegetae, stood around in the cold northwesterly winds. Spargises' bodyguard was under the command of Parasades, decked out in all his gold in honour of the Dumae chief.

Nikometros looked around him at his other companions. Tomyra stood a few paces in front of him, wrapped warmly in richly coloured robes decorated with many gold ornaments. He watched the back of her head, catching glimpses of her soft skin and raven hair under her hood as she moved. *What do I really feel for her?* he wondered. *And what does she feel for me? Do I dare say anything?*

Tomyra talked to the Egyptian slave Ketherennoferptah in a low voice. The old man stood beside her, writing quickly on a parchment with a reed pen. Alongside him stood the young Scythian servant, clasping the same wicker basket Nikometros had seen a few nights ago. Nikometros smiled at the sight. *No doubt his cat is in there.* Spargises and Timon stood on either side of Nikometros. The chief was dressed in

211

his most ornate robes, bedecked with gold and enamel jewelry. The rich apparel and jewelry jarred with the piece of chewed-over dried meat in his hand.

A low murmur came to Nikometros' ears as the wind eased, backing to the west. He glanced round at the bodyguard of Lions surrounding them. Mardes walked slowly from man to man, checking equipment and exchanging a few words. The young Persian had fully embraced their new life-style. His unruly military-cut hair now flowed in luxuriant waves over his shoulders, a full beard and moustache hiding his face. Gold and enamel ornaments bedecked his tunic and leggings. It was only his slim supple grace that distinguished him from the Scythians of the bodyguard. Several of the chief's personal bodyguards stood just behind his Lions, their attention fixed on their commander.

Timon plucked at Nikometros' tunic. "Something is happening over there." He pointed to the west where the crowd was surging forward and cries of lamentation rose afresh. "Yes, I can make it out. It's a wagon with a mounted escort."

Spargises leaned over, chewing noisily on his dried meat. "That will be the bier with the body of Serraces. He has been visiting the other villages of the tribe, showing himself before his burial. Now the main ceremonies will start." He belched and gestured to one of his personal warriors who hurried up to him. "Prepare the chest of gifts." The man saluted and slipped through the guards to the rear.

The crowd parted slowly as the wagon bearing the chief's body slowly bumped over the uneven ground toward them. A small group of men and women waited in front of, and slightly to one side, of the Massegetae visitors. Nikometros could make out the figure of Nemathres, though the man looked very different from the day before. Large clumps of his hair had been hacked out, leaving the remainder sticking up unevenly. Bloodstains covered the sides of his head and chest from the wounds in his ears and forearms. The men standing alongside Nemathres were similarly shorn and mutilated. The women, though less bloody, were almost bereft of hair and their fine stitched robes hung in tatters. A low moan of grief went up as the wagon halted before them.

Nikometros edged down to stand between Tomyra and Ket. The old Egyptian slave looked up at him with bright, twinkling eyes and a gentle smile. Nikometros smiled in return then touched Tomyra on the shoulder. "My lady, is there any significance to the wounds the kin have inflicted on themselves?"

Tomyra turned her head and nodded a greeting. "Yes, Niko. The ears are cut to show their grief at hearing the news of his death. The arms that defended him in life show symbolically the wounds of their fight to keep him from dying." She shook her head. "That is all though. He died of an illness, a fever, so they will not inflict further injury on themselves. Illness is sent by the gods, usually Oetosyrus. We can mourn a man's passing but we cannot fight the will of the gods."

Ket gave a low cackle. "And what is the will of the gods? If a man dies of fever it is their will. If he gets better, it is also their will. But what if a man is cured by a healer? Does the healer do their will, or is the healer a god too...a more powerful one?"

"Hush! You forget yourself." Tomyra reprimanded the old man, before touching his arm gently. "We will discuss these matters another time." She turned to Nikometros. "Remember he is a scribe and a priest,

Niko. Lugartes gave him to me because he can read and write. He is writing down the burial customs of the Dumae for me. In many ways they are similar to those of our People but there are some differences."

Several warriors lifted the bier bearing the body of the chief from the back of the wagon and laid it on a richly woven mattress. Nemathres and three other men stepped forward and fell to their knees beside the corpse. They clasped its rigid limbs and cried out...

"...Nemathres and his brothers greet their father and lord, returned from his last journey around his lands," muttered Tomyra. Ket scribbled furiously, dipping his pen into a small bottle of ink hanging from his belt.

The grieving men rose and turned toward the crowd. A young girl in rich robes walked forward slowly, an older woman supporting her by one arm. Her head hung on her breast, her long, dark hair covering her face. Behind her walked three other men. They staggered as if drunk and were steadied by other men just behind them, leading several horses. Nemathres brought the young girl to the foot of the bier and spoke to the corpse...

"...he introduces his father to his youngest wife." Tomyra glanced at Nikometros. "He has been away on his last journey some forty days. He may have forgotten who she is." She frowned slightly. "She is beautiful and will accompany her husband in death."

The brothers brought the other men forward and Nemathres moved from man to man, talking in a low voice...

"...his cup-bearer who will continue to serve him fine wines and plentiful supplies of koumiss. The next is his cook as the journey to the other world is long and he will need sustenance. His head groom to take care of his favourite horses. They too will go with their chief."

Nikometros looked at Tomyra aghast. "Do they go willingly or are they forced?"

Tomyra shrugged. "The servants have always known their fate if their lord should die. They will continue to serve their master." She looked across at the young girl swaying gently at the foot of the bier. "What young girl looks for death so early though? She has been drugged and is unaware of what is to happen."

"It happens, young lord," muttered Ket. "Even in the Land of the Gods, my beloved Egypt, men willingly follow their king into his tomb. Service of the immortal gods is a worthy calling."

The men and young girl were led off to one side as the horses were brought forward. All were a uniform reddish colour, with long manes and tails combed and braided, their coats gleaming. Rich cloths flapped around their sides in the cold gusts and ornate headdresses tossed as the horses plunged and pulled against the ropes. The stallions were led up first, followed by several plump but less richly attired mares. Nemathres moved from horse to horse, quieting them with gentle movements of his hands, whispering to them and feeding them a handful of grain...

"...these are his father's favourite war-horses. Each one has carried him in battle and will be needed by him again. They will be sacrificed and buried with him. The mares are to provide him with new foals."

The warriors led the horses off in the direction of the tomb. Nemathres beckoned and a number of richly dressed men pulled a low cart up beside the bier. Slowly and with much reverence, the body was placed on the cart and beautifully embroidered cloth

215

draped over it. The cart moved off towards the tomb, small bronze bells affixed to poles at its corners, tinkling and jangling with every bump. The mourners followed, their red-rimmed eyes downcast.

Spargises leaned across to Nikometros. "Come, brother. It is time for us to pay our respects before the interment." He started forward then turned back to address the captain of his bodyguard. "Parasades, stay here. My brother Nikomayros shall represent the tribe with me today. Leave your guards here, Nikomayros. It would be unseemly to openly mistrust our hosts." He walked on, with Tomyra and Ket beside him. A single warrior of his bodyguard accompanied them, bearing a small wooden chest. Parasades watched them leave, a troubled expression on his face.

The chambers of the tomb lay open to the skies despite a fine rain now falling. Nikometros looked in awe at the elaborate rooms and halls carved in the dark earth. Every wall was faced with timber, and heavy tapestries softened the harshness of the scene. Carpets disguised the packed earth floors of the chambers. Furniture and household goods filled several chambers entirely, though others were arranged as if it was intended the chief should use them. Already the body of Serraces lay on a bed within the deepest chamber.

Nemathres caught sight of Spargises and his companions and walked over to them. "Greetings, Spargises son of Masades. You honour my father by your presence." He turned to the others. "My lady, my lord Nikomayros, I thank you." He bowed.

Spargises gestured to his man. "Nemathres, son of Serraces, please accept these grave gifts on behalf of your esteemed father."

Nemathres bowed again and gestured to his own men who relieved the man of his burden. "My thanks. Perhaps you would like to pay your respects in person?" He turned and started down a long ramp leading down into the tomb. Spargises and Tomyra followed with Nikometros and Ket bringing up the rear.

The tomb seemed even larger when they reached the bottom of the pit. Large horse stalls led off to the left. Grooms bustled around, leading the horses into position and making sure food and water was present. Corridors led to a kitchen and storerooms, together with small chambers for the servants. A more sumptuous passage opened out into a suite of fully furnished rooms.

The body of Serraces lay on a bed, propped up with cushions and pillows. Nemathres stepped up to the corpse. "Father, Spargises son of Masades, of the Massegetae greets you and brings gifts." He paused as if expecting a reply then gestured to his men to put the box at the foot of the bed.

Spargises held his right hand out in front of him, clenched his fist and jerked his hand downward. "Farewell, Serraces. May the Mother take you to her breast." He turned, nodded at the others and left the chamber.

A shadow fell across the chamber. Startled, Nikometros turned his face up into the fine drizzle. Men balanced on the walls, carrying lengths of timber, now started to roof over the chambers. Already the light inside the tomb had dimmed and faded. Nemathres gestured toward the exit.

As Nikometros passed down the corridor, he heard a soft muffled cry. He turned, slowing. Nemathres put a hand on Nikometros' arm and shook his head. "It is his wife. She accompanies my father on his journey." Nikometros looked troubled but said nothing.

A stench of blood and ordure greeted them when they reached the ramp again. The horses now lay in their stalls, blood soaking the packed earth and straw beneath them. The last of the mares still kicked spasmodically as the warriors wiped their weapons carefully before turning and walking wooden-faced into the dim interior of the tomb. Nemathres saluted them gravely as they passed.

Nikometros emerged into fresh air and watched as the villagers tamped earth down over the timbers covering the tomb of Serraces burying the dead and the yet-living. Tomyra stood to one side talking rapidly to Ket who busied himself with his parchments. The old slave's companion held a large piece of greased cloth above him, preventing the raindrops from ruining the writing.

"...the tomb will remain open while the burial feast takes place. Then a great mound of earth will be raised over it. The tomb remains undisturbed for a year then it may be reopened and sacrifices made. Customs vary here. Some tribes do not reopen the tomb but just sacrifice more horses and sometimes prisoners too. In the meantime..."

"Just a moment, my lady...yes, I have it." The old man raised his hand to catch Tomyra's attention. "Everyone knows where the tomb is, my lady. Is it guarded to prevent grave robbers?"

Tomyra's mouth fell open. "They would not dare!" she snapped. "No man would risk the anger of the Gods by desecrating the tomb. What are you thinking of?"

"Forgive me, my lady. In my land, the tombs of the kings are plundered almost as a matter of course.

We put grave robbers to death when we catch them but the terrors of the afterlife are perhaps not so great when you are starving."

Tomyra looked at Ket sadly. "I think you must come from a godless and desperate land, Ket, despite you calling it the land of the gods."

A bustle of activity interrupted them. Villagers brought large trestles out onto the freshly turned earth of the tomb, covering them with cloths and platters filled with cold meats, bread and pitchers of koumiss and wine. Nemathres picked up a large flask of wine and, chanting an invocation to the Great Goddess, poured it slowly onto the ground where it rapidly drained away. As soon as he finished, others moved forward, picking up cups and drinking, grabbing handfuls of food. Within minutes, the area above the tomb filled with a seething mass of people, drinking and eating.

The rain grew heavier with the passing time, but few people noticed. The food disappeared rapidly and great vats of koumiss were brought out. The drinking continued steadily, people breaking into drunken song, or fierce argument. Occasionally the arguments deteriorated into brawling fights. The contestants fought loudly, encouraged by the yelling crowds, until one or other of the fighters collapsed unconscious or in a drunken stupor.

Nemathres remained close to his Massegetae guests. "My people overcome their grief through drink and unruly behaviour. Besides, noise will chase bad spirits away before we seal the tomb." He signaled to his own bodyguard, who immediately began the task of clearing the area of drunken revelers. Groups of villagers were led away to stacked tools and, with much grumbling, started to haul more soil and stones over the trampled site of the tomb.

Nemathres looked up at the heavy cloud cover. "I think the rain is easing. It is time to light the fires again." He called his bodyguard to him, issuing rapid instructions. "Tell the priestess we are coming. It is time." He smiled at Tomyra. "I think we could all do with some hot food and besides, we need to purify ourselves."

Nikometros nudged Ket as they walked toward the village. "What form does this purification take? There doesn't seem to be enough clean water around for washing, even a ritual washing."

Ket cackled. "Something quite different, young lord. You will think yourself one of the gods after this purification." Nikometros could get no more out of him.

The priestess' hut was large. The entrance flaps were tied back allowing the gray light of the day to penetrate all but its farthest reaches. The priestess herself was old, her wrinkled brown face lined with gray hair. Her eyes had a milky sheen to them and she stared past them when they approached.

Nemathres saluted her, speaking softly. "Greetings, old mother. It is time. My father has been sent to the Great Goddess. Will you light the fires for us again?"

The old woman muttered and sucked her teeth noisily, fussing with her robes. Delving into deep pockets, she brought out a piece of iron and an old polished flint. She crouched down over a bronze basin filled with dried moss and became motionless, staring straight ahead.

The silence dragged on then just as Nikometros shifted uncomfortably she started a low crooning. Her voice rose steadily in volume and her body started swaying. She struck the flint and iron together repeatedly, sparks cascading into the dried moss. Tendrils of smoke appeared and she bent over the bronze basin, blowing gently. Small flames shot up with a soft crackling sound, and she gathered the burning moss in her bare hands. Standing up, she held her hands aloft, flames leaping high as she cried out. "Tabiti! Great Goddess! Come back to your People."

The priestess dropped to her knees again, depositing the fiery mass in the basin and adding dried twigs from a pouch. The flames crackled loudly and spread. The old woman looked intently at the flames, holding her right hand in them for a long moment before sitting back. Nikometros stared at her. She gave no indication of pain but sat on her heels, rocking gently and singing softly to herself.

Nemathres picked up the basin and started transferring burning twigs to other pots of dried moss and kindling. Villagers picked up the pots, carrying them off. Nikometros squatted down beside the old woman and gently took her hand in his. To his astonishment, it was free of all blemishes, untouched by the flame.

Tomyra stepped quickly to his side and plucked at his tunic. "Niko, rise I beg you, quickly!" Nikometros looked puzzled but rose. "It is death to touch a priestess unbidden," she whispered. "Especially during a ceremony." She looked round quickly then relaxed. "No one has seen you. The old woman is blind. If she claims to have been touched I will say I did so." Tomyra held up a hand to silence his protest. "I am permitted."

Nemathres turned away from the bronze basin, leaving one of his men to continue handing out the life-giving flames. "The purification booths are being prepared. Normally it would take many hours to heat the rocks but we will use a copper plate over a wood fire instead. The smoke is as pure and the gods will still be present." He led them out of the tent, crossing to a small felt booth held up by crossed poles. Gaps around the base showed a brazier within it, topped by a heavy copper plate that already sizzled and spat as the occasional raindrop found its way in through the hole in the roof. Thin curls of smoke escaped, held low over the village and pulled to the east by the gusty winds.

Nikometros looked at the booth askance. "Do you mean to stun us with smoke? I have seen farmers collect honey from wild bees, stunning them with smoke but I have never seen men willingly do it to themselves."

Tomyra smiled. "I promise you will enjoy this smoke, Niko. The gods of air and fire combine to let man see as the gods do for a short time. Come, do as I do." She took a handful of small, dark shiny seeds from a pouch attached to one of the poles, and ducked under the flaps of the booth. Nikometros shrugged and followed, as did Timon, helping themselves to handfuls of the small glistening seeds.

Ket shook his head. "I think not. I have talked to the gods before. The presence of the gods at my age might overwhelm me. Besides, I must look after my Bubis." He stroked a bulge in his robe that responded with a low rumble of contentment.

Spargises grinned and nodded to Nemathres. "I will willingly partake, my friend. Will you join us?"

Nemathres shook his head. "I must see to my people before I can purify myself. Enjoy meeting the gods. I will see you later." He watched as Spargises took a handful from the pouch and entered the booth, before leaving.

Nikometros made a place for Spargises around the brazier. Tomyra smiled across at him then threw her handful onto the hot copper plate. "Hemp seeds," she explained, as the first of them cracked and started smoking. "Throw yours on and breathe the smoke. Hold it for a few moments then breathe out." She demonstrated.

Spargises threw his seeds on the plate when Nikometros hesitated. Timon grinned, leaned across the brazier and took a deep breath of the smoke. A moment later he exploded in a paroxysm of coughing, doubled up and retching. Nikometros grinned in turn, slapping him on the back and helping Timon to his feet. He gingerly sniffed the sweet smoke, held it a moment and released it. Throwing his seeds on, Nikometros breathed again as the smoke thickened and curled about the enclosed space. His eyes watered and he coughed, wondering why this was supposed to be a joyful experience.

Both Tomyra and her father composed themselves, breathing the smoke in, holding it for a long moment before exhaling slowly. Their expressions calmed and smiles creased their faces. Nikometros leaned over the copper plate again, taking shallow breaths. The itching in his lungs and throat eased and a feeling of lightheadedness came over him. The sight of Timon still coughing filled him with mirth and he laughed softly.

"Shallow breaths, my friend," he told Timon. Nikometros leaned back and looked up through the smoke hole. Wisps of pale gray smoke curled gently against the darker gray of the overcast skies and the soot-darkened fabric of the booth. *What wonderful colours and patterns it makes*, he thought. *It reminds me of something, but what?*

223

Tomyra's visage swam through the smoke towards him, her eyes closed and a calm expression on her face. Nikometros felt suddenly as if he stood to one side looking at himself. He watched fascinated as the four people in the booth leaned forward once more, breathing in the smoke. The tall, fair-haired man snorted and he felt himself laughing with him. *Of course, that is how I look. How strange!* A feeling of great contentment swept over him. He turned to Spargises and saw a short, broad man with a smiling face and an enormous mustache and beard expand around him. He felt waves of friendship sweep over him and he embraced the man. He knew the other man in the tent too, but he could not quite remember his name now. He grinned at the man, delighted when the man grinned back and hugged him.

Nikometros moved around Timon until he stood next to Tomyra. She opened her eyes and reached out to touch his face, stroking his cheek. He looked at her intently, trying to hold onto thoughts that formed and broke up repeatedly. "My lady," he murmured. "To-myra, To...my...ra," he enunciated slowly, the syllables flowing off his tongue like honey. "You...you are beautiful, my lovely young Scythian priestess. I think I have loved you from the very first time I..." Nikometros' voice trailed off, confused. "When did I see you first, my beautiful lady? I think you have been with me forever."

Tomyra's face showed her struggle to control her own thoughts and tongue. "Ah, Niko, my great warrior. Is this you I hear, or the gods letting me hear what I most desire?" she whispered. "The Great Mother revealed you to me in prophecy. She said we would one day be..." Tomyra blushed and put her hand to her mouth, her eyes widening.

Nikometros grinned inanely, his senses reeling and peered across the smoky booth at Spargises. "Brother, you have a beautiful daughter and I love her. I love her and I want her..."

Tomyra gasped and gripped Nikometros' arm, swinging him around. Nikometros stumbled and fell against the brazier, almost upsetting it. Spargises shook his head, trying to clear enough smoke out of his head for a very important thought. "Niko, my brother." He paused, shaking his head. "The smoke makes us say strange things, so I must warn you, as a friend and a brother." He scratched his beard, carefully examining his fingernails then turning his hand over to stare at his knuckles. "What was I saying? Ah,...Do not ask for what you cannot have, my brother in blood. No man can claim my daughter for the Mother has already claimed her. If I had another daughter..."

"Please, Niko. It is the smoke talking." Tomyra whispered, clutching Nikometros' arm. "Do not say anything else, I beg you."

Nikometros gazed down at her, puzzled. *What have I said that is so bad? I only said I loved her...that I loved her and wanted her...O perdition! She is a priestess and sacred!* He flushed and stammered an apology.

Spargises waved a hand dismissively, taking control of his thoughts with an obvious effort. "I think we have adequately purified ourselves. I suggest we stop before someone says something unforgivable." He looked seriously at Nikometros. "Do not be concerned, my brother. What has taken place here today was spawned by the smoke of the gods and goes no further. If action follows not on thought then...then your words are as smoke upon the wind. Forgotten." The chief lifted the edge of the felt booth for Tomyra then ducked outside himself.

Nikometros and Timon followed. The cold, damp air cleared Nikometros' lungs, racing like an icy freshet through his head. The stifling lightheaded feeling left him, to be replaced by a comfortable sense of well-being. He looked about at a number of similar booths, the sweet, burnt odour of the hemp seeds hanging over the whole village. Men staggered from the booths, many roaring with laughter or singing. The whole mood of the village had changed.

Spargises peered at Nikometros. "Come, brother. We should return to our camp. The Dumae will choose another chief in the next couple of days. We can return then. I have much to discuss with them." He swiveled on his heel and marched off, calling to his bodyguard. Tomyra followed for a few paces then stopped and waited for Nikometros to catch up.

Mardes approached with the Lion bodyguard and saluted. "All present, sir." He glanced at Timon who stood clutching at the sides of a booth. "Is everything all right, sir?"

Nikometros nodded. "Yes, Timon will be all right but look after him until he regains the use of his feet."

Mardes nodded and moved to support Timon. "Must have been damned strong wine to affect you so fast. I don't suppose you have any of it left?" he asked hopefully.

Nikometros looked at Tomyra who was still standing, arms by her side, gazing at his face. He smiled tentatively, opened his mouth to speak then closed it again. He took a couple of steps toward her. "My lady, I...I would talk to you later."

Tomyra stared intently into his eyes and nodded. "My father says your words are as smoke upon the wind, but I have not forgotten them." Her lips moved briefly again then she lowered her head. Turning, she ran after her father and Nikometros watched her go.

Did her lips really say that? Or is it just that I want her to say it? Dear gods and goddesses everywhere, if it can be, let it be!

Chapter Nineteen

Tomyra's heart beat faster, her fingers fumbling with the clasps of her dark green gown. Stagora, her ancient nurse and attendant, muttered crossly as she tried to push the young woman's hands away. "Let me do this, my lady. You will tear this beautiful material."

"Do it then, but hurry, old woman." Tomyra smiled. "He will be here soon." *Great Mother, what are you leading me into?* She raised her arms as Stagora fastened the last clasp at her neck, shaking her dark hair out in a wave over her shoulders. "Quickly, Stagora. Set out the wine and the cushions. Make sure the braziers are full."

The old woman hurried to obey, muttering constantly. "Quickly, Stagora. Do this, Stagora. Do that. It is as if a suitor was calling, not just your father's brother come for his language lessons." She stopped short, looking back at Tomyra suspiciously. "My lady, you will act in a manner befitting your position?"

"Of course, Stagora." Tomyra flushed, turning away to hide her face. "You know how I enjoy reading the poetry scrolls with him."

Her old nurse looked hard at Tomyra's back, noting the tension in her shoulders and sighed. "Like your mother indeed. Just remember your greater Mother, child."

A challenge rang out from the entrance, and a moment later a guard ducked his head through the entrance hangings. "The Lord Nikomayros, my lady." Nikometros stepped inside and bowed to Tomyra, smiling.

"Greetings Nikomayros." She turned back to the guard. "Thank you, Lyartes. You may leave us. We will not require your presence tonight."

Lyartes looked troubled. "Er...my lady, I am required to guard you at all times."

"Do you think the lord Nikomayros, my champion, is unable to defend me?"

The guard flushed. "Of course not, lady. I only meant...well, the person of the lady...I mean, you...yourself." He stuttered in his embarrassment. "You should not be left alone in the presence of a man, my lady, even one such as my lord, lady," he finished in a rush.

Tomyra smiled, gesturing at the old woman behind her. "I commend you for your zeal, Lyartes; but I am not alone. My nurse will be present at all times. There will be no unseemly things happening here tonight." *Great Mother, forgive me. But it is no lie, what I do is not unseemly if it comes from you.*

* * *

Lyartes bowed and backed out of the tent hurriedly. Turning, he almost collided with another man. Grasping his spear firmly he rasped out a challenge.

"Only I, Lyartes. Is all well?"

"Yes, my lord Parasades. The lord Nikomayros is with the priestess." He licked his lips. "My lord, I am dismissed for the night."

"She is alone with him?" Parasades asked sharply.

"No, my lord. The old woman, her nurse, is present."

"Very well then. You have been dismissed."

Lyartes saluted and hurried off into the night. Parasades stood silently, staring at the hut's entrance, listening intently to the murmur of voices within it. He stroked his beard thoughtfully, and then slowly withdrew into the shadows.

* * *

Nikometros smiled and moved closer to Tomyra. "Tomyra, I have longed for your summons. I..."

Tomyra held up her hand, stepping back as she whispered. "Softly, Niko. We must wait." She raised her voice. "You are indeed welcome, Nikomayros. Let us take some wine and begin our lessons. I thought that we might examine further our customs." She gestured towards the cushions. "Come, Stagora. Pour us some wine."

The old woman came forward with a copper pitcher and two ornate cups. Setting them down next to the cushions, she carefully poured a stream of rich red wine into both cups. She set the pitcher down and retreated into the shadows.

Tomyra glanced round at her, reaching into the folds of her gown. She took out a small, earthenware phial, pouring a stream of dark fluid from it, into the pitcher. She looked up at Nikometros and then quickly stirred the wine with one finger. She licked a drop from her finger and nodded in satisfaction. "Stagora," she called.

"What is it, my lady?" grumbled the old woman.

"It is a cold night. You may have some wine to warm those old bones."

The old woman hobbled over rapidly then returned to her seat in the shadows, grasping the pitcher of wine. Slurping noises immediately ensued.

Tomyra smiled fondly in the direction of the old woman. "She does love her wine, when I allow her to have it," she whispered.

"What did you put in it?"

"Only poppy juice. She will sleep soundly tonight."

Nikometros looked into Tomyra's eyes, seeing them soften and glisten in the flickering light from the oil lamps. "Tomyra. Tomyra, did you mean what you said silently to me today?"

"And what did I say to you today, my champion?" she asked boldly. Her eyes dropped after a moment and she flushed. Tomyra smiled tremulously. "Do you really doubt my feelings for you, Niko? I have known from that first day, when you almost killed me in battle that the Mother had brought you into my life for a purpose." She turned as a soft thump came from the shadows. "A moment, Niko." Tomyra rose and went to the old woman's side. Stagora lay on the floor, between two cushions, breathing noisily. The wine lay pooling beside her. Tomyra carefully poured out the rest of the wine onto a patch of earth and draped a rug over the stain. She eased the old woman onto the cushions and settled her comfortably under a thick wool robe. *Great Mother, keep her safe and give her deep sleep.* Tomyra kissed Stagora's wrinkled forehead then swiftly moved back to Nikometros' side.

Nikometros reached up and took her hand, guiding her to the cushions beside him. "Tomyra, you know I love you, I always have, but this is dangerous for you."

"For you too, my barbarian warrior. Remember, it is death to lay even a hand on the sacred person of the priestess. Aaah!" She shuddered as Nikometros slid his arm around her.

"Would you rather then I left, my love?" Nikometros smiled, turning her face to his, smoothing her raven hair from her eyes.

Tomyra leaned back on his arm, her dark eyes searching his pale ones. Gently she shook her head. "No, my love, my Niko. Do not leave me."

He relaxed, smiling, and lowered his head to hers. His lips brushed hers then again. He looked into her

231

eyes. "I love you, Tomyra." Nikometros kissed her deeply, tasting the spices and herbs of her cleansers.

Tomyra drew back for an instant then, her pulse racing, returned his kiss. Like a caged animal freed for the first time, she threw herself into that first kiss, hungry for more.

Panting, she at length drew back, her cheeks flushed, eyes gleaming. Nikometros grinned and reached out for her. She leapt to her feet and stood looking down on him. Moving slowly, keeping her eyes fixed firmly on his face, she walked to the first lamp and snuffed it. Nikometros stood then reached out and snuffed the other lamp. Deep shadows swept over the inside of the hut, lit now, only by the dull red glow of the braziers.

"Come, Tomyra." Nikometros reached out his hand to take hers in his.

She laughed softly. "The blood of my mother, of the Sauromantians, burns hotly in my veins, Niko. Think you that I am as other women, to be taken as a prize, as a right of conquest?" She advanced a step, the glow from the brazier behind her throwing her gowned body into outline. Tomyra reached up to her neck and undid the clasps of her gown, letting it fall in a heap around her ankles. A thin shift covered her body, the dim red light showing her soft curves and finely muscled limbs. "I will not be taken, Niko. Rather, I give myself willingly to my chosen man."

Nikometros swallowed then stepped forward, loosening his leather tunic coat. Tomyra reached up slipping it from his arms, and drawing herself into his embrace. They kissed fiercely, heads moving feverishly. Nikometros sank to his knees, pulling the young girl down beside him onto the cushions. They kissed again, her hands running over his smooth skin, feeling the power in his arms and chest, fumbling with the cords of his leggings. He reached down and drew her shift upward, his hand smoothing her thighs.

Tomyra cried out suddenly, her legs locking tight and her hands clutching his arms. "Oh, Niko, I am sorry." She leaned against his chest, her voice muffled and shaking. "It seems my blood runs thin after all. Treat me kindly, my lord. I am yours."

Nikometros pulled her head back gently and kissed her trembling lips and moist eyes. "Tomyra, my love. You mean more to me than my life itself. Thy hurt is my hurt, thy pleasure, my pleasure." He reached down once more; cupping her breast in his strong, calloused hand and drew her close.

* * *

Outside the hut, deep in the shadows, Parasades watched, noting the sudden extinguishing of the light, the sullen glow of embers all that remained. He stood, stroking his beard, deep in thought. A little later, his head lifted as a quick, high cry of ecstasy pierced the still air, quickly silenced. A troubled look crossed his face and he turned away.

Chapter Twenty

The weeks following the purification ceremony were hectic. The bereaved tribe had, after much debate, decided that Nemathres was a worthy successor to his father as chief of his tribe. He was duly consecrated by their priestess and installed in the position. His first act as chief was to enter into an alliance with the Massegetae. In no small part, this was due to the increasing reputation of Spargises and his barbarian war leader. Several smaller tribes also sent emissaries to the Massegetae, pledging their support in return for peace and a share of the spoils should war with the western horse-peoples ensue.

Nikometros sang softly to himself as he groomed Diomede. The early morning sun sparkled on the dew, and a cold breeze delayed the clouds of biting insects. *By the gods,* he thought, *these colder days are good after the heat of summer.* His hand hesitated over the horse's flanks as he remembered the previous night and the several nights before it. His pulse quickened at the memories and his song faltered, a grin slowly growing on his face. Lost in his thoughts, he jumped as a hand clapped him on the shoulder.

"Nikomayros, my friend, have you so little to do that you can stand around all day?"

Nikometros looked up into the amused eyes of Parasades. He flushed, grasping his friend's forearm. "Welcome, Parasades. I had not thought to see you return so soon. Your tasks went well?"

"Well enough. Come; talk with me as we walk. Spargises requests your presence immediately."

Nikometros fell into step alongside the tall Scythian warrior. "So, the talks with the western tribes were fruitful?"

"Yes. They all sought our friendship. It seems that word of our powerful champion has spread far beyond our lands, and they seek the protection of our army against the western horsemen. Wherever I went, I heard talk of the deeds of the Lion and his Companions."

Nikometros glanced at Parasades, grinning. His smile faded at the expression on his friend's face. "What is wrong?"

Parasades shrugged. "Perhaps nothing. The Massegetae have always been a proud and strong people. It saddens me a little that the tribes now fear something new."

"But the Lions are Massegetae, they are of your tribe."

"My tribe, Nikomayros?"

"Our tribe, of course, my friend. You know I am ever mindful of the honour of being one of the People. But the only new things are the battle tactics that have conquered tribes like the Jartai. Surely you do not fear these new things?"

"Fear? No." Parasades scowled briefly. "Nikomayros, do you not know how powerful you have grown in the last few months?"

"What do you mean, Parasades? I am blood-brother to Spargises, but that brings no power. I command my own company of horsemen in battle, as do you. I train other companies, but I do not command them."

The Scythian warrior shook back his long greasy hair. "And what of your influence? Our chief listens to the counsel of his advisors, but does what you say. Hundreds of Massegetae warriors would willingly obey your every command, would be proud to be led by you. As for our priestess...I wonder whether she does not also alter her allegiance...never mind, Niko-mayros. Talk to our chief once again then tell me you have no power." Parasades stopped beside the entrance of a large hut and swept back the entrance hangings.

A small group of guards just inside the hut looked up and grinned at Nikometros. Beyond them the hut was crowded with men. Spargises looked up as the noise level dropped. "Nikomayros, brother! Come, stand beside me." He gestured to his guards. "Bring wine for our Lion."

The crowd parted for Nikometros as he pushed his way toward the chief, accepting the cup of rich, aromatic wine thrust into his hand. Most of the warriors around him were smiling and raised their cups in salute, though a few looked sullen. A few paces behind the chief stood the imposing bulk of the chief's son, Areipithes. He glared briefly at Nikometros before turning his back on him to talk with two of his own advisors.

Spargises held up his hands for silence. As the conversation died away he clasped Nikometros by the shoulder. "Friends, you have heard the good news. Our prowess has gained us the respect of all tribes — of the Massegetae and many others. They look to us for leadership in war, and war we shall have. The western horse-tribes have been harassing our outliers and herds. They have refused to treat with us, and we shall grind them into the dust this coming spring. Our great armies, trained so well by my brother, the Lion, will crush them. We will take their herds, their gold and their women."

The crowd of men broke into loud shouts and cheers, brandishing their weapons, or clashing swords together. Spargises raised his hands again, and as the shouting died away, continued. "We must, of course, be united in our efforts. It is important that one who understands the new ways of fighting be at the forefront of our attack. Such a man must lead our armies against the foe."

A low buzz of conversation broke out, several groups of men losing their cheerful looks as the chief's words sank into their minds. "My brother Nikomayros has proved himself many times over in battle and in leadership. I have consulted with my advisors and counselors," he raised a hand as the murmuring increased in volume, "...and have decided to name Nikomayros as joint war leader with my son Areipithes against the western tribes."

"No! You cannot! That honour is mine alone by right." Areipithes pushed forward, his face suffused with blood. "I will not share my position with a barbarian."

Spargises turned on him with a roar of anger, throwing his cup to the ground. "You are not chief of the Massegetae, and if I say this man, my brother, is war leader with you then you will obey!" He turned, gesturing to his guards, "Remove this man from my presence until he regains his manners."

The guards hesitated a moment then slowly advanced. "My lord," one of them muttered, "it is not seemly that you should quarrel with your war leader."

"Get him out of here, you fools, before I strip you, and this upstart son of mine, of all your duties and privileges."

Parasades stepped up to the chief and laid a hand on his arm. "My lord, please listen."

Spargises swung round, his swollen face still livid with anger. "And what do you have to say, Parasades?" he grated.

"Just that you push things too fast, against all custom." He held up a hand as the chief opened his mouth to shout once more. "Please, my lord. None doubt the worth of this man," he gestured at Nikometros. "...Your sworn brother. But think, I beg you. Your son is a stalwart warrior, and has been sole war leader for many years, without any disputing his right to do so. You slight him by forcing him to share the honour with another. Give Nikomayros high honour, by all means, the gods witness he deserves it. But let Areipithes, a Massegetae by birth, and your only son, retain his position as leader of our armies."

Spargises took several deep breaths as the silence in the hut grew. Nikometros stood silently to one side, looking questioningly at Parasades, who met his gaze levelly. At length, Spargises said in a low voice, "Are you challenging me, Parasades?"

Parasades shook his head. "No, my lord. It has never been my ambition to be more than a counselor and warrior of the People. I seek only what is best for the tribe."

"Then do not presume to contradict your chief. I have made my decision. Nikomayros is joint war leader with Areipithes. If my son will not share the honour then let him step down." Spargises swung round on his heel, searching the faces of the men around him. "If any dispute my decision then you are no longer of the People. Depart now."

The room was silent for a long time. At length an aged counselor murmured, "As our lord wishes, so shall it be." A number of others muttered agreement, but Nikometros noticed nearly a third of those present just looked down and said nothing.

"Now leave me, everyone. I will rest before I consult the priestess." The counselors bowed and left the hut, followed by the men. Areipithes motioned to his followers and strode out, casting a menacing look at Nikometros as he left. Nikometros hesitated then walked rapidly after Parasades, catching up with him just outside the hut.

"Parasades, my friend? What has happened that you turn from me like this?"

He looked sadly into the Macedonian's face. "Did I not say that you were powerful? A powerful man can act for the common good or turn his hand to evil things. Two powerful men give rise to nothing good for those around them. I like you, Nikomayros, and feel privileged to call you a friend, but I cannot stand by and see my people betrayed, even innocently." Parasades walked rapidly off, leaving Nikometros gazing open-mouthed after him.

Chapter Twenty-One

A howling autumn gale shook the tent flaps, sending gusts of cold air skittering around the room. A brazier glowed fitfully in a corner of the hut, giving off more smoke than warmth. Areipithes sat moodily on a felt cushion to one side of the brazier, a bronze cauldron filled with coals, on the ground in front of him. He rubbed his hands together over the coals, feeling the cold absently as he debated his problem mentally. To his other side sat two men, wrapped in thick felt tunics and leggings. One, a thin, unkempt individual kept his eyes fastened on the chief's son, awaiting his commands. The other was tall and burly, bearing many badges and gold ornaments. This man regarded Areipithes with an expression of disdain.

At length, Areipithes yawned and stretched, fixing the two men with a dispassionate stare. "Why am I surrounded by fools and traitors, Scolices?

The smaller of the two men squirmed uneasily. "Er, I don't know, my lord."

"My question does not require an answer," replied Areipithes. "I am merely thinking aloud." He rose to his feet in a single, lithe movement and strode over to the brazier. "If my father were not chief, who would the People choose as their next one?" The silence was unbroken; save for a muffled booming as the tent leathers shook in the storm winds. "Well? Answer me."

"My lord?" Scolices leapt to his feet, his companion rising slowly behind him. "I'm sorry, my lord, I thought..." The man cleared his throat noisily, pursed his lips to spit before thinking better of it, and, after a few moments, swallowed convulsively. "The situation has changed my lord. With the Jartai and Dumai now traveling with us, fewer men know of your great leadership skills, your bravery, your..."

"Enough, you fool. Do not seek to flatter me. What of the Greek? Will the People follow him?"

Scolices glanced nervously at his companion. "Er...he is popular, my lord. His victories, and the unnatural way he trains his men, and leads them to success makes many believe the Mother favours him. And now he is made war leader with you..."

Areipithes scowled. "Enough!" He stopped and looked hard at the other man before continuing. "He must be removed and soon. I will not wait forever before assuming my rightful place as sole war leader and..." he hesitated a moment, "...chief of the Massegetae. The People must be given no other choice as leader." He started pacing up and down the hut, kicking cushions out of the way.

The tall and burly man smoothed his moustache with one hand and coughed discreetly. When Areipithes swung round on him the man smiled pleasantly. "My lord, there is a way."

Areipithes slowly advanced on the man, holding him with a fixed stare as he did so. Though a tall man himself, Areipithes found himself staring levelly into the man's eyes, saw the crinkles of amusement in their corners. "Just why are you here anyway, Parasades?"

"First, let me see if I have your problem firmly in my mind." Parasades turned on his heel slowly and deliberately, ignoring the look of fury on the face of the chief's son. "The Greek, this Nikomayros, arrived at a time that you were contemplating challenging your father for leadership. You were, however, unsure of your support by the elders of the tribe. The Greek allied himself to your father, seduced the priestess, your sister..."

"Half sister, curse you."

"Of course. He then proved himself a remarkable fighter, a charismatic leader, and a brilliant general. The Massegetae are now far more powerful, having taken over and taken in other tribes, allied themselves to others. When next we face an enemy, as we will shortly, it will be with him as war leader alongside you. Now, even if your father should die, the People will probably not accept you as chief." He turned to face Areipithes again. "They may, however, make the barbarian our next chief. Or is 'king' a more fitting title for so powerful a person?" He laughed briefly. "You do have a problem."

Areipithes ground his teeth, his hands clenching by his sides. "You have an answer?"

"Oh, indeed I do. The question you must answer first is, 'Why should I help you?'"

Areipithes stared hard into the other man's eyes, seeking to dominate him. After long moments he dropped his gaze with a grimace. "Very well then. You will help me because I am the only son of Spargises. I am war leader of the Massegetae, and the only one to lead our tribe to victory over the western horsemen."

Parasades kept silent, smiling softly. Areipithes cursed. "Because you hate this barbarian, though you make a pretence of being his friend, and wish to see him dead." The man continued to stand silent. "Curse you then," ground out Areipithes between clenched teeth. "So you have other reasons. I do not need to know them so long as you rid me of the barbarian."

Parasades barked out a laugh and started pacing in turn, throwing his arms about to make his points. "You have made no secret of your hatred for the Greek, even when it became clear your father valued him. This was your first mistake. Then you tried to throw a wedge between him and the priestess, using the woman Roxana. No doubt hoping to get your father enraged at him." He shook his head. "Another mistake. You should, rather, be encouraging them to grow closer. Spargises is too cunning a leader to throw away an asset like the Greek just because his daughter is upset. However, if his daughter was compromised, the tribe's sacred priestess violated..." Parasades stopped, turning to Areipithes with his face neutral. "Do you believe the Greek is totally loyal to the People, or does he yearn for his own kind?"

"He is loyal to my father...and my half-sister," Areipithes said slowly, "But I believe his first loyalty is to his Macedonian friends."

"Yes, yes, certainly," broke in Scolices. "Even at the start, he was concerned not to wage war on the Greeks." He flushed, finishing with a mumble. "His crony, that Timon, has said he misses his former life."

Parasades nodded. "Soon we will be nearing our winter quarters near Urul in preparation for the spring campaign against the westerners. We will also be close to the Greek garrisons on the Oxus River. I think the Greek could be persuaded to take his woman and flee."

"That would remove the barbarian, I grant you, and my sister is but a small loss to the tribe for we can get another priestess; but I want him dead."

"Then ensure that he is caught. Even the good Spargises, faced with the defection of his blood brother, the desecration of the holy priestess, and, who knows, maybe even the theft of some precious items, would put him to death. Then the way is open for you to become sole war leader again."

Areipithes nodded slowly, his brows knotted in concentration. "Why do you tell me this? I thought the barbarian was your friend."

Parasades pursed his lips and shrugged. "I admire many of his abilities, and were he truly of the People, I would help him to the chief's seat or even a throne, despite your wishes. He is a foreigner, however. We should be led by a warrior born of the Massegetae, someone whose loyalties are totally Scythian."

"And, of course, you would seek the good will of the man who will be our next chief."

Parasades smiled and bowed slightly. "If you would replace the chief you must convince more than just me. I am not sure that our People would prosper with you as leader, but better a son of the Massegetae than an upstart foreigner."

Areipithes scowled. "We shall see. With the barbarian dead, I shall take my father's place. The tribe knows I can best any who come against me."

"Perhaps. In the meantime I would suggest that you cease your efforts to drive the Greek and our priestess apart. Let their own inclinations rule them. I will ensure the Greek has opportunities to accomplish his Goddess-cursed plans, and also an opportunity to escape with her."

The chief's son nodded slowly. "Very well. And when he does...?"

"I will catch him in the act and deliver him to your father. You will stay out of it until all is done." The man smiled again and turning, walked to the hut's entrance. "One more thing," he said, turning back. "Try and keep out of his way. With you absent, he will be less on guard." He stepped back, letting the felt entrance hangings swing shut behind him.

Areipithes gestured to Scolices. "Make sure he is followed, but discreetly. Bring me word of who he sees and talks to."

Scolices nodded and left the hut.

Areipithes stroked his beard and moustache, staring at the empty doorway. *Do I trust Parasades? And if I do not, what must I do about it?*

Chapter Twenty-Two

The valley of the Oxus lay spread out below him. Nikometros sat comfortably on his stallion's back, guiding him with a gentle pressure of his knees as the horse picked its way along the crumbling ridge top. The river itself meandered several stadia away, a thin ribbon of gray metal almost lost among the shingle banks and scrubby trees still clad in tatters of red and gold. A thin, biting wind swept in from the north, causing Nikometros to gather his cloak around himself, grateful for his thick felt tunic and leggings. He looked back at his troop, standing stolidly in the lee of an old riverbank where, despite the shelter, their pennants bearing the emblem of the lion head and arrow cracked and snapped in the stiff wind.

A rider detached himself from the troop and trotted up, saluting as he came alongside his commander. "Sir, the scouts are back. They report no sign of activity to the north or south." The rider was likewise clad in full Scythian dress, though sporting a full beard and moustache. The accent of his speech betrayed his Macedonian origin.

"Thank you, Timon. We will continue on to the agreed meeting place." Nikometros squinted up at the lowering cloud, trying to judge the position of the weak winter sun. "At least five spans to sunset. We can have camp set up and a hot meal prepared by the time the others arrive." A smile drifted across his face at the thought.

* * *

Timon turned in his seat and gestured the horsemen onward. "Aye, sir. I'll send some men forward as a precaution though." When his commander nodded, he rode off to intercept the others. *Thank all the gods he has at last acted on his desires. Both wanted it to be, so why wait so long?* A smile creased his face as the thought of Nikometros and his priestess brought to mind his own tempestuous affair with one of the priestess' own maidens, Bithyia. *These horsewomen are bold and know their own minds, not like the soft females of home.* He grinned broadly, taking up his place at the head of the company of Lions. Timon signaled to Lythures, a young Jartai warrior, explaining his task. The warrior in turn picked a handful of men and galloped off, angling down the shingle banks toward the distant river.

Timon considered the men in the troop once more, ever mindful of the need for discretion. Each man had been hand-picked, carefully sounded out, as had the women in Tomyra's guards. Nikometros trod a dangerous path, loving the sacred priestess of the Mother Goddess, and an incautious word or casual comment to another tribesman could spell death for all concerned. It was only a matter of time before they were found out, but Timon was determined to protect Nikometros until then – and after if possible.

* * *

The sun sank low over the river, filtered through gaunt-limbed trees, and dimmed by the wood smoke that rose from several cooking fires. Small hide lean-tos surrounded the fires, and men lounged in them, polishing weapons or mending equipment. Some tended spits over the fires, turning haunches of meat as fat sizzled and flared in the embers, filling the air with the aroma of cooking meat. The horses, groomed and hobbled near the stunted trees and scrub, whickered and snorted softly as they fed. Almost unseen were pairs of men, a hundred paces out from the camp, in hollows scooped out of the shingle, and sheltered by felt cloaks. They scanned the surrounding country for any sign of the enemy.

The first stars in the eastern sky were struggling to break through the cloud cover when a sharp challenge came from the south and, a few moments later, by a muffled greeting. Soon, a body of riders could be made out trotting in along the river, splashing through the shallows toward the camp.

Nikometros leaped up from his seat by a fire, striding to greet the riders. Tomyra jumped down off the red mare, and threw her arms around him. The other riders, bearing pennants with a stylized owl, looked away discreetly, as did the men running up from the lean-tos. Nikometros failed to see them, his attention centred on the young woman in his arms. "Tomyra, my love. You are safe? All went well with you?"

Tomyra laughed gaily. "Of course, Niko. My Owls are more than capable of looking after me. They have been trained well by your man Timon...though I think he looks to train more than just warriors."

Behind her, Bithyia sniffed loudly. "It is a matter of some dispute as to who is training who, my lady."

Nikometros laughed loudly. "Timon! Come attend to your fierce Owl." He turned to a group of men beside him. "The philosophers tell us the mating of a lion and an eagle produced the Gryphon. Perhaps a Lion and an Owl will produce another such rare creature."

A roar of laughter followed Timon and Bithyia as they ran arm in arm into the dark. Nikometros turned to Tomyra. "Come then, my lady. Your supper is prepared."

Tomyra grinned, taking his hand. "Good, my stomach growls to be filled." She leaned close and whispered, "Another part of me also desires to be filled, my lord." Tomyra saw the expression on Nikometros' face and giggled. "Am I too forward, dear Niko? Would you rather I played the coy maiden like the town girls?"

"By the gods above and below, I would not! Now come and eat, we will see about the other later," he grinned. He led the smiling woman to a lean-to in a copse of trees somewhat removed from the main camp. A small metal cauldron bubbled on a low fire, releasing tendrils of appetizing steam. Nikometros spooned a generous portion onto ornate copper plates and squatted beside Tomyra, handing her one. "Only mutton, I'm afraid, but Agarus swears the mixture of herbs he provided will make it worth eating."

Tomyra nodded, her mouth full. Swallowing, she wiped her mouth with the back of her hand. "He's right." She immediately started eating again.

For a period the only sound was the scrape of wooden spoons and daggers on the copper plates, and the distant rise and fall of conversation from the main camp. At length Nikometros pushed his plate away with a sigh, followed a moment later by Tomyra. She belched in appreciation and leaned back against a tree-trunk, stretching her limbs. "By the Mother who sustains us, I needed that." She grinned at Nikometros. "Well, at least one of my desires is satisfied."

Nikometros eased himself over with a smile. She leaned across and kissed him, licking a small spot of gravy from the corner of his mouth. He responded fiercely, his hands searching, and for a while they shut out the sounds of the river, the wind and the encamped men and women. A roar of laughter from the camp roused Nikometros, and, clasping Tomyra tightly, he led the way into their lean-to.

Nikometros woke to the sounds of soft footsteps in the gravel near the river's edge. He listened intently, his hand on his sword then relaxed as he heard the familiar muffled challenges and replies of the guards changing shifts. He looked over at Tomyra, sleeping beside him, her body dimly visible by the embers of their fire, naked and vulnerable. He reached over, pulling the furs over her, and rose quietly, ducking under the entrance flap to stand, naked himself, in the darkness. He looked towards the eastern horizon, noting the faint, pearly luminescence that heralded moonrise. He sniffed the air, smelling distant rain. A low rumble of thunder far to the north made him tense for a moment, before he remembered that was downriver. He stretched and crawled back into the lean-to.

"Is all well, Niko?" Tomyra sat up, the furs slipping to her waist.

"Yes, love. The relief guard woke me."

Tomyra ran her fingers through her hair unselfconsciously, pulling at the knots with a grimace. "I heard thunder."

"To the north. The rain will not affect us."

"I wonder who has angered the gods. Perhaps it's my brother Areipithes." Tomyra grinned mischievously. "I wouldn't be sorry to see him terrified by some god."

Nikometros snorted. "And perhaps it is just a storm. I have told you before, Tomyra, thunder is not caused by angry gods, but by clouds striking together."

"Oh, Niko. That is foolishness. Clouds are soft, they would not make a noise."

"A great philosopher told me this. Well, not told me, exactly, but I heard him expound on the matter."

Nikometros thought back to his youth. "When I was a boy, a servant on my father's farm found a white fox cub. Alexander, who was only a youth himself, had let it be known his tutor wanted such prodigies. My father sent it to him, and sent me along too." Nikometros tossed his head gently, smiling. "My father thought philosophy a waste of time, but he wanted me close to Alexander. He could recognise greatness and wanted me remembered."

"And what happened?" Tomyra lay down, looking up at Nikometros through a veil of her hair.

"Alexander was polite and seven years later, when I joined his army in Asia as a groom, he made me one of his Companions."

"I meant with the philosopher, Niko. The thunder, remember?"

Nikometros grinned. "I never met him, but I heard him talk. He never believed in anything he couldn't see or touch. He said we couldn't see gods, but we could see clouds hitting into each other. Sometimes they hit hard enough to make sparks, he said, like flint and iron. This is the lightning."

"I think your father was right, Niko. Philosophers are a waste of time. How can anyone doubt the presence of the gods...and goddesses too? Do you doubt the power of the Mother?"

Nikometros shivered slightly, his arm hairs prickling. "No, I have had her protection." He slid under the furs, and propped himself on one arm, leaning over Tomyra. "I have also seen the power of her very human priestess," he laughed. "And the power she has over men."

Tomyra reached down. "Power over one man, at least," she said with a smile. "Now, your priestess commands you to make a sacrifice at my altar." She

251

pulled him down on top of her, and for a while they were in total agreement.

The distant thunder grew slowly louder, and flickers of lightning lit up the lean-to. Nikometros lay back on the furs, watching the flashes and listening to the thunder rolls. *Why does the thunder come after the light? Surely the noise of clouds hitting produces the sparks? Perhaps Tomyra is right after all and it is an angry god.* He pondered for a few moments then gave up. "Tomyra," he whispered. "Are you awake?"

"Yes, Niko," came the sleepy reply.

"That night your father brought me into the tribe, you prophesied. What did you see for us?"

"What makes you think I saw anything, Niko? I vaguely remember talking about glorious battles and great victories, and a king of gold. All the sorts of things men are interested in."

"You also hid something. You stopped and looked flustered, as if you had seen something you shouldn't talk about."

The silence dragged on so long, Nikometros thought Tomyra must have fallen asleep. At length she sighed deeply. "The Mother said you would be my lover for a time. She also said I would be separated from you and dishonoured. For you, though, there would be great glory."

"No, Tomyra!" Nikometros sat up, an agitated expression on his face. "I will not, would not, leave you. If you are dishonoured through our love then I will share your fate."

"My love, my wonderful Niko. If the Goddess has ordained it, it will be so." She reached out a hand to stroke his face. "Let us enjoy our time together."

Nikometros gripped her arm. "Tomyra, there is a way. Come with me to my people. Let us find the

252

Macedonian camp on the Oxus. I am a cavalry officer. They will take us in and give us the army's protection"

Tomyra stared at him, round-eyed. "To be what, Niko? A captured woman, following the army? Here at least I have position and honour...at least for a while longer."

"As my wife, Tomyra. Alexander favours marriages by his officers to women of the other nations. He believes it gives the conquered people hope. We can be together, in honour and happiness."

Tomyra looked away, shivering. "I would be giving up everything; my father, my people, my way of life."

"Not quite everything."

She gave Nikometros' hand a quick squeeze, flashing him a smile. "Of course, my love. I do not doubt you. It is something I must think on though. I must pray to the Mother."

"Very well, but, Tomyra, don't take too long. We are near to the Macedonian camp now, but when the tribe moves east toward Urul, we will be moving farther from safety each day."

"And what of your companions? And of my Owls? Your Timon will not want to leave Bithyia."

"I will talk to him. If he wishes to stay with her, he can."

"We are surrounded by tribesmen, Niko, every day and night. Even if we wanted to, we could not escape unseen. Our companies are loyal to us, but also to the tribe. Will they let us go?"

"I will sound out some I can trust. Be sure in yourself, Tomyra. We can escape whatever fate the Mother has for us here, and make a new life among my people." Nikometros rose and pulled on his clothing, strapping on his weapons. "I must check the guards, Tomyra. Get some sleep, and think on what I have

said. If we have to move, we may have to move fast."
He bent, kissing her head then ducked under the flaps
into the stormy night.

Chapter Twenty-Three

Parasades sat inside his tent, brooding. Outside, his Leopard pennant fluttered and cracked in the chill, northerly wind. His guards, stamping their feet against the cold, huddled in the lee of the tent, talking quietly amongst themselves. Parasades drew his dagger and lightly ran his callused thumb up the blade. *Needs sharpening,* he thought. *So many things need my attention. And what do I do about the Greek? There is no doubt now that he and the priestess are lovers. That alone seals his death.* He dropped the dagger point first into the turf. Withdrawing it, he started to pick the dirt off the blade. *And hers. Do I want to encompass their deaths or should I remove them by helping them escape?* He blew on the blade to remove the last specks of dirt and sheathed it.

Rising, he stepped outside the tent and motioned to one of the guards. "Bring my horse." He mounted, and, kicking it into a trot, set off in the direction of Nikometros' encampment. Parasades rode through a scattered military encampment spread out over an area measuring several stadia in length. The women, children, and the vast herds of cattle and horses were already over the horizon to the east, making steady progress toward winter quarters in Urul. Each company of the combined Massegetae and Jartai tribes had set up temporary huts and tents, complete with latrine trenches and horse lines. Until Spargises was certain there would be no incursions by the western tribes, the army would remain near the Oxus River, ready for action.

Spargises' own hut was roughly in the middle of the camp, with the joint war leaders, Areipithes, with his Wolverines, and Nikometros, with his Lions, on opposite sides. The priestess, with her Owl company,

255

remained close to her father and to Nikometros, while Parasades and his Leopards were stationed further out, past Areipithes' camp.

So it was that Parasades, as he rode to talk with Nikometros, passed close to the Wolverine camp. He was surprised to see a much larger camp than he expected. Despite the large number of huts, and greater number of tents, hardly anyone was moving about. The horse lines were packed with mounts, overflowing the rough shelters, jostling each other. Parasades looked curiously at the chaos then turned toward them. At once, several men emerged from a tent, catching at his horse's mane. Parasades drew back on his reins, startled. "Curse you, what do you think you are doing?"

"No one is to approach," grated the leader of the group. "Now turn around and depart."

"Do you know who I am?"

"I know you, Parasades. I could not care less if you were the barbarian Persian king himself. No one passes here unbidden."

"We shall see about that," retorted Parasades. "Where is Areipithes?"

"He will not see you. He is not here, now go." The other men started fingering their weapons, slowly spreading out around Parasades.

Parasades controlled his mount, circling tightly. "I shall see our chief about your insolent behaviour, and your company leader." He kicked his heels, riding back into the main encampment. *What don't they want me to see? And why do they have so many horses? There must be at least three for every warrior.* He pursed his lips in irritation, looking around him as he rode, looking for anything else out of the ordinary. Except for the lack

256

of men moving around, and the many tents, there was nothing to see.

Parasades passed the huts of the priestess and Spargises, answering cheerful greetings from female guards and the chief's personal guards. He forgot his worries, exchanging friendly banter with one of the Owl riders. He waved a farewell as he passed from the huts of the priestess toward the Lion camp. *I never thought women would make good warriors, but those Owls are shaping up nicely.* He grinned. *Some nice shapes, too!*

A loud challenge brought his thoughts back to reality. A trio of young men neatly attired and bearing lances topped with the Lion banner, confronted him. For a moment, Parasades sat there, looking down at them, not sure why he was doing so. He drew in a sharp breath as he realised what he looked at. *By the ice demon's frozen testicles, they have shaved themselves. They look like women...or Greeks.* Disturbed, he slid off his horse, asking for Nikometros.

Nikometros looked up from polishing his armour as Parasades entered the hut. He rose slowly and walked toward him. "I had not thought to see you here." Nikometros watched the other man's eyes. "Do you come in friendship, Parasades?"

"I have never ceased being your friend, Nikomayros." *Even if I must bring about your death, I would grieve for the loss of a fine warrior and trusted companion.*

"Toss the horse-buggerer out, sir. I wouldn't believe a word he says anymore," growled a voice from the other side of the room. Parasades looked round, startled, to see Timon advancing on him, stave in hand.

Nikometros held up a hand. "Enough, Timon." He looked coldly at Parasades. "Why are you here?"

"I need to talk to you. In private."

"Timon stays. Say what you came to say."

Parasades looked sourly at Timon then shook his head. "Very well." He looked around the tent. "Do you mind if I sit down?" He gestured at a tattered blanket draped over a stool in the corner nearest the smoldering brazier. Without waiting for a reply, he walked over and sat down.

Nikometros waved Timon back to his place and stood over Parasades. "I repeat. What is it you want?"

"Do you believe me now when I tell you, you are powerful? You are now joint war leader of the combined Massegetae and Jartai tribes. Your company of Lions is one of the most disciplined and...what is it your men are doing, making themselves look like women or eunuchs?" He shook his head again. "Never mind, I don't want to know. Just tell me this; with all your power and influence, do you realise how quickly that can all vanish?"

Timon started forward again. "That son of a horse thief is actually threatening you, sir."

Parasades shook his head. "Not threatening. I seek only to make you aware of certain realities." He took a deep breath. "You are aware that the penalty for violating the sanctity or person of the priestess, the representative of the Great Goddess, is death. No exceptions, even the chief would forfeit his life. The same would apply to other men violating the sanctity of her maidens – Bithyia for example."

Timon swore softly. Nikometros stood over Parasades, grimly staring down at him. "I am aware. What is this to me?"

"I have certain knowledge that you and the priestess are lovers."

Nikometros hesitated a moment. "You are lying. You cannot have certain knowledge."

258

Parasades sighed. "You are too trusting, Nikomay-ros. When a man comes to you and says he wishes to join your company, you welcome him without questioning his motives." He rose to his feet and leaned close to Nikometros. "I have two of my men serving in your Company. They are ready to swear by any oath that the priestess has on many occasions, slept in your tent with you."

"Being in the same tent does not mean..."

"Nobody would believe such an action was innocent."

Nikometros stood stunned. "The priestess is not to blame," he whispered.

Parasades grimaced. "She came willingly, by all accounts. You know as I do, that the blame is equally hers...and the punishment."

Timon stepped forward, his hand on his dagger's hilt. "If he dies, sir, none need find out. I can question our men; I'll find these two men of his."

"Did I say two? Perhaps it was more. You can be certain though, that Areipithes also has his spies. It would indeed surprise me if he was not aware of your flagrant indiscretions."

Nikometros flushed then started pacing agitatedly. "Why do you tell me this? Why have you not publicly accused us already?"

"I am undecided as to what result would serve the tribe best. Undoubtedly the just solution is to let the law take its course. On the other hand, I have come to realise that the death of his daughter may well unman our chief. I would not like to see his son Areipithes challenge him at a time such as this."

"You surprise me, Parasades. I thought you and he made good company for each other."

Parasades snorted. "Areipithes would rapidly bring disaster on our People, were he chief. He is selfish and bloody-minded." He shook his head. "There is no one in the combined tribes that could yet replace Spargises, but if he is to remain strong, he must have a strong war leader. Areipithes leads well in war, he is Massegetae born, and is accepted by most warriors. By your very presence, you weaken Spargises' position and spread dissent."

"Spargises is my blood brother. I would do anything for him."

"Then you have a choice. Either accept death for violating the priestess, along with his daughter, and weaken his hold on the tribe; or flee to your own people, with or without your lover."

Nikometros looked up, startled. "Go back to my garrison? Would this not have the same effect of weakening Spargises' hold?"

"Our good chief would be extremely angry at your betrayal, but having a focus for his anger will keep him strong."

"And what of Tomyra?"

"That is your decision. Abandon her, and I will not accuse her. Unless Areipithes does so, she will retain her position and influence. Or take her with you. Spargises will be very angry, but there are others who can take her position, Lynna for example, the Jartai priestess."

"I would have her safe with me, but she must make the decision."

"Ask her then, Nikomayros, but hurry. If Areipithes makes his move, you and she are dead. If you are still here at sunrise in three days time, I will accuse you myself."

Nikometros stared hard at the Massegetae warrior. "You did not have to give me this chance. I thank you." He thought for a moment. "We cannot leave from the camp. Too many people are watching. However, there are reports of wild pig in the foothills. I will take some of my men on a hunt."

"Good. When you are judged to be missing, say at dawn on the third day, I will lead the pursuit myself, to the south along the river. Go any way but this." He nodded at Timon. "I would advise certain others to leave with you." Parasades turned on his heel and strode from the hut.

Chapter Twenty-Four

After a night of hurried consultations, Nikometros casually announced at dawn that he intended to take a few of his men south to the foothills on a boar hunt. Timon and Mardes would accompany him, together with Tirses and Berinax of his Lions company. Several warriors cast envious looks at the selected hunters, hanging about Nikometros as he made the final preparations, dropping broad comments about how much they would like to go on a hunt. Nikometros smiled and changed the subject and, when his small party left the camp, they were accompanied only by wistful glances.

Tomyra and a small group of her Owls rode out of camp about an hour later, in the opposite direction. Her announced intention was to seek certain wild herbs along the river edges that would lend a piquant quality to the pork the hunters would be certain to bring home. Out of sight of the outlying patrols, the Owls angled round in a wide circle, heading toward the agreed rendezvous.

Beech forest clung to the lower foothills, drifts of fallen leaves deadening the sound of horses' hooves as they picked their way slowly up the rough game trails. Arriving in the lea of a crumbling cliff face, Nikometros bade his companions dismount. They started a small fire and sat, out of the wind, the flames warming them as they waited. Hours passed, the sun moving unseen behind the gathering clouds.

Tirses sniffed the air and looked up at the overcast sky, wrapping his cloak tighter about him. "Smells like snow," he said. "Hope it doesn't come before we're over the mountains."

Timon grunted. "We'll manage. What worries me most is what direction we take. Are you sure you know where the garrisons are, Niko? It's been nearly a year."

Nikometros nodded. "I have a good idea of the direction. I'll know more when we get further south."

"What's that?" hissed Mardes, raising a hand to silence the conversation. "I thought I heard something."

The others listened, hearing the gentle sough of wind and the creak of tree limbs. The horses whickered gently, rustling the leaves as they shifted.

"Horses," Berinax said, pointing back down the trail. He casually strung his bow and stuck three arrows into the ground in front of him, fitting one in readiness. Tirses, after a moment's pause, did likewise. The sound of riders came louder, more distinct, then into view came four horses, their riders sitting upright and looking eagerly about them.

"Tomyra!" Nikometros called, grinning with relief. He hurried forward and helped the priestess from her mare, holding her close. Bithyia leapt from her horse and embraced Timon while the other two Owls nodded warily at Mardes and the two Massegetae Lions.

"Come, my love," Nikometros urged, drawing Tomyra toward the smoking fire. "Warm yourself for a moment. We cannot delay long, but you can at least have something to eat."

Tomyra smiled wanly and allowed herself to be seated. She refused food but sipped at a cup of koumiss while the others repacked the horse's saddlebags and prepared for their journey.

"Niko," said Tomyra. "I feel terrible sneaking out like this. My father will be...I don't know...angry maybe. Certainly he will grieve. For my part I miss him already."

"I know, my love, but how else can we do it? He would not willingly let you go and if he thought we had become lovers he would be forced to execute us both. That would hurt him worse than this." Nikometros took her hands in his. "Tomyra. I would not bring hurt to you. If you want to go back to your tribe, say so. I will leave you here and return to my people alone."

Tomyra jerked her head up, her eyes widening. "Don't even think it, Niko," she cried. "I made my choice long ago. My place is with you, wherever that takes me."

Nikometros smiled and kissed Tomyra. "Then come with me, my love. I will take you back to my country, to Macedon."

Mardes coughed discreetly, interrupting the lovers. "All is ready, Niko," he said. "We should be going."

Tirses extinguished the fire, smothering it beneath wet leaves as Nikometros and Tomyra mounted. The party moved out slowly, turning toward the mountains, moving in single file. The horses picked their way over the rough trail, hooves slipping in the wet leaves. The land rose, leaving the beech forests behind and exposing the riders to the chill wind from the north. Wrapping themselves tighter in their cloaks, they forged steadily upward. Toward sunset, the riders came to a broad ravine that cut through the crumbling rock of the mountain range.

Nikometros called a halt, pointing to a shallow scallop in the cliff face. "We'll stop here for the night. This cave will afford us some protection."

Timon looked doubtful and stared back the way they had come, out over the beech forest to the plains below. "Are we far enough away, Niko? They are sure to pursue us."

"Not yet, but we will be by the time the alarm is given. Besides, Parasades won't raise the alarm until the dawn of day after tomorrow and has sworn to lead the pursuit along the river, not up into the mountains."

"What about the ladies?" Timon asked. "They'll miss them a lot sooner. They were only supposed to be heading to the river."

"So where will they look for us?" enquired Tomyra, smiling. "Do not worry, Timon. The Goddess will protect us."

Mardes started a small fire in the shelter of the rock wall while Berinax searched for more firewood, riding back down the trail in search of logs and branches. The two Owls tended to the horses, feeding them handfuls of grain and watering them from a folding leather bucket. Groomed and hobbled against straying, the horses settled contentedly for the night. Bithyia and Tomyra searched through the saddlebags, clucking with dismay at the lack of foresight by their men folk. In the end, they heated wine in a small iron vessel, crumbling cheese and honey into it.

"Not much," remarked Tomyra, "But it will be hot and tasty. A crust of bread and it will suffice."

"Maybe tomorrow I can find a rabbit or two," said Bithyia. "There should be some still in these hills."

They ate as darkness fell, banking the fire with logs to last through the night before curling in their cloaks to take advantage of the warmth. Nikometros sat up, keeping watch until the moon rose, dim behind the overcast. Tomyra sat with him, huddled close for warmth, her head on his shoulder. For a long time they sat in silence, staring out over the dimly seen mountainside to the invisible plains of grass below.

"It does not seem like only a year," Nikometros said quietly. "I feel I have known you all my life."

"In a way you have," replied Tomyra. "The Goddess sent you to me because our fates are joined. I have known this almost from the beginning."

"Then you knew more than I. But of course, I did not have a god telling me the future."

Tomyra sat up and looked to see if Nikometros made fun of her, but seeing only his gentle smiling eyes, snuggled back into his arms. "I don't see the future, Niko. Only what She reveals to me."

"And what has she revealed for you?"

"Only a life." Tomyra sat silently for a long while, as the cloud cover shredded, sending patches of moonlight scudding over the dark earth. "The love of a man, pain and sorrow, joy, distant lands and...and..." She shook her head. "In the end, blackness."

"All men and women are mortal, my love. It is our lot," Nikometros said gently.

"It isn't the blackness of death, Niko. That's not a sorrow if it follows a full life. No, this is more like a withdrawal, as if the Goddess forsakes me."

"Why would she lead you down this path, only to leave you?" asked Nikometros.

"I don't know but it's worth it if I have you, my Niko." Tomyra stared up at her lover, her eyes fierce and hungry. "Don't leave me, Niko. Never leave me."

"Never. Not while the gods leave breath in my body."

A muffled crunch of gravel behind them brought Nikometros to his feet, his sword out. Tomyra moved rapidly to one side, her hand darting to the dagger in her belt. A shadow loomed against the dim glow of the embers and a low chuckle echoed off the cliff face.

"By the gods," said Timon. "I'd hate to be trying to sneak up on you two."

Nikometros shook his head. "Give us a bit of warning next time," he replied sourly. "I feel jumpy enough without you adding to it."

Timon snorted. "There's nothing out here to worry about, Niko. Maybe a few bandits but we can cope with those easily enough. They won't tackle armed men."

"You're probably right. Well, I'm for bed if you're taking over the watch."

A thin rime of ice covered the ground at sunrise. The sun had little warmth and the party gathered shivering around the embers of the fire, breaking their fast with bread and cheese. Packing up their baggage, they mounted their horses and turned them uphill once more toward the indistinct border between Scythia and the Persian province of Sogdia.

The ravine narrowed and steepened, forcing them to ascend the side via a narrow goat track. They emerged onto a shoulder of the mountain and moved south and west across the slopes. Presently the track dipped into bare-branched scrub and stunted trees.

"Are you sure this is the right way?" called Tomyra. "We seem to be going downhill again."

"No, I'm not," replied Nikometros, frowning. "I told you I can probably find our way once we are over the ridge into Sogdia, but till then I'm just trying to go in the right direction."

Berinax, at the rear of the file of riders, gave a low whistle. He gestured back along the trail. "Someone is following us," he hissed.

Nikometros pointed at members of the party then to the scrub. The riders slipped from their horses and led them off the trail into such cover as they could find. Tying their mounts they hurried back to the trail with bows and swords at the ready, and hid as best they could. They waited.

A horse came into view, its rider keeping his eyes fixed on the trail as he followed the tracks. Behind him came another horse, then several more. All the riders were armed and vigilant, scanning the land around them as they rode. The leader abruptly reined his horse in and sat back, looking straight at Nikometros' hiding place. The other riders crowded around him, staring into the scrub.

Nikometros cursed quietly and stepped out, his sword still in his belt but his hand ready. Trying to remain hidden, the others in his party drew back on their bows, preparing to defend themselves against attack.

The man on horseback threw back the hood of his cloak and laughed out loud. "What, Nikomayros?" he guffawed. "Have you mistaken me for a pig? I am insulted."

"Taxicus," said Nikometros flatly. "What are you doing here?"

"I might ask you the same thing, Nikomayros." Taxicus stopped laughing and his eyes narrowed as he saw Timon, Mardes, and the two Scythian Lions with bows drawn. "You will not find pig this high in the mountains."

Nikometros said nothing, just staring at the Massegetae commander.

"They told me you had ridden out to hunt pig, Nikomayros. I brought my men to join in the sport." Taxicus gave a silent finger signal and his men spread out, easing their bows from their backs. "Instead I find my esteemed war leader halfway to the border and ignoring obvious pig sign in the forests below. I have to raise the question of your loyalty, my friend."

"We took a wrong turn, Taxicus, that is all," Nikometros replied. "As you can see, we're heading back down into the forests." He signaled, and his friends emerged from the scrub, their bows still drawn but pointing at the ground. Timon and Mardes lowered their swords.

"I don't know how you hunt pig in your home land, Nikomayros, but I scarcely believe you intend to stab it with your sword. Unless you are going to sit back and watch your men kill it for you?"

Nikometros shrugged, his eyes watchful. "Different ways, Taxicus," he said. "Now, if you will excuse us, we shall get back to the business at hand."

"I think not, Nikomayros. I have it in mind to keep you company on this...ah, hunt. I wouldn't want you to get lost in these hills."

"Thank you for your concern but your presence is not required..."

"You mistake me," snapped Taxicus. At his silent command, his men whipped their bows up, training the arrows on the five men in front of them. "I will take you back to face Spargises or cut you down where you stand. Your choice. Now, put down your weapons."

Nikometros stared at the dozen men confronting him, their arrows aimed unwaveringly at their hearts. Feeling sick, he opened his mouth to order his men to disarm.

"Would you kill your priestess, Taxicus?" Tomyra stepped out from the bushes with Bithyia and the other two Owls.

Taxicus stared, gaping. "My lady," he gasped, knuckling his forehead. "What are you doing here?"

"What is it to you where I go? I am accompanied by my champion and by my handmaids. I answer only to the Great Goddess."

"But...but they said you went to the river." Taxicus frowned. "How is it you are here?"

Tomyra smiled. "The herbs I sought were not to be found by the river, so I came to the forests seeking others. Instead I found the lord Nikomayros and his friends. They were good enough to call off their hunt in order to escort me." She advanced toward Taxicus and laid her hand on his horse's neck, stroking the animal as it snuffed and pushed against her. "Now that you are here, I feel doubly safe. You may of course join us as we return to camp."

Taxicus bowed his head. "Of course, my lady." He signaled to his men to put their arms up. They obeyed but continued to eye Nikometros with suspicion, keeping their bows handy.

Tomyra turned and walked back to where Bithyia stood, her women having brought the horses out of cover. As she passed Nikometros she glanced at him and whispered.

"We shall have to return, Niko, but we can try again."

Taxicus led the way back down the slopes toward the beech forests. Behind him rode Nikometros and Timon, then the Owls and Lions. Bringing up the rear, watchful and armed, rode the company of Taxicus' Eagles.

Timon spoke in the gutter patois of the Macedonian army. "This is bad, Niko. Didn't you say Parasades was going to denounce you at dawn tomorrow?"

Taxicus swiveled round, a look of baffled fury on his face. "What are you saying?" he growled.

Nikometros smiled and shook his head. "Just discussing inconsequential things," he said in Scythian. "The hunt, the weather, that sort of thing." He turned back to Timon, dropping back into Macedonian. "Yes. We shall have to leave by then."

Taxicus gave an angry snort and turned his back. Timon bared his teeth at the man's back. "Let me kill him, Niko. A swift strike to remove the snake's head and his men would not be so troublesome. We can take them."

Nikometros shook his head. "There are too many, even for you, my friend. We must wait until we get back and try and sneak out under cover of darkness."

They emerged from the beech forest by early afternoon and headed out into the grassy rolling plain toward the Massegetae camp. Soon, outriders and patrols spotted them and galloped up, making jovial enquiries about the success of the hunt. Nikometros put on a brave face and joked that he and his men had become lost and how Taxicus and his men had come to their rescue. The Eagles grinned and made the most of their sudden fame, though Taxicus remained sullen and silent.

When they at last reached the outskirts of the camp, Taxicus led his men off with scarcely a backward look. Nikometros excused himself from the interested attentions of passers-by and rode close to Tomyra.

"We must leave tonight, when it gets dark," Nikometros said.

"We would not get far," replied Tomyra. "I will talk to my father, Niko. He loves me and will not punish us. He will let us go, I know."

Nikometros shook his head dubiously. "Be careful, Tomyra. Approach the subject delicately and sound him out before you tell him. If he reacts badly we may have to make a run for it."

Nikometros left Tomyra by her tents and rode off towards his own camp. Parasades watched him, having been alerted by one of his men. He frowned, his forehead wrinkling in thought.

Chapter Twenty-Five

Spargises welcomed his daughter into his hut after dinner. He got up from his padded stool by the brazier and lamp where he sat mending his armour and greeted her.

"Welcome, daughter," he said. "Come and sit with me."

Tomyra smiled and embraced her father before pulling up another stool to the brazier and sitting down. She refused his offer of koumiss and sat and watched him as he worked the leather of his armour.

Spargises worked silently for a few minutes before looking up. "Taxicus came to see me tonight."

Tomyra tried to look unconcerned. "Oh? What about?"

"He says he found you and Nikomayros high in the hills near the southern border of our lands. He thinks Nikomayros was trying to flee back to his people."

"What a strange thought!"

Spargises watched his daughter carefully. "There is no truth to it?"

"Father, you know Nikomayros holds you in the highest regard. He loves you and our people both...as do I. Do you imagine we would betray you?"

"No, Tomyra. I know your love for the People. And for the Goddess." He shrugged. "Nikomayros though? I sometimes wonder how civilised he has become. At times he still seems like a western barbarian."

"That's nonsense, father, as well you know." Tomyra paused then continued quietly, watching her father from the corner of her eye. "Besides, would it be so terrible if he left?"

Spargises looked up from the shield he worked on. "Leave? My blood brother? I thought you liked Nikomayros."

"I do, but at heart he's still a Greek. Why not send him back with an embassy to his king Alexander? That way he would benefit our tribe and his."

"An interesting thought, Tomyra. I'll have to discuss that with my advisors." He bent over his shield again, picking up his dagger.

Tomyra sat and watched him for several minutes, thinking how to broach the subject of her own departure.

"Do you still miss my mother?"

"Ehh?" Spargises grunted. He looked up from his efforts to drive the point of his dagger through the leather strap of his shield. "What was that you said, daughter?"

"Just that you never talk about her anymore, father. When I was a little girl, you would often tell me stories of how you met and the things you did. I wondered whether you missed her."

Spargises laid down his shield and dagger carefully. "Yes I do, Tomyra. I doubt there are many days I don't think of her." His eyes lost their focus and he smiled gently. "Every time I see you I'm reminded of her, child. You're so like her in many ways."

Tomyra stepped forward eagerly and knelt beside him. "How am I like her, father? Tell me."

"You have her eyes, Tomyra, green as the Mother Sea. Her hair was beautiful like yours, black as night, but longer. You also have her form, daughter. She was tall and willowy when first I saw her." He sighed, and ran a hand over his face. "She stood tall, defiant, though the slave-traders had used her cruelly, tried to break her. She was so different from the soft, weeping

274

creatures around her. I walked up to her and looked her in the face." Spargises grinned, lost in his memories. "She spat at me! Such spirit." He reached out to grasp Tomyra's arm and squeezed it. "I bought her and brought her home to Urul. She escaped twice before I could convince her I meant her no hurt."

"And you fell in love?"

"Yes, I fell in love with my fierce warrior maiden from the shores of the Great Sea. I was only young, barely twenty summers, but I already had the burdens of chieftainship. My wife was newly dead, and I had a young son to care for. Yet, all these things were as nothing. I had to have her."

Tomyra smiled as the familiar story unfolded, once again. "And my mother, how did she feel?"

"The blackness of her ordeal was slow to lift, but lift it did. Within a few months she came to love me and we wed." Spargises smiled fondly at the young girl beside him. "And after a time, the Goddess blessed us with a daughter."

Tomyra gazed into her father's eyes, squeezing his hand. "Father..."

"All too soon my joy passed from me." A tear formed in the corner of one eye. "Now all I have are my memories, and a daughter to bring them back to me." Spargises brushed his eyes with the back of his hand. "Once I had a son, too, though he has withdrawn from me." He sighed again, deeply. "I failed Areipithes, my child, when he needed me most. Now I pay for my failure."

"Father, you have not failed in anything. A man makes his own choices in life. He cannot forever blame the hardships and unfairness of youth."

"Perhaps you are right, Tomyra. I hope that one day he will see that I love him still. I would like to have grandsons around me one day." He smiled wryly. "Seeing as how my daughter chose to serve the Goddess, rather than bear sons."

Tomyra flushed. "Father, I..."

Spargises held up a hand. "I don't blame you, child. Your mother was consecrated to the Great Goddess in her own land before pirates plucked her from her service. The Goddess takes what is Hers, and it is not for men to question Her ways."

"Father, you know I love you?"

Spargises looked at Tomyra, noting the strain in her voice and her failure to hold his gaze. "I know, Tomyra. But there is something else...?"

Tomyra stood, wrapping her arms around her waist. She started to pace. "Father, the Goddess calls all of us in different ways. You, she called to be chief of our People. She called me to serve her for a time. She even called..." she smiled quickly, "...One of the western barbarians to her service."

Spargises rose. "You said the Mother called you...for a time. What do you mean?" He spoke slowly, puzzling out the meaning. "Those who serve the Goddess do so for life. They are consecrated."

"Yes, father. So we have always understood. But times change, ways change, as we have seen since Nikomayros came to us."

"Nikomayros? This is about my blood brother again?" Spargises frowned, thinking back to the cleansing ceremony with the Dumae. "Has he acted in an unseemly manner in any way?"

"No, father. He has followed the wishes of the Mother in all things."

Spargises relaxed, his face becoming clearer. "Then what are you saying?"

276

Tomyra stopped pacing and faced her father. She lifted a hand toward him then dropped it to her side again. "The Mother has spoken to me. She bids me leave the People. I must obey her."

"What?" Spargises shouted. "You cannot leave. It is unheard of." He stepped up to Tomyra. "And you are my daughter," he went on in a gentler tone. "I cannot let my daughter go alone into the world."

"Yet I must obey the Mother. She has hidden the future from me, father. I cannot say why I must leave, so please do not question me on this." Tears trickled down Tomyra's cheeks now. "I love you, father, but I must go, and secretly. I only told you so you would not think the worst when the news came to you."

Spargises paced up and down, agitatedly. "If the Mother commands then it must be so." He held his right hand palm-down over the ground as he spoke. "However, you cannot leave alone, daughter. I will send a company of my best warriors with you. Let me see, perhaps Taxicus, with a score of his Eagle Company. I know he will protect you."

"Father, I have my own warriors, the Owl Company. I cannot leave on the bidding of the Mother accompanied by men."

"Nonsense, daughter. I allowed you your Owls to please you, but you must have proper warriors with you."

A commotion outside the hut interrupted the chief. A blade slashing through the cords tying the entrance flaps followed shouts of agony. Areipithes burst in, his right hand gripping a bloody sword. Behind him, several men pushed into the room, all armed, some with fierce expressions on their faces, others looking frightened.

"By the infernal gods, Areipithes. What is the meaning of this?" Spargises pushed in front of Tomyra, his hand fumbling at his side for his dagger. He scanned the faces behind his son. "Falaces, Pyricus, Lemurtes...I did not summon you, why are you here? And who are these others?"

"You have betrayed my honour too often, Spargises. I will not stand by and see my battle honours stripped from me to be given to some barbarian. You are removed as chief of the Massegetae. The elders of the tribe," Areipithes waved his blood-stained hand nonchalantly at the frightened men beside him. "Will ratify me as interim chief until I can call proper elections." He smirked. "Do not think to call your guards. I have control of the camp already."

"You are a fool, Areipithes, if you think the Great Goddess will allow this." Tomyra stepped forward, holding up both hands. "The Mother herself will curse these actions."

"Silence her!" Areipithes waved his men into the hut.

The bearded warriors hesitated. One muttered beneath his breath, "She is a priestess, we were not told."

"I call on the Great Goddess, Three-fold, Mother of all men..."

Areipithes cursed and strode forward. He lifted his other hand and struck Tomyra in the face, throwing her to the ground. "Take the bitch, she is no priestess. She lost that right by her whoring."

The men hesitated a moment longer then moved toward Tomyra as she struggled to rise. Spargises roared with rage, grabbing vainly at his side for the dagger. He remembered too late it lay beside his shield on the ground. He gripped Areipithes, trying to

278

wrest the sword from his hand. They swayed back and forth across the room, the others backing away, watching the struggle with varying degrees of fear and interest.

Areipithes dropped his sword, hitting his father on the side of his head with a fist. Spargises staggered, falling to one knee. He shook his head, grabbed his dagger from the ground and launched himself at the other man.

Tomyra pushed against her captors, screaming imprecations. A tall man, with an air of authority, standing to one side of the melee, strode forward, pushing into the chief as he lunged at his son. Spargises staggered past, missing Areipithes, who grabbed a lance from one of the men. He turned, steadied himself and cast the lance with a fluid motion. The spear flew straight, catching Spargises below the ribs, driving him back into the shadows, agony on his face. For a moment, there was a stunned silence then Tomyra screamed once, high and piercing.

Areipithes turned with an oath. "Silence her, you fools. We do not want others coming to her aid now." A warrior holding her clasped his hand over her face, stifling her renewed cries and sobs. A strip of felt was proffered, and a horsehair rope, and soon she lay, bound and gagged at Areipithes' feet. He nudged her with one foot. "That is your proper place, whore. Think on it before you die."

"What should we do with her?" Pyricus asked.

Areipithes turned to the tall man beside him. "Take her outside and kill her then bury her body."

The tall man bristled. "I am not your servant, Areipithes. You may wish to be chief of this lice-ridden tribe, but I, Dimurthes of the god-born Serratae, take orders from no man."

279

Areipithes' face darkened. "You may hold us in low regard, Dimurthes, but you westerners were not slow to ally yourself with me in return for us not waging war on you."

Dimurthes scowled. "We do not fear you Massegetae, but there is one I would have dead. The one you call the Lion of Scythia."

Areipithes spat on the ground. "You shall have him. Even now, my men search for him. I will give you his head myself, to make into a drinking cup."

"As for the woman, she is beautiful. You say she has lost her maidenhood and no longer serves the Mother?"

"That is so. She soiled herself with the barbarian, and deserves death. If you want her, take her and use her then kill her."

"Perhaps I will." He gestured to his men. "Take her outside and tie her to a horse. Deliver her to my company." Dimurthes turned back to Areipithes with a sneer. "With your leave then, chief of the Massegetae, we shall withdraw across the river." He swiveled on his heel and left the hut, hard on the heels of the men bearing the struggling body of Tomyra.

Areipithes turned to the cowering elders of the tribe. "Convene a council meeting. You will formally elect me chief tonight. You can also tell that girl Lynna, the Jartai priestess, that she is now full priestess of the combined tribes. She will consecrate your choice."

"My...my lord," quavered an old grizzled man. "We cannot convene the council. We need more than just us few." He looked quickly around him at the others, who started to nod agreement. "We need a majority of elders, at least six more, to make an election lawful."

Areipithes scowled. "Do you defy me?" He glared at the councilors, smirking as they dropped their gazes. "No, of course not. You haven't the courage." He turned to the entrance flap and peered out into the night. "Tareses, get in here with your men." The guards filed in and formed a line as Areipithes swaggered past them. "Tareses, you and your men deserve a signal honour for your service tonight. You are hereby made councilors of the People." He turned back to the old men. "There, you have," he glanced at the guards, "eight more councilors. Now get out and convene that meeting."

The old men looked at one another then bowed and filed out of the hut. Pushing past them, as they left, came Parasades. He stared around the hut, taking in the signs of struggle, the presence of the Wolverine guards. He started at the sight of a body in the shadows, striding to the stiffening corpse of Spargises. He turned and stared at Areipithes. "My lord, that was ill done."

Areipithes shrugged. "It is done. Now you must decide whether you take advantage of the situation." He looked hard at Parasades. "I have cut through the problem. The Greek will be dead shortly, and there is no one to oppose me."

Parasades looked shocked. "Patricide is god-cursed. No good can come of this, Areipithes. I want nothing to do with it." He pushed past Areipithes and disappeared into the night.

Areipithes stood and watched him leave, stroking his beard and thinking. He snapped his fingers at Tareses, who stood in one corner, fingering the rich drapes adorning the walls of the hut. "Take your men and kill him, Tareses. Bring me his head."

Chapter Twenty-Six

Parasades stood in the darkness outside the hut, his mind reeling. A man standing in the shadows coughed, causing him to turn, his hand grasping for his sword. As he drew the blade, the figure stepped forward into the small patch of light spilling from the rent edges of the hut's entrance flaps. "Partatua?" he said, belatedly recognizing one of Spargises' older councilors. "What is your part in this?"

The old man beckoned. "Hurry, Parasades. Areipithes has bid us summon the council to elect him chief. There will be more bloodshed over this before morning."

Parasades grasped the old man by the throat. "What did Areipithes pay you to help him murder his father?"

Partatua plucked feebly at the hand on his throat. "Not so, not so," he wheezed. "We could do nothing with his guards there." He twisted his head around, gazing fearfully from side to side. "And Serratae. Many of them."

"What?" Parasades dropped the old man, who stumbled back, clutching his throat. "What did you say? Our enemies here, in camp?"

Partatua nodded. "Their leader himself, Dimurthes led his men to do Areipithes' bidding. Spargises is dead and our priestess carried off by Dimurthes. Our People have been betrayed, Parasades. You must rally the tribe."

A flood of light spilled out from the hut as Tareses pushed past the flaps, illuminating the two men outside. With an oath Tareses drew his sword and lunged at Parasades. He ducked, drawing his own sword and, half turning, aimed a backward cut at his foe. Tareses stepped back, avoiding the blow but stumbling into the first of his men following him. For a moment, the entranceway was filled with jostling men, striving to draw their weapons.

Parasades clutched the old man by the shoulder, and pushed him away. "Run, there are too many!" Partatua almost fell, and then turning, broke into a shambling run, Parasades beside him, cursing.

Sharp commands rang out behind them, as the darkness began to envelop them. Something flicked by Parasades' head and, without thought, he jinked to the left. Another shadow hissed to his right, followed by a thump and a cry. He looked over his shoulder to see the old man spread-eagled on the ground, the shaft of an arrow between his shoulder blades. For a moment, he hesitated, and then sprinted for the blackness as more arrows arced toward him.

Panting, he crouched by a crudely fenced latrine pit as his pursuers stumbled in the darkness, shouting and thrusting swords and spears into the shadows. A flicker of torches appeared and Parasades, bent double, ducked around the latrine and ran quietly in the direction of Nikometros' camp.

By the time he reached the outskirts of the camp, shouts and cries could be heard clearly behind him, spreading through the camp. Warriors were milling around in the open space in front of Nikometros' hut, holding weapons and torches, talking and gesticulating. Parasades hesitated then covered his face with the hood of his tunic and walked out into the midst of the crowd. He touched one of the men on the arm. "What is happening, friend?"

The man shrugged. "I do not know. There is something amiss, but no sound of battle. No doubt the officers will tell us shortly." He pointed. "See, here comes the Persian now." Parasades saw Mardes, the Persian companion of Nikometros hurry towards the group, two guards in attendance.

Mardes raised his arms for silence and waited for the noise to die down. "Lion Company, form ranks." There was a hurried shuffling as the men sorted themselves into rows, expectant faces turned toward the speaker. Parasades unobtrusively joined the end of one of the rows. "There is fighting in the sector of the camp around the chief and his son," went on Mardes. "I am told that spies have entered the camp. The Wolverines are hunting them. The chief, through his son, has requested you to stand down and wait with your officers while these men search our camp and the surrounding area."

The men around him muttered and grumbled. "What of the Lion?" one of them cried. "He would not let that filth search our tents. Where is Nikomayros?" Others raised their voices in agreement.

"He knows of this matter and will be here shortly. Do you want him to find the chief's orders disobeyed?"

The muttering increased in volume then died down. Officers ran down the lines picking out their men and ordering them back to their tents. Parasades casually attached himself to one group heading in the general direction of Mardes. As he neared the Persian, he stopped and called to him. "Ho, Mardes, I would talk with you."

Mardes looked startled for a moment before recognizing Parasades. "My lord Parasades. What are you doing here? All Company commanders are ordered to stand by their men."

"I must speak with your commander at once. Where is he?"

"My lord, he will be here shortly. He is attending on the priestess I believe. He will return now that the chief has ordered it."

Parasades swore violently under his breath. "Mardes, listen closely. Spargises is dead and the priestess taken, possibly dead also. Traitors have let the enemy into our camp."

Mardes' jaw fell open. With an effort he gathered his wits, and swallowed. "What must I do then, sir?"

"Alert your men, order them to arms, but do not wait for the Wolverines. They have orders to kill your commander." Parasades turned his head toward the increasing noise. The sound of many running feet could be heard. "Move them south along the river. I will try to find Nikomayros. Go, you fool!" Without waiting for a response, Parasades melted into the night while Mardes turned and bolted for the nearest tent.

The sound of running feet, and shouting, increased in volume, the light of flickering torches illuminating the weapons in the hands of the approaching men. Groups ducked into tents as they came, some emerging almost immediately. In other tents, screams and cries erupted, followed by flames as the tents were torched. Parasades stood in the shadows of a hut, hoping to be bypassed. The horde rushed past him, intent on the Lion camp ahead. Parasades waited a few moments and stepped out. He was nearly thrown to the ground by two men bursting out of the hut entrance.

With a shout, the first of the men were onto him, sword flashing. Parasades twisted desperately, kicking out at the man. His foot connected, drawing a howl of pain from his opponent as the man dropped his sword and clutched his side. He dragged his own

285

sword out and parried a spear thrust by the other man. He backed up as the man stabbed at him cautiously, not seeming eager to close with him. The hurt man held his side and leaned against the wall of the hut. "Ho, comrades, to us! We have one," he called weakly.

Parasades parried again desperately. The man called again in a stronger voice. An answering shout came from the darkness. Parasades threw his sword toward the face of the man with the spear, and as he flinched, drew his dagger and leapt forward, grappling with him. The man hung onto the spear reflexively, and Parasades swept his fist upward, driving his dagger into the man's belly. Leaving his blade in place and the man screaming, Parasades reached down and grabbed his sword again, sprinting away as the hurt man's calls brought a response.

Swiftly orienting himself as he ran, Parasades angled eastward, toward the priestess' camp. *How am I to find one man in this confusion? I dare not call out.* He slowed, looking about him, seeking any who might talk before trying to kill him. Twice he stumbled over corpses, and once hid as a party of armed men hurried by.

Great Mother, help me.

Parasades came to a halt near the priestess' darkened hut, listening. The only sounds were distant shouts and screaming. A red glow suffused the sky over the southern camp, where it seemed a battle raged. He groaned despairingly, and heard a low, echoing moan from the hut. He stepped forward cautiously, sword in hand, lifting the entrance flap and peering into the dimness.

A small hand reached out feebly for him and he started. He dropped to one knee, feeling with his free hand. He got up and stepped back outside, looking around. A smoldering cooking fire yielded a brand, and cupping it in his hands, he re-entered the hut, blowing on the guttering end.

By the dim light Parasades made out the form of a frail young woman, clothed in warrior's leathers and the armband of the Owl Company. A pool of blood soaked her chest and the ground beneath her. Her eyelids fluttered and she moaned again, more weakly than before. Parasades knelt beside her, lifting her head gently. "Lady?"

The woman coughed blood and drew a slow, quavering breath. Her eyes opened and she tried to focus on the man kneeling above her.

Parasades leant closer. "Lady, I must know where the Greek is, Nikomayros. Have you seen him?"

She coughed again. "My lord Nikomayros? Is...is that...you?" She struggled to raise herself on one arm. "Why...are...My lady is with...her father. Men came, my lord." Her breath came raggedly. "Strangers. I did not tell...them where you...are to meet."

Parasades cursed. "Lady. It is urgent. Where is Nikomayros?"

The woman clutched at his arm, her breath whooping as she struggled for air, blood dribbling down her chin. "You must...return, my lord." A paroxysm of coughing racked her tiny frame. "She awaits...you." Her eyes bulged, her fingers digging into Parasades' arm.

"Where? Where does he...where must I go?"

"One..." She took another great breath and choked on the blood. The woman sank back, her head lolling, "...Rock." Her fingers relaxed.

Parasades let her head down onto the ground gently. "Go with the Mother, little one. Let us hope you tell the truth."

Chapter Twenty-Seven

The monolith known as One Rock stood cold and bleak in the plains nestled by the foothills to the south of Urul. Gusts of wind brought light drizzle from the lowering clouds above. Two horsemen sat quietly by the rock, sheltering as best they could from the weather, each wrapped in their own thoughts. One of the horses stamped, shifting in protest at the enforced inactivity, jolting its rider from his reverie. Nikometros leaned low over the neck of his mount, stroking the horse's neck gently. "Patience, Diomede. They will be here soon." He sat upright and turned to the other man. "I am worried, Timon. They should have been here by now."

"They will be here, Niko. They must be cautious and arouse no suspicions."

Timon sounded calm, but Nikometros knew he was as worried as he. "We should have waited, and ridden out with them. It isn't right leaving Mardes the sole responsibility."

"If we'd been seen, we would've been challenged. Too many would suspect something if they saw you and Tomyra leaving the camp together. It's better this way."

"You're probably right, but it makes the waiting no easier, my friend."

Time passed. A faint glow could be discerned in the eastern sky, the stars paling as dawn approached. "Something is wrong, Timon. We must return."

Faintly on the wind from the plains came the sound of hooves. Timon grinned. "At last!" The smile slipped. "Sir! That is the sound of many horses."

Nikometros listened intently, loosening his sword in its sheath. "They're also coming from two directions, the camp and the river. They may pass us by, but I fear we are discovered my friend," he said grimly. "We cannot flee, let us hope we can brazen it out."

They waited, as the light slowly gained in strength. *At least it is better to die in the light of day.* A light mist flowed softly around them, swirling as a group of riders approached. Nikometros peered at them then suddenly relaxed, and grinned at Timon. "They are Owls. It is Tomyra and Bithyia." He frowned. "Why have they brought so many others with them?"

The riders came to a ragged halt beside them, Nikometros and Timon searching the faces of the young women. Tears streaked many faces and several swayed in their saddles from wounds. A tall young woman pushed to the front. "My lord Nikomayros. Thanks be to the Mother, we have found you."

Nikometros nudged Diomede close to her. "Where is Tomyra, your priestess? What has happened?"

The young woman drew herself up and saluted. "I am Sarmatia, sir, sworn attendant to my mistress. She..." Her stern demeanour faltered. "My lord, we are betrayed. Our lord Spargises is dead and my mistress has vanished, none know where."

Nikometros sat stunned then looked around at the small group of riders with growing horror. "You left your mistress in danger?"

"My lord, we were dismissed when she went to her father's hut. When the fighting broke out in the camp, Bithyia came to us and bid us ride here to meet you."

"Bithyia!" Timon pushed to the front. "Where is she now?"

Sarmatia shook her head. "She said she would bring our mistress, but that we must find you."

A shout came from the back of the party. "Sarmatia...my lord. Riders approach."

Nikometros and Timon swung round, their swords in their hands, the Owls tiredly forming a ragged line, lances at the ready, as a disciplined column of horsemen rode up the slope. The first rays of the new sun caught the leader.

Nikometros cursed and drove his stallion forward, sword raised. "Parasades. So you would betray us and murder your chief?"

Parasades reined his horse back, ducking under the blade. "No, my lord!"

Two riders immediately behind him shouted and rode at Nikometros from either side, jostling him with their shields as he struggled to bring his mount around. "My lord," they cried. "He is innocent. It is us, my lord, your own Company of Lions."

Nikometros lowered his sword, looking at the gold lion head patterns on the shields and pennants of the column of men. The features of the two riders became clear and he recognised the smiling features of Mardes. He turned and looked at Parasades grimly. "And what of you, Parasades? What part have you played in this betrayal?"

Parasades pursed his lips. "I admit I plotted to remove you from power, Nikomayros." He hurried on as murmurs of anger rose from the ranks behind him. "I believed, and still believe a Massegetae should rule us, but not Areipithes. He is god-cursed, Nikomayros. The demons of night will hunt him down for killing his father."

"And what of Tomyra? Has she...has she also been killed?"

Parasades hesitated. "No, my lord." He held up a hand and hurried on. "She remains in great danger though. She has been taken captive."

"By whom? Areipithes?"

"Again, no. Areipithes could not do this alone. He has sold the Massegetae honour to the westerners, the Serratae. They have carried her off to their own lands."

Nikometros groaned. He dropped his sword and put his head in his hands.

Timon rode up. "What of Bithyia? Do any have word of her?" He looked around at the riders.

Mardes nudged his gelding alongside Timon. "My friend, I saw her briefly as we rode toward the river. She and two others rode by us, fast, to the west. They did not hear our shouts, and we could not pursue." He laid a hand on Timon's arm. "She is in the hands of the Mother Goddess, my friend."

Nikometros looked up, his eyes wild. "I must ride to find Tomyra."

Parasades grabbed his arm. "Nikomayros. Think. You command more than just yourself. Others rely on you, would you desert them?"

Nikometros stared at him then a shadow passed across his face and he shuddered. "You are right." He looked around him, and then rapped out a string of commands. "Sarmatia. We camp here for an hour. See what provisions we have and tend to the wounded. Mardes, send two men out toward the camp to make certain we are not discovered." He struggled to remember the name of the eager young Lion in front of him. "Tirses, isn't it? A promising junior officer, if I remember rightly. You are promoted to senior officer rank. Organise the men; see they are fed and the horses rested. No fires though."

Nikometros dismounted and beckoned to Timon, Mardes, Sarmatia and Parasades, drawing them aside. "Parasades, your chief is dead. What are your intentions, and where do your loyalties now lie?"

292

Parasades shrugged. "Death releases us from our vows. However, I love my People and do not wish to see them suffer under Areipithes. Our desires are the same, I believe."

"And you, Sarmatia? What will you do?"

"Seek my mistress, my lord. My Owls may not be as skilled with arms as the men of the Massegetae, but we are loyal and will serve the Lady unto death."

Nikometros smiled. "Well said." He turned to Timon and Mardes. "I release you from your duties, my friends." He held up a hand. "Let me finish. I will seek out Tomyra in the western lands, and I suspect Timon will wish to follow me, to search for his Bithyia."

Mardes looked stricken. "I, too, my lord. I will accompany you to the land of the dead, should it be necessary."

"No, Mardes. I have another task for you. A harder one, but vital. I will give you a letter, a dispatch, to the commander of the garrison in Sogdia. You must find him and tell him of the situation. The border was stable under Spargises, but anything could happen now." He looked at the uncomfortable expressions of Parasades and Sarmatia. "I am sorry. I still have a duty to my commander and to the people south of here, as well as to the loyal Massegetae. I seek to prevent bloodshed."

Parasades nodded. "Very well. I shall accompany you, Nikomayros. I know the land to the west of here. For two days travel at least." He smiled grimly. "I have raided that far into their lands." He waved towards the men sitting on the turf, eating bread. "One or two of them know the land as well, I expect."

Nikometros stared hard at Parasades, gauging the man. "So be it. Ask my Lions for two volunteers to come with us." He turned to Sarmatia. "I must ask you to stay, lady. There are others of your mistress' Company, who are now alone, leaderless. I ask you to search for them and care for them. Do not let Areipithes hurt them."

Sarmatia scowled. "If you insist, my lord. But, when I have secured my full Company, I will follow my Lady. I must." She turned on her heel and strode back to her warriors.

Nikometros signaled to Tirses. "You are ranking officer of the Lions now, Tirses." He slipped his armband off, the sword cut still fresh in its metal. "Take this as my authority. Gather any who would resist the parricide Areipithes. I promise you, we shall return with the priestess, and remove the usurper." He thought for a moment. "One other thing; if you can, go north and find Nemathres of the Dumae. There is a slave called Ket in his hut. Ask him if he will release him into your care." He smiled at the confused expression on Tirses' face. "He is special to me and to our priestess."

Tirses saluted then took the armband and hurried back to his command.

Nikometros dug into his bags, drawing out parchment and a quill pen. He grimaced as he saw the writings of Homer on the back of the sheet, remembering he had borrowed some of Tomyra's old scrolls. Thinking for a few moments, he wrote quickly in a cramped hand, filling the page with his report. He handed it to Mardes. "Take this my friend. Give it to no one but the garrison commander." He embraced Mardes. "Take care. I would see you again."

Nikometros turned to Timon, and then called out to Parasades as he selected his volunteers. "Come, time is wasting. We ride." He grasped Diomede's mane and vaulted onto the horse's broad back. He raised a hand and waved, digging his heels into the stallion's flanks. The five horsemen thundered down the slope toward the Oxus, in the cold winter sunlight.

Chapter Twenty-Eight

Hands tied in front of her and feet tied below the horse's belly, Tomyra fought to stay upright. Her face and body ached from the beatings of the previous night, and her tongue gingerly probed the loose tooth in her jaw. Her gown was ripped and dirty. She knew she was bleeding still from the savage assault of the leader, Dimurthes. He had taken his pleasure with her, trying unsuccessfully to make her beg for mercy. Thinking of her brother Areipithes had given her the strength to maintain her hate, her silence. She would not let him see her cry; she would not give in to her overwhelming grief.

She looked about her carefully, noting the men riding watchfully on either side of her. The column of men stretched ahead of her, and by careful movements of her head, she could make out many more behind. After fording the river the night before, the band of riders moved up through scrubby willow and alder, heading north and west into the lands of the Serratae.

Father, I will grieve for you. And you, my love, my Niko. Are you out there somewhere?

She reached out with her mind, feeling a slow pulse of power from the land around her.

Great Goddess, she prayed. *You brought us together, help us now.*

A feeling of warmth flowed over her and she smiled. The man on her right shouted and struck her. She swayed in her saddle, her face carefully neutral again.

He will come for me, I know it. My Niko, I love you.

The story of Nikometros and Tomyra will
continue in 'The Golden King'.

About the Author

Max Overton has traveled extensively and lived in many places around the world – including Malaysia, India, Germany, England, Jamaica, New Zealand, USA and Australia. Trained in the biological sciences in New Zealand and Australia, he has worked within the scientific field for many years, but now concentrates on writing. While predominantly a writer of historical fiction (Scarab: Books 1 – 6 of the Amarnan Kings; the Lion of Scythia trilogy; the Demon trilogy; Ascension), he also writes in other genres (A Cry of Shadows, the Glass House trilogy, Haunted Trail, Sequestered) and draws on true life (We Came From Königsberg, Adventures of a Small Game Hunter in Jamaica). Max also maintains an interest in butterflies, photography, cryptozoology, the paranormal and other aspects of Fortean Studies.

His other published books are available at Writers Exchange Ebooks:

http://www.writers-exchange.com/Max-Overton.html and all his books may be viewed on his website: http://www.maxovertonauthor.com/

Max's book covers are all designed and created by Julie Napier, and other examples of her art and photography may be viewed at www.julienapier.com

CPSIA information can be obtained at www.ICGtesting.com
Printed in the USA
LVOW01s1523140214

373766LV00016B/498/P